Praise for 

"He's done it again, paired the playful with the apocalyptic and made my brain spin in his galaxy. REWIND is a book you want to spend time in. I read slower as I reached the last pages because I didn't want it to end."

— Kirk Lynn, author of *Rules for Werewolves*

"Greg Shemkovitz's *Rewind* is a powerful mix of paranoia and hi-tech malfunction set in a near-future dystopian city. A gripping story which radically destroys our tech-friendly narratives and remind us that behind the nodes, the diodes and the numbers, human lives are at play. A vital read in these "A.I. positive" times."

— Seb Doubinsky, author of *The Sum of All Things*, *The Horror*, and *Paperclip*

"In the vein of Kazuo Ishiguro, Shemkovitz delivers a literary science-fiction novel that transcends genre conventions to explore the fragile nature of identity. Shemkovitz's detailed, character-driven approach to storytelling will leave readers utterly immersed in the protagonists' fight against technology for their very existence."

— Eric Z. Weintraub, author of *South of Sepharad*

Also by Greg Shemkovitz

Lot Boy
REMIND

 REWIND

A NOVEL

GREG SHEMKOVITZ

Denver, Colorado

Published in the United States by:
Spaceboy Books LLC
1627 Vine Street
Denver, CO 80206
www.readspaceboy.com

Cover design features CC0 images freepik and Cristian Grigore from Pixabay

First printed November 2024

ISBN: 978-1-951393-40-3

To the future.

"We say stand together!
Not to fight, just to exist."

—Operation Ivy

PART ONE

There's an entire world under this city. Everyone talks about the rats, especially now that those little rodents make more appearances as the water keeps rising. But nobody talks about all the kids out there, all of us Haydens. Probably just as many of us living underground as there are rats.

CHAPTER ONE

Struggling to breathe, Step reaches for the door across the restroom. Mouth gulps like a goldfish out of water. Knees buckle. Body slips down the wall until limbs pile over themselves. But there is no pain, just cold welling up as if drawn from the tile floor now pressed against Step's face. Lines of tile grout trace toward the door, as panic gives way to calm. Resignation. This is it.

Is this it?

Shoes come into view. A sudden shift of weight to the heel. A gasp. Step tries to push an arm toward this person. And the shoes scuffle out again. The door swings closed.

Is that Haddy shouting from the other room?

Step knows allergic reactions. Nothing ever this bad but close, and more times than Step can remember. Hayden's don't usually have the luxury to be picky, scrounging as they do. Just another problem to solve like any other on the street. Add a body like Step's to the algorithm, and you have more room for errors like this.

Another pair of shoes arrives. Worn black leather. "Damn," says a voice. A knee drops to the floor, a hand barely touches Step's arm. "An ambulance is coming," the person says, and seems to look around before standing up again. Step can't get a clear view of their face. "I'm–" The person opens the door. "Stay put." Backing out the door, the person says to somebody else, "It's okay. It's okay. Just some Hayden but we–" and the door swings closed.

Step pulls on a thread of air. Barely that. But it's enough. Or the lightness in Step's head says so. *Be calm. Resign. This may be it.* Step's mind jolts awake again with primal thoughts–one part *help me*, one part *kill me.* Step always seems to listen to the part that brings the most suffering: *help me.*

Do what you can, Step. Details. Gather the details.

Step knows to read body signals, take note of what's wrong, what's off. As consciousness fades, take down every last detail. That's Step's greatest strength, and a wizard granted this power.

—

When Step was a little boy–*that's how long ago*–maybe even before Step knew what a wizard was, one appeared like a ghost out of nowhere. Eyes closed tight against some terror, probably a group of other Haydens, and the wizard just game into being before Step's eyes. There was no setting in this vision. No lair, no castle, no foggy forest. Just black. That's what Step always sees. Blackness all around and this wizard robed in an ocean of vibrant colors swirling and shimmering like waves across light fabric.

This first appearance was before words. Step was that young. And the wizard had no name. Still doesn't all these years later. Step doesn't remember if the other Haydens were mocking him for being a boy or harassing him the way they always did back in Hayden House. No matter the reason, this wizard appeared for the first time. He said, "I will protect you," and granted Step the power of confidence. Step could feel it almost immediately, a certain carefree calm, a feeling as euphoric as this hallucination.

Like all other Haydens, Step has no memory of having parents. And like most Haydens, Step has no recollection of arriving at Hayden House to live among a population of feral girls whose biological parents cast them away in hopes of having a male child to pass along the family name. Yet, Step could carry the family name, given the chance.

But over the years, slipping in and out of foster care and back into a world of budding women, Step was forced to learn everything himself about the male body, about navigating the world as a nameless boy, and how to survive on his own. And the wizard helped. Step was alone to fight factions of rival groups within the Haydens, never accepted or protected by any. When he was ten, a group of them tied him to the bed and stripped him of his clothes. He cried for help as they painted his genitals with nail polish. In his mind, he tried to escape somewhere safe, and the wizard appeared again. He said, "You are never alone," and granted Step the power of fearlessness. Step would remember that night as the last time he cried.

Then Step met Haddy, a girl he saw as carefree and knowing. They became good friends. She walked with purpose. She always showed confidence, even when she carried her duffel bag out to the car of another mysterious foster family or when she returned months later as if having finished a long, daunting job and was happy to be back. Haddy carried herself differently.

On hot days in System City, when yard dust kicked up like a cloud under girls at play and bored Haydens began to circle Step like sharks, Haddy would sometimes take him by the arm and escort him to a safe spot inside. Sometimes she'd outright confront the biggest among the group, shove them, take a punch or two before letting go completely to some carnal rage before Miss Ula Mae or some older, wiser Haydens pried her off. She was fearless and self-assured.

Step often wondered what made him unable to act this way, if being a boy meant that your feelings were all gentle and passive. But he was angry like the others. He was tired of having no future, no home beyond Hayden House. He knew how to live without most things and he stopped worrying about danger until he faced it. But Step felt like he lacked something the girl Haydens possessed, a certain primal kinship.

Meanwhile, other boys came and went from Hayden House but infrequently. They usually arrived as older child runaways, instead of being abandoned. And they never seemed to stay long. Most were recruited into street gangs or decided to run away because they couldn't handle how rough the girls were.

At night, while the girls slept in bunks strewn across large rooms separated by ages (infants through two years, three through seven years, eight through eleven, and so on), Step lay awake in a cot in the hallway by the kitchen. He often snuck down the hall to peek in on quiet commotion that unfolded in different bunk rooms, like when a couple of girls decided to gag a Hayden who'd just returned from foster care and beat her with shoes and boots. Or the time when some girls tried to sneak past Step and raid the kitchen for food. Step kept his eyes cracked just enough to ensure that they wouldn't attack him. Rarely did he sleep, and instead took in the whimpers of younger, scared girls or the groans and panting from dark corners. He often sat in the hall outside a room and scanned the dark gathering of bunks for signs of nightlife. The mystery of what made these girls tick seemed never to appear in these moments of calm, as much as he hoped. But he watched anyway.

After several years, Step began to wonder how long he could stand living in Hayden House. He thought about what it might take to escape like the other boys or if maybe doing something drastic, like cutting himself, would send him away somewhere safer. One night, he crept from his cot to the dark, cold kitchen. He didn't know what he was looking for until he noticed the knife block. But when he tried to take one, he found that the blades were locked in by a bar that stretched across the knife slots. He tried the smaller ones, which wiggled but did not come loose. Could he poison himself? He searched for a cleaning closet but didn't know which one of these locked doors held chemicals.

Defeated and back at his cot, he pressed his face into the cool, limp pillow and growled quietly to himself. He would not cry. But perhaps on the brink, his eyes tightly shut, the wizard once again appeared. Only, now he was a teenager and no longer cared to see the wizard.

"Go away," he said.

The wizard said, "You belong."

"Just kill me," Step said.

Again, the wizard, in his robe shimmering with light, said, "You belong." Step let out a groan and the wizard repeated, "You belong." And without knowing how or why, Step felt something much stronger than those previous powers. It would be months or years before Step heard the term intersectionality or knew the idea of his interconnectedness with the world around him. Each power was a feeling, a knowing, but not an understanding. And Step knew that belonging among the Haydens meant more than being one of the girls or some *freakboy* or whatever he'd long thought of himself by this point.

For months, Step carried their self with this newfound feeling. Taunting and insults from the other Haydens seemed trivial and only compounded those previous powers of confidence and fearlessness. Then one autumn morning, Miss Ula Mae, the Hayden House mother, brought a group of them to a nearby park. Most times the Haydens knew to behave if Miss Ula Mae was around. But this time, emboldened by this freedom away from Hayden House or because Miss Ula Mae was distracted by the cool breeze against her napping face, a faction of teen Haydens cornered Haddy and Step. Before Haddy could defend herself, a couple of girls seized her by her baggy hooded sweatshirt. Another three girls made a wall to keep Step at bay.

"C'mere," said one girl. Her name was Mallory. She had a thin nose Step wanted to break. She produced scissors from her jacket and yanked at Haddy's hair, which had already been crudely cut to flop long on one side. Apparently Mallory didn't like that so much.

"Let me go," Haddy snarled.

"Do it," said another girl, peering back to make sure Miss Ula Mae was still sleeping.

"Yeah, Mal. Cut it," said another.

Step struggled against the wall of girls and was promptly shoved to the ground. "Back off, freakboy," said one of them over their shoulder. Sitting there behind the legs of three Haydens, Step felt powerless. What good was living if this was what Step and Haddy had to deal with every day. Step clenched two fists of mulch, scrunching eyes against the violence of Mallory and her scissors.

That's when the wizard appeared again and said, "Know yourself," and granted Step the power of seeing what others ignored. Step knew just then that what this meant was more than knowing one's self but of knowing what others see or feel. Knowing the world around.

Step's eyes opened to Mallory struggling to keep a hold of Haddy's hair while Haddy tried to jerk free.

"I'll cut your hair or I'll cut you," Mallory said to Haddy. "Your choice."

"Mallory," Step called out. "Mallory. Hold on one second." Nights alone in that cot, listening and wondering. It all came to mind. How Mallory hunched over herself in group therapy. How she guarded her tray at meals. Step recalled every moment.

Step put out a hand for help from one of the girls but it was quickly slapped away. Unfazed, Step stood while the others froze in puzzlement.

"I see you at night," Step said.

"What?" Mallory shot back. "Creep!"

"Why do you twist your blanket around your hand as you fall asleep?" Step asked, moving through the wall of now dumbstruck Haydens. "That something you did as a baby?"

"What the hell are you talking about, freakshow?" Mallory said.

"Back off," said another girl.

Step looked at her and said, "Oh, yeah. Walda, that's right. You snore."

The others couldn't help but laugh nervously.

"What?" Walda said, and she was clearly ashamed.

"No, no," Step said. "Not loud. Just quietly. Like a faint crackle in the back of your throat." Step was in her face now. "I have to be real close to hear it." He leaned a little to demonstrate how close. "You snore so softly," he whispered.

"Gross!" cried Walda.

"I see it all," Step said. He looked at another girl in the group. "You talk sometimes in your sleep."

"Screw you," said the girl. "No, I don't."

"No?" Step said. "It's mostly vowels." He imitated her slack-jawed nighttime chatter. "I'll let you know tomorrow what you say tonight." Step's eyes turned back to Mallory, whose grip on Haddy's hair had loosened. "Or maybe I'll just get some scissors of my own. And maybe I won't stop with just your hair."

"What the hell?" Mallory muttered in terror.

Step put out a hand to help up Haddy. As they walked away, Haddy turned to the group and said, "Sweet dreams, ladies."

When they reached a safe place, Step vomited from nerves, and they both laughed.

—

Step lurches awake to find a nurse looming, a pair of surgical scissors drawing closer. Step's body is still weak, no panic or fight left inside. The nurse slowly draws the flat end of the scissors under some tape that holds the IV tube to Step's forearm. As she removes the IV line, Step thinks about the warning signs of low blood pressure—lungs filling with fluid or the brain growing tired and foggy. Step catalogs these feelings to be ready for the next allergic attack.

"You won't need this anymore," says the nurse, pulling the IV rack away.

"Where's Haddy?" Step asks.

"Who's that?"

"My friend. You know, the one here earlier today."

Haddy had come by earlier at some point. Step can remember

that now. She was really clingy like something awful had happened.

"Oh," said the nurse. "That girl. I don't remember her name. Can't even think of her face anymore, what with all that's going on."

"What's going on?" Step says, not so much to the nurse.

Step remembers seeing something on the news when Haddy was here. But it's vague now. Something about their chips getting scrambled, the System all out of whack. Step looks at the nurse's face and says, "Greta Eichenbaum." That's the name that the System has given the nurse. At least that's what is being fed into the chip in Step's head.

"Maybe," the nurse says. "I'd have to look in the mirror. But my name's really Natalie Holmes. Or it was." She chuckles to herself. "I've had maybe three names since this morning."

Step looks around the room, searching for signs as if something has to stand out when such an epic event has occurred. But it's so quiet and unassuming from this hospital bed. How can the System be broken and Step feels nothing different? This has to be a dream.

"Where's Haddy?" Step asks again.

"That girl?" says the nurse, wrapping up the tube and pulling down the IV bag to throw into a trashcan across the room. "She left here with some official-looking men. Real duds, if you ask me. But they seemed like they knew her pretty well."

"Did she bring my porto?"

"I don't know," says the nurse. She goes over to a drawer where Step's clothing is put away. "Yes," she says, and lifts his porto into view. "It's dead though. I can charge it after I'm done here." The nurse goes back to disconnecting intensive care equipment.

Outside the window, the sky is gray and heavy-looking above a crowd of tall buildings. Step glances around the room again for signs of Haddy. But nothing shows.

"She seemed to know something about what's going on out there," the nurse says. "She wasn't the least bit fazed by all this... what are they calling it... Name-a... Name-ageddon." The nurse laughs to herself.

Step remembers now. Something happened to the System that feeds identities to everyone's chip. Haddy didn't explain much but acted resigned to it, like she had already come to terms with it. Of course, Haddy's tough. Probably tougher than any other Hayden out there. Step knows better than anyone.

"She's fried," Step says, recalling that Haddy suffered a pretty bad accident not long ago and her chip no longer works. "That's why she doesn't seem–"

"Oh," says the nurse, cutting Step off. "I'm sorry to hear that." She adjusts the sheet to cover Steps bare feet, and Step immediately sticks them back out. "Maybe she's better off then," says the nurse. "It's driving the rest of us crazy."

Thinking about Haddy, Step gets flashes of their dinner the other night and what had led to this hospital stay. She had seemed unsettled for so many weeks, like somebody was following her. What happened that night?

Step ordered veggies. Always veggies. Haddy ordered... *come on, Step. Details.*

Seafood! Haddy ordered that smelly, nasty seafood dish. But that wouldn't hurt Step.

Eyes now closed, Step tries to place a visual of the restaurant and all the people there. It was swanky. That's right. And where were they sitting? What was unusual? *Come on, Step. Remember.*

Did Haddy mess with her porto the whole time? What was the weather like? Was it loud in there? How did the wait staff react to Haydens being there? What did–*wait.* Something on his porto. A message. It read, *What does the mantel clock say?*

What the hell does that mean?

CHAPTER TWO

In the remote hills of Pennsylvania, fissures and cracks seep sulfur dioxide and carbon monoxide from fires that have burned for decades in the mines below, creating a haze that, on still mornings like this, lingers among the pines like an eerie, gray fog below a pale blue sky. Beyond the silhouettes of trees glows a tiny cluster of concrete buildings called the colony. Its founder, the elusive fugitive Reuben Mayfield, known to residents simply as Paul, has just calmly departed for System City.

Because of his contributions to the System's software development, Mayfield's history of abusing young women has been overlooked by System City's governing body, MIND. However, Agent Stevenson has taken it upon himself to bring Mayfield to justice. With the unlikely ally Hadley Hayden, Agent Stevenson was able to track Mayfield to this location, only to be ambushed and captured by two of Mayfield's soldiers. Now tied to a chair before a small camp of colony residents, Agent Stevenson watches dust settle from Mayfield's getaway car.

"Is he safe?" one of the soldiers asks. Agent Stevenson doesn't look up to find out which one is asking. He's given up on cooperating now that Mayfield is gone. To make matters worse, Mayfield took Hadley Hayden as a hostage. So, he's failed on two missions: to capture a fugitive and save his Hayden friend.

The soldier steps closer and grabs Agent Stevenson by the shirt with a yank, pulling a button loose. "I said, is he safe?"

"Back off," says one of the residents. He's a tall, burly man who seems nearly unfazed by a gunshot wound to his knee that this very soldier inflicted. Agent Stevenson looks the resident in the eyes. The System tells Agent Stevenson that the man's name is Opal Marks. He knows this is not true, and that moments ago, before Mayfield executed a long-awaited plan, the System had a very different name for this man and for everyone else in System City.

The other residents, still reeling from their host's sudden evacuation, become antsy and begin to approach the two soldiers for answers.

"I still don't get what the hell just happened," says a resident. "Paul messed up the System or something and then he peaces out?"

In a few keystrokes, Mayfield brought down the System's identity recognition program that everyone has grown up under. Until that moment, everyone knew each other's names. Identities were fed to them through a chip implanted in their brains at birth. And now, all that has been scrambled. Nobody is who they appear to be.

"So, everyone is just messed up now, huh?" says another resident.

"Not us," says another. "For once, I'm glad I'm fried." At some point in the residents' lives, their chip were damaged or "fried," as people like to put it. It's the reason Paul, or Mayfield, invited them to the colony. Only, they thought they were being rehabilitated. Instead, Paul was fishing their memories for an encryption code that would gain him access to the System.

"Quiet," says the soldier standing over Agent Stevenson.

"Okay," says a resident. "I'm confused. The System is messed up? But what does Paul stand to gain from that?"

"Quiet," the soldier says a little louder.

Agent Stevenson understands. It's the perfect way for a fugitive to hide in plain sight. Just make it so nobody can ever place your face with the fugitive's name.

"Can we please get to the matter at hand?" says the resident with the wounded knee. "If you haven't noticed, there are two pricks with guns about to–"

"Shut up!" yells the younger soldier, sweeping a pistol across the group. "Just shut up."

The group goes quiet but before the soldiers can establish order again, a resident says, "Well, then who's in charge?"

The younger soldier points his pistol at the resident forcefully but looks to the other soldier, maybe for permission to shoot.

"One of you better think about taking the reins," says the resident with the wounded knee.

The soldiers look at each other briefly. Everything has happened so fast, from Mayfield scrambling the System to rushing off with a hostage, and now their brains are no doubt telling them the wrong names for each other. Agent Stevenson can see the unease in the younger soldier's face. The older soldier, who is standing over Agent Stevenson, glances back to the third among Mayfield's cronies.

Agent Stevenson has known him until moments ago as Weston, a jack-of-all-trades gofer and henchman for Mayfield. Weston stands quietly beside the tire tracks left in the gravel by Mayfield's getaway car. Agent Stevenson can see sweat glistening from the man's shaven head, his eyes showing a hint of fear or confusion. He's been quiet this whole time, perhaps still processing that his boss has left him here to deal with the fallout.

"What now?" asks one of the residents again. "If you all can't make up your minds about who's running this show then we might have us a problem."

"Who's holding the gun?" says the younger soldier, presenting his pistol. "Be quiet."

"What's even happening?" asks another resident. "What are we doing here? Was all this crap we've been doing just for Paul to mess up the System and bail?"

"Shut!" yells the older soldier at the top of his lungs. With the residents quiet, he lowers his voice and says, "Up." He turns his attention back to Agent Stevenson and says, "Tell me. Is Mayfield safe?"

Agent Stevenson isn't going to answer, but Weston does, "Yes, he is." Agent Stevenson looks up to see Weston walking toward the group.

"He's perfectly safe," Weston adds, gesturing to the soldiers and their guns. "This is unnecessary."

"I don't give a raccoon's ass about Paul," says one of the female residents. "I want to know what's going to happen to *us*."

"Who's going to run the colony?" asks another. "Are you taking over, Weston?"

And another says, "I can't go back there. The city isn't for us fried." He begins to choke up and says, "I just can't," before another resident pulls him aside to comfort him.

"Actually," another resident says. "I think we'd be fine."

If they're to believe Mayfield, the virus that was released into the System will continue to scramble identities every six hours when the database updates, causing mayhem for people across the city. All infrastructure will be seized by confusion. Those with the greatest advantage are the people who live off the System, the fried.

"We're not dependent on some faulty chip in our heads," says another resident.

"They're not going to shut up," the younger soldier says to his colleague.

A pistol barrel under his chin slowly directs Agent Stevenson to look up at the older soldier looming over him. "What about this guy?" asks the older soldier. "Can't seem to get you to make a peep."

Agent Stevenson looks the soldier in the eyes and he suddenly sees it. He can just tell. No system needed. He knows this man, maybe not by name but he knows him well enough by the way he carries himself. This soldier is a former MIND agent.

"I bet you can make him scream," the younger soldier says.

Agent Stevenson smirks. "What now?" he says. "When does Mayfield's command end?"

"He speaks," says the older soldier. He presses the barrel of his gun into Agent Stevenson's skin. "Is there a trap for him?"

"Did you defect for the credit? How much?" asks Agent Stevenson, keeping eye contact with the soldier. "Or had you already given up on your oath before Mayfield found you?"

A grimace crawls across the older soldier's face. He slowly parts Agent Stevenson's lips with the barrel of his gun, metal sliding smoothly against the agent's teeth and forcing his jaw open wider. Agent Stevenson can't help but give a small grunt of discomfort. The soldier studies his prey for a sign of fear, until his eyes drop to the opened button in Agent Stevenson's shirt. He parts the collar further with his other hand to reveal a faint gray tattoo peeking through the agent's chest hair. It reads, *2388*. The soldier's eyes grow curious and then hesitate before looking back into Agent Stevenson's eyes.

"Paul... I mean, Mayfield will be fine," Weston says with strained authority in his voice.

"How do you know?" asks the younger soldier.

Weston looks at the younger soldier and his gun. Agent Stevenson can tell that Weston is uncomfortable. He licks his lips. He moves his hands from his hips and folds his arms across his chest before using them to gesture while saying, "This was his plan all along. Have you ever known Mayfield to put himself in harm's way?" He turns to the older soldier and gestures to lower the gun. "He'd have asked one of you to go with him. Don't you think?"

"What about Haddy?" asks a resident.

"I'm sure she'll be fine too," says Weston. "Let's all take a deep breath." To the older soldier, he says, "The residents and I are going inside. Please join us."

After a moment of hesitation, everyone looking at each other for agreement, the residents begin to slowly move toward the cafeteria.

"Wait a minute," commands the younger soldier still holding the group at gunpoint. "Nobody's moving."

"Let 'em go," says the older soldier. "Nobody's a threat but this one." He straightens up and positions his gun against Agent

Stevenson's temple.

"Don't do it," Weston says.

"Go," commands the younger soldier with a wave of his gun. "Go to the cafeteria. Now!" He looks to Weston and says, "Round up the rest of them."

Weston and the younger soldier lock eyes. After a moment, Weston moves on.

When the group is gone, the two soldiers convene over Agent Stevenson. The younger one says, "What the hell are we doing here? We're just the watchers, for crying out loud."

"That's a really good question," Agent Stevenson says.

Known as the watchers, these two were hired by Reuben Mayfield to protect the colony from outside danger such as encroaching wildlife or, in this singular instance, the trespass of an unwanted guest like Agent Stevenson. Their days have been spent watching from different vantage points on the hills above the colony. But now that Mayfield's mission is over, Agent Stevenson knows that whatever purpose they had must have left with his fugitive.

The older soldier nods to Agent Stevenson and says, "Twenty-three eighty-eight."

It takes maybe a second for this to sink in but the younger soldier lowers his head with this news. He curses to himself and turns away. "Twenty-third class," he says, shaking his head. "Dammit."

The older soldier backs away, gun still pointing at Agent Stevenson. It's clear that he doesn't know what to do.

"I'm guessing you're, what, twenty-eighth?" says Agent Stevenson. "Maybe thirtieth class?"

"Twenty-seventh," the soldier says, tepid pride in his voice.

"And you?" says Agent Stevenson, sizing up the older soldier. "You have to be twelfth or older. Practically OG."

"Ten fifty-two," says the younger soldier. "Ain't I right?"

The older soldier lowers his gun.

"Honor above all," says Agent Stevenson, beginning the MIND Academy creed.

"And all in the name," replies the younger soldier. The older soldier keeps his eyes locked on Agent Stevenson's.

A calm breeze picks up momentarily, sending wafts of sulfur past the three men. Agent Stevenson hasn't moved in his seat but keeps his eyes trained on the older soldier's eyes. "No sense asking what you go by then," he says. "Ten fifty-two will do just fine."

The younger soldier lifts layers of clothing to expose a scarred chest and the number *2701* tattooed in the same position as Agent Stevenson's. "Top of class," he says.

Agent Stevenson nods in appreciation of their shared experience. He knows what these men have been through, the work they did to earn those tattoos and the honor they must have shown at some point in their lives. He could test their allegiance to MIND or their oath to humanity, ask them to atone for aiding Reuben Mayfield, a known sexual predator and now cyber terrorist. From where he sits, tied to a chair in the middle of nowhere, Agent Stevenson might want to leverage any of those appeals to set himself free. Instead, he says, "That girl. She didn't ask for any of this."

"That Hayden?" says the younger soldier. "Hell."

"Is that what the System tells you?" asks Agent Stevenson. "Not anymore."

"What's she to you?" asks the younger soldier.

"She's an innocent girl."

"Seems to me she had a lot to do with this mess," says the younger soldier.

"An unwitting accomplice," says Agent Stevenson. "A powerless pawn. What's that make the two of you?"

The older soldier finally holsters his weapon back under his jacket and scans the hillside.

"Do you actually think he'll ever come back?" says Agent Stevenson. "His whole plan was to safely return to System City."

"I don't know," says the younger soldier. He's more anxious than his older colleague and paces toward the gravel where Mayfield's car rolled away. "I just... I don't know."

"I won't lie to you," says Agent Stevenson. "You untie me and I'm going after Mayfield. But that's my charge and it has nothing to do with you two."

The older soldier says nothing, just rubs his chin slowly.

"I could use your help though," says Agent Stevenson.

"I'm not going back there," says the younger soldier. "I'm not going to face what's coming."

The older soldier remains quiet.

"If not me." Agent Stevenson nods to the cafeteria building where Weston is guiding the last of the residents through a door, and says, "then these folks could use your help." Agent Stevenson knows the older soldier is watching those people now, a haze of regret forming in his eyes. "Seems to me your reason for being here has come to a conclusion. And now you got yourself a colony with no purpose. Maybe the two of you can help set it in a new direction."

"Wait," says the younger soldier, his finger pointed as if to shush somebody. His eyes seem to search for something. He moves to the older soldier's side. "Yeah. You know. This could work."

"It's been working all this time," says Agent Stevenson. "But imagine what two MIND Academy grads can bring to this place."

"That Weston fella knows the logistics," says the younger soldier. "Hell, he *is* the logistics."

"I have no reason to come back," says Agent Stevenson. "And nobody from headquarters ever needs to know you're out here."

"These folks have been running this place just fine," says the younger soldier, now clearly trying to convince the older soldier. "It'd be nice to come down from those hills."

"You served well, Ten fifty-two," says Agent Stevenson. "Now let me finish my duty."

A grimace settles on the older soldier's face as if he agrees but doesn't like it. The way he locks eyes with his captor says everything Agent Stevenson needs to know. Still, if there was any doubt, the old man nods and says, "Twenty-three eighty-eight."

CHAPTER THREE

The news camera pans a street somewhere on the Upper East Side to show nothing out of the ordinary. A reporter's voiceover says, "Less than 24 hours in and people are trying to make the best of this new normal."

Cut to a far-off shot of a street vendor organizing her stand. "And life goes on in System City."

Cut to a bus passing by and then a bank entrance with an armed officer standing outside. "Essential workers make sure that public transportation, hospitals, and banks are operating. But everyone remains vigilant."

Cut to a woman in athletic attire, catching her breath as a microphone peaks into the shot. The voiceover says, "Names have been removed for the sake of this report's longevity."

The woman says, "I was Fred this morning. I'm Harriet now." She laughs. "Who knows who I'll be at dinnertime."

The voiceover says, "Many are taking it in stride."

A montage of city scenes pan across the screen. "They're calling it the Great Glitch. Name-ageddon. The System Scramble. But its cause is still unknown. MIND officials say that it isn't an issue with software code."

Cut to an official-looking man standing outside of MIND headquarters in downtown System City. He says, "The people of System City know not to panic. They know this is just a minor hiccup. Besides, it's a simple issue of availability. It's not a bug. Not a glitch."

Cut to an aerial view of the city. The voiceover says, "Just yesterday we felt secure. Our names were what they've always been since birth."

Cut to a homeless man holding a tattered cardboard sign that reads, *In System We Trust.*

"The System. It's what keeps us safe," says the voiceover. "Know your neighbor, know yourself. That is until the next time you look at your neighbor and their name has changed again."

Another montage of city scenes pans across the screen. "According to outside monitoring groups, this was bound to happen."

Cut to a person whose image has been blurred. In an altered voice, they say, "This is big. Nothing like this has happened in System history. And I can tell you that not even the backups are working. Data has failed us."

The voiceover says, "And what happens when that failing data is our identity?"

Cut to a boy holding a basketball. He says, "I think it stinks. My friends keep calling me the wrong name!" The camera pulls back to show the boy's friends. One says, "The System's all jacked up. Nobody knows nobody."

The voiceover says, "This all has people asking, 'How do we know anyone if we can't place their name?'"

Cut to an older woman feeding pigeons. She says, "You can't rely on some computer to keep us connected. It's got to come from here." She puts her hand over her heart.

The voiceover says, "In our hearts or in our minds, officials are working hard to restore what connected us all this time."

Cut back to the official-looking man at MIND headquarters. "We're handling it as quickly as we can. But rest assured, we're handling this blackout... No, no. Call it a brown out." He nods as if pleased by this explanation. "Yes, it's more like a brown out. A rolling brown out."

Cut to brief shots of city scenes. Commuters walk along a sidewalk. Cars move slowly down an avenue. A large dog on a leash plods through the park. The voiceover says, "Black, brown. Glitch or bug. How long will it last? Nobody quite knows. But the people of System City are resilient. We're moving on with our lives."

Cut to a butcher behind the counter at his shop. He says, "We got this. We're strong."

The voiceover says, "Strong indeed. Even stronger together."

CHAPTER FOUR

Thomas Karp doesn't need the mirror to adjust his tie and smooth down the crisp collar of his light blue MIND Academy uniform. But he uses this time to study his face and burn it into his memory.

"Thomas Karp," he whispers to himself against the name that his chip is telling him. Similar to a trick of the eye–like a mirage or an illusion in shadows–his mind is telling him one name while he *knows* his real name. But it feels to him like "Thomas Karp" is the illusion.

The frosted window in the dormitory bathroom has gradually lightened behind him, and soon other cadets will shuffle into the bathroom for last-minute morning care before meeting for drills outside the cafeteria. Unlike the others, Thomas gives himself thirty extra minutes to make sure that his uniform is presentable and that he's awake and limber both mentally and physically. It's Tuesday, which means oatmeal and toast for breakfast, much less of an incentive for cadets to behave during drills. If only they saw food as fuel the way Thomas does. Maybe then they would put less stock in their meal time. Instead, more than likely, a few will act out for a laugh, forcing an extra round of drills as punishment. Everyone will groan despite drills being mostly symbolic at their level. Upperclassmen have been doing these drills for the last six years out of routine. With muscle memory and years of conditioning, Thomas and his fellow cadets can do these wall sits and minute planks in their sleep. The uniform, training bells, morning drills, and, to some extent, Tuesday hijinx, are all part of the routine. With the exception of their scrambled names, life inside MIND Academy has not changed much with the anarchy they hear rumors of beyond academy walls. Thomas takes comfort in the routine. He looks himself directly in the eyes and says, "Thomas Karp."

If there's one thing he can never prepare for, Thomas knows that it's life outside the academy. He trusts that everything he has learned will prepare him to be a stellar agent and handle the most extreme cases that System City can throw at him. But he worries sometimes about living without routine and what he will do off duty to keep a regimented lifestyle, if he even can.

Thomas returns his hair brush, toothbrush, and toothpaste to his bathroom caddy. He picks up the caddy, gives one last tilt of the head to spot any facial hair at the jawline (more out of hope than caution), and heads for the bathroom door. He has three more minutes before the first training bell and the hall becomes mayhem with boys scrambling for the bathroom, hopping on one foot while they work their pants up a leg, blinded by shirts half over their heads, hair matted in all directions. And the stench. Thomas cannot stand the smell of his classmates in the morning or anytime for that matter. How any of these guys will be among a graduating class of 100 agents is beyond Thomas. To him, filth and failure go hand in hand. In moments of weakness, Thomas has allowed himself to lecture his roommate, Carl, on this very topic, citing homeless people as a prime example of human dereliction. Second to the homeless are Haydens, who Thomas will refer to as "functional failures" because some of them still find work, despite being mostly intolerable.

But Thomas often cuts himself off before going too far. References to Haydens lead to thoughts of his biological sister, Hadley, whom he wishes he could forget entirely. His biggest secrets are not only that he has a sister who is a Hayden but that he has also met her on two occasions. And those two occasions remain the scariest moments of his life.

The first time he met Hadley, he was still in primary school. His parents had been arguing for a week or so in hushed voices, and

Thomas could hear the occasional reference to a baby. His father had always been a sad man, slowly shuffling in from work as an overnight custodian downtown. He dragged himself out each night the same way, slouched in his beige coveralls. His form of arguing was tired and dismissive. "Jeanne, please," he often pleaded. "Be happy with what we have."

Mrs. Karp usually maintained a cheery demeanor while helping Thomas–*her Little Tommy*–get ready for school and making sure to be back from her part-time job as a metals cleaner before he got home. Before she passed away, she was Thomas's world. He was the first to notice her getting sick, even as she tried to mask her paling complexion with makeup and diminishing energy with exaggerated enthusiasm. When the argument about their daughter was coming to a head, his mother was not yet showing these signs. But Thomas sometimes lumps those events together because he could hear the same desperation in her voice when she talked about reconnecting with their daughter. "I'm sorry, Joe. I just wanted to meet her."

"We can't take her back," said Mr. Karp. Thomas could hear that his father was trying to be compassionate but he, too, sounded desperate. After all, the law limited households to a single biological child, even if the System City population continued to grow despite these measures. Nevertheless, Mr. Karp was a fervent rule follower, which was something Thomas admired most about his father.

"I know, I know," said Mrs. Karp. "Don't worry. She already has a foster family anyway."

"Okay," said Mr. Karp. "So, please let this go."

"I just—"

Thomas could see from across their small living room and into the kitchen that his father had her wrapped in his arms. She was sobbing into his shoulder, which is how many of their arguments ended. Thomas was reading through sight words on his porto at that moment. In his memory, Thomas remembers the contrast between the complex moment in the other room, and the simple, almost trivial language on his porto screen—a chart that read "the, is, and, that, of, an, it..."

This should have been the extent of his memory concerning his sister. But not long later, on his way home from school, he found her lurking outside his home. He knew that this girl had something to do with his parents' strife because of what he gleaned from their arguments, something about an orphan named Hadley. Now, as he saw her, the chip in his head told him that her name was Hadley Hayden. And Thomas knew that this last name was assigned to all orphans who passed through Hayden House.

Thomas remembers thinking that she was suspicious-looking with her baggy, stained prep school shirt, like she was trying to pass as something more than an orphan. He was confused whether a girl raised in an orphanage could end up going to a prep school. He always just assumed what his porto stories told him, that orphans were all criminals. But if his mother wanted to meet this girl so badly, then Hadley couldn't be dangerous. So he reasoned.

"Would you like to see where I live?" she asked him. The thought of the two of them venturing about immediately made his skin tingle. Thomas remembers this as the exact moment when he felt that he could be independent. For the first time, he could do something without his mother. How great would it be to have a sister that could show him the world?

But his reluctance got the better of him. After all, he knew nothing about Hadley. Here she was trying to convince him to join her. She even took him by the hand. But Thomas ultimately declined.

Then Hadley said something that Thomas will never forget. "I just thought you were grown up enough to hang out with me."

Until this moment, Thomas could only walk alone to his school down the block or visit his friend Schmidt's house around the corner. But he had never ventured alone beyond his block. Neither of his parents had taught him how to navigate their neighborhood, let alone any other parts of their corner of Queens. So, as he watched Hadley walk away toward the train back to Manhattan, Thomas realized that this might be his only opportunity for adventure.

He quickly caught up close enough to keep this mysterious girl in his sight, but far enough back that she might not see him. After a few blocks, they reached the train platform. The turnstile pinged credit from his porto, and Thomas immediately cringed at the thought of what trouble he would face when his parents found out. But the damage was done and he could do nothing to reverse it now. So, he made sure to board the same car as Hadley but at the other end. This would allow him to see where she exited and he could stay close behind.

As the tall city skyline drew closer, everything became darker until the train was underground. At their stop, Thomas followed Hadley up to the street and was immediately seized by the image of buildings stretched to the sky. He had seen it before a couple of times on trips to Central Park or to a museum. But how could he ever get used to this view? And there were so many people around. Hundreds, maybe thousands. He could so easily be swept up in the river of people and carried who knows where.

"Oh, Thomas," Hadley said. "I didn't see you there." He'd been caught. Both horrified and relieved, he decided that he should probably stick with her, wherever she was going.

Eventually, they ended up at what Thomas remembers now to be Madison Square Park. He'd seen pictures of different parks around the city or from other cities. He didn't know. And this one looked a lot like what he had seen, only there was something off. There was a group of people gathered in the park, mostly spread out but all their attention was on the center of this gathering. Thomas could vaguely see that a bunch of them were boys in prep school uniforms and a bunch more were, based on their unkempt appearance, probably Haydens. From where he stood, he couldn't hear voices getting loud. But he could feel that something was about to happen, maybe because Hadley had stiffened up and became alert. If a Hayden is suddenly on guard, there must be something wrong.

And then it erupted. A huge fight broke out. Bodies on bodies.

Dust kicked up. Shouting and crying. Some people ran from the scene but more and more kids came from out of nowhere with pipes and chains, charging toward the brawl. Thomas might have thought he was safe at first. But as the numbers grew–Haydens leaping over shrubs to get in and prep school boys practically multiplying–Thomas found himself in the thick of it. One teenage boy with a paddle came rushing toward them, knocking Thomas down as he ran after Hadley.

Thomas was tangled in his school bag, and he scrambled to get loose before darting toward some bushes at the edge of the park. Hadley was nowhere to be seen now and he worried that something bad happened to her. Later, Thomas would realize that this concern was foolish. She was the one that led him to this danger. But in the moment, Thomas couldn't make out her voice among the crying and screaming. He shouted for her, "Hadley!"

When the police finally arrived, people started to flee. Thomas crawled his way through the bushes along the fence, flanking the park, as police zip-tied and dragged Haydens into lines along the curb to be arrested.

Once the police had the park under control, Thomas snuck back to get his bag. It was dirty and must have been trampled. He quickly pulled out his porto to find that the screen had been broken. Messages from his mother were barely legible through a web of cracks. He tucked it away and quickly walked down the block, turning wherever looked safest, until he was lost in a throng of busy people. All the buildings appeared the same, and when he looked up, the sky seemed to be shrinking as the peaks of skyscrapers closed over him.

Eventually, his mother found him blocks away too scared to move.

That afternoon would mark a turning point in Thomas's understanding of the world. That was what happened when you stepped outside of your routine. He may have heard stories about how dangerous the city could be, even with chips and the System keeping everyone mostly at bay. But he never would have expected that he might happen upon such violence, and so suddenly. Looking back, that's what Thomas fears the most, when expectations are broken, especially the expectation that he will be safe or that he will live to see tomorrow.

Even when Thomas was accepted to MIND Academy, he was still nervous to go to the city. His father made sure that Thomas was fully invested in the choice to train at the academy, making him record his own application video, take after take in his bedroom. Thomas had to imagine how he would contribute as a MIND agent and consider the real possibility of life beyond his home. If it weren't for this exercise in speculation, Thomas might have crumbled under a panic attack when his father escorted him into the city and to a life with new routines and unknowns. By this point, Mrs. Karp had become weaker and bedridden. She would not live much longer after Thomas left.

Academy life turned out to be just what Thomas wanted. With strict routines, tight schedules, and clearly defined chores, Thomas was able to expect, if not predict, every moment before it happened. With the exception of one evening, Thomas's time at MIND Academy had been one of tightly controlled bliss.

It just so happened that the one evening that broke that mold happened just a few weeks ago and centered around Hadley.

His class had finished up floor duty. That's when the class splits into fours and walks the entire academy dorm building, floor by floor, up and down each stairwell, checking that doors and windows are locked and that everything is in order for shutdown. Thomas's crew included his roommate Luke, a stocky kid from New New Brighton, Angel, a fast-talking funny kid from near where Thomas grew up, and Christopher, a tall kid that Thomas often thought was older but seemed sometimes to be more childish than the rest.

Somewhere around the seventh floor, Thomas received a message on his porto. It came from their commanding prefect, Douglas Dorchester, who was somewhere on the top floor now, awaiting reports from their floor duty inspections. The message read, "Change of duty: B Squad form a search party to find a missing first-year cadet. Kyle Grady. Last known location: the cafeteria for dinner. Search blocks east of the academy." Thomas assumed that other squads were assigned the other cardinal directions. So, he seized the opportunity to lead his group.

"Ok, boys," Thomas called down the hall to his squad. "Change of duty. Gather 'round."

"Funny stuff," Luke said, still walking the hall.

The others kept inspecting doors.

"Check your portos," Thomas said. "Douglas sent instructions."

They each casually glanced at their portos.

"Nope," said Angel.

"Not me," said Christopher.

"Nada," said Luke.

Thomas studied the message he received. "Then I guess I'm in command on this mission," he said. "Line up."

More out of curiosity, the others slowly walked back to Thomas. A door next to Thomas opened and a young cadet half in pajamas peeked out. "What's–"

"Back inside," Thomas barked, pointing at the confused boy.

The boy closed his door. Thomas led his squad a few steps down the hall and, in a hushed voice, gave them the details.

"So," Luke said, "we gotta go out now and look for this kid?"

"No way," said Angel.

"Come on, Angel," said Christopher.

"Those are the orders," Thomas said.

"Nope," said Angel. "I'm not going out there. This is bull." Thomas would have normally agreed with Angel. This seemed suspicious and well outside their regular routine. But it wasn't normal for cadets to wander off. It seemed that the younger boys were less-and-less cut out for the rigors of MIND training, and maybe they needed the upperclassman to step up to set an example.

"Dinner was just over an hour ago," Thomas said. "There's no telling where this Kyle kid might be but I think we can cover from here to the river, then break north and south in twos to work our way back."

"I'm sorry, Tommy," Angel said. "I'm out."

"It's an order," Thomas said.

"I'll take it up with Douglas," said Angel. "I don't like this."

"Fine," Thomas said. "Fine. You keep on floor duty."

Thomas waved the other two to follow him down the stairwell. Suddenly they were on a mission. Under the echo of their feet shuffling down the steps, Thomas could hear the other two laughing to each other. At the bottom of the steps, Thomas stopped them and said, "Guys, can we take this seriously?"

The two looked at each other and then at him.

"Yeah, sure," said Luke.

"Fine. Yeah. Whatever," said Christopher.

Thomas led them down the first floor and around a corner so that they would emerge from a side door that faced east. He could sense the importance of this moment, and soon he was walking more swiftly. This was his moment to shine. That is, until he opened the door to the nighttime outside. Massive buildings loomed overhead, their facades aglow with LED signage and grids of lit windows. Walls of light stretching into the dark sky. Thomas suddenly felt the unknowns of this mission. Kyle Grady could be anywhere out there, and now it was up to Thomas and these to misfit cadets to find him. And suddenly Thomas just wanted to be back on floor duty.

Wherever that anxiety was coming from, Thomas closed his eyes and shoved it back down inside when Christopher and Luke stood at loose attention before him. Thomas looked down the block each way. "You two take that way, I'll take this way," he said. "Perimeter the block and meet on the other side."

"Who is it again?" Luke asked.

"Kyle Grady," said Thomas. They would know him when they saw him. The System made sure of that. "Approach him with caution." The two boys gave him a strange look, and Thomas didn't know why he added that. It just sounded like something he should say.

They crossed the street and split in each direction, taking their respective streets around the block heading east. As he walked, Thomas scanned the dark entryways of buildings, noting any movement around piles of trash by an alleyway. He thought about how Kyle Grady got away. Was he taken? Why would anyone want to leave the academy? Thomas stopped for a moment and traced, with his eyes, the length of a building across the way. His eyes were drawn skyward again, where the rooftops came together above like teeth. Why would anyone choose to throw themselves into the wild like this?

Thomas found Christopher and Luke waiting around the block, playfully pushing and shoving each other. They must have hurried, and Thomas wondered if they were taking this charge seriously. But as he watched them tease each other like little kids, Thomas couldn't help but notice how out of place these two looked in the big city. They weren't adults and certainly not Haydens. The three of them seemed so small and vulnerable out here.

"No Kyle," Luke said.

"Let's keep going," Thomas said. They crossed the street. "Slow it down this time."

"Yessir," said the other two, mocking Thomas.

They split up. Alone again, Thomas walked his side of the block on alert, as if the farther away from the academy they got the more dangerous it became. As he approached a group ahead, he stiffened to prepare for the worst. Instead of looking them in the face, he kept his head down and watched them on the peripheral of his vision. None of them seemed to notice he was there.

When he rounded the corner on the other side of the block, Thomas looked across the street to find the entrance to Madison Square Park, and immediately his heart began to race. He knew the park was there but some part of him pushed it much farther away in his memory. Images of that day flashed in his mind. The dust. The bodies. The screaming.

"You alright, Tommy?" Christopher asked. The two were coming toward him now.

A feeling of nausea welled up and Thomas swallowed it back down as best he could. Thinking about that day made Thomas sick, but when he remembered why he had been there in the first place, he started to feel angry. He had let his guard down and trusted a Hayden.

"Yeah, man," said Luke. "You okay?"

"Let's keep going," Thomas said, and led them across the street. He could feel his legs and arms shaking now. That fear he suddenly felt was beginning to melt into something more primal, like he was in danger all over again.

"Maybe Angel was right," Luke said, as they entered the park. "This is weird. Like, why are we even out here? Why would Douglas tell us to do this?"

A tangle of tree limbs kept getting thicker above them the farther they stepped into the park. Strange noises came from dark corners of the park like they were deep in the wilderness.

"This is messed up," Christopher added. He flinched at the sound of something ahead. "What's that? This place is crawling. I've never been down here at night."

"Shut up already," said Thomas, now considering that maybe Douglas sent them by mistake or he was testing Thomas somehow. "Who knows why the hell he sent us."

"Sent you," said Luke. After all, only Thomas received the message.

The three of them slowed down and became more alert. Luke turned on the flashlight on his porto and Thomas immediately gestured for him to put it away.

"Dude," Christopher said, peering down the path. "That's a Hayden."

"How can you tell it's a Hayden?" asked Luke.

As they slowly continued down the path, Thomas knew who they were approaching. He could feel it boiling in his blood. None of this made sense, not the message from Douglas or the fact that cadets would be sent out at night to find some first-year kid. Being here in Madison Square Park, the rage began seething inside him. Thomas knew the person he was walking toward just had to be Hadley. "It's her," he said, sure of himself.

"No way, man. What are you doing?" said Luke.

There she was, Hadley Hayden, a mess of a teenager sitting on a park bench at night. Alone and withered like discarded trash, exactly how Thomas expected to find her again.

"It's actually you," he said. He walked up so close to her that he was practically on top of her. "Time hasn't been very good to you."

With time, Thomas had grown to resent Hadley so much that the young woman he saw before him now was not worn and haggard enough for what his imagination allowed. He had hoped for her to look worse.

"This Hayden," Thomas said, watching fear creep into Hadley's eyes. "She tried to teach me a lesson."

"Haydens are scum," said Luke.

"Yes," Thomas said. "Yes, they are."

For weeks now, Thomas has thought about that moment, playing it over and over in his head. Hadley's terrified face lit by the city light that clawed through the laced tree branches overhead, the false bravado in her voice giving way to a quiver as she pleaded for forgiveness. But when she tried to point out their similarities as brother and sister...

Thomas still regrets the way he lost control of his emotions, the rush of power he felt when taking her porto and smashing it on the ground before her. Had he not been stopped, he doesn't know what he would have done.

Hadley kicked him in the knee and tried to run just as a stranger came out of nowhere and blindsided Luke. Thomas struggled with the man, never getting a good look at his face. He had on a peacoat and beanie. Thomas squirmed away and took off running. He leapt over the bushes to find Hadley pinned under Christopher.

"Run!" Thomas yelled and kept going. He didn't look back but would later learn that the man attacked Christopher with a small metal club.

Standing alone at attention out front of the MIND Academy cafeteria, Thomas once again thinks about that night as he waits for the rest to gather for their morning drills. He thinks about Hadley and wonders if they will cross paths anytime soon or if another seven years will pass before he has a chance to confront her. If she's still alive, that is.

As the world outside falls into chaos with a scrambled System, Thomas is thankful to know where he belongs and what is expected of him. Even if the System tells others that his name is something else, he knows that he is Thomas Karp, a young man of promise, a future agent, and top of the forty-third class at MIND Academy. He stiffens with pride just thinking about all that he has accomplished so far and the potential he has going forward. Nothing at all like some scumbag Hayden.

CHAPTER FIVE

Cammy Hayden sees blood. Sitting at her small desk in a corridor on the twelfth floor of Boylan, Boylan, Trapper, and Boylan, Cammy swipes at her iWindow to reschedule a meeting for her boss, Frances Boylan, daughter of partners Edna and Sydney Boylan and niece of partner Lawrence Boylan. As her finger slides across the iWindow in front of her, Cammy can see a smear of blood on the back of her hand. She quickly pulls her hand down and out of sight and covers it with her other hand. Only, when she looks at either hand again, there's no evidence of blood.

Uncle Larry, as Frances Boylan often refers to the fourth partner, walks by, and Cammy flashes a quick smile. Through the calendar and spreadsheet on her iWindow, Cammy can see Uncle Larry's stone face as he nods in passing. He's still warming to the Hayden in his office, even if her last name is no longer Hayden due to recent events. Over these last few days, Cammy has started to feel a sense of belonging that she simply couldn't when her last name was Hayden. It has taken her years to move up at Boylan, Boylan, Trapper, and Boylan and become Frances's assistant, having paid her dues in the data mining unit a few floors down, perhaps paying more than the average non-Hayden.

Cammy's role used to be to scan clients' System data and social media activity to flag incriminating evidence that would hurt their case. This involved reading posts and viewing pictures that seemed always to be either completely mundane or totally awful, but never in between. Her job also involved scanning purchases and location history, which was an easier task because it cut out the nuance of language and imagery. Cammy still wonders if any of her colleagues in data mining ever took the time to scan her history, suspicious of what that Hayden has done in the past. Of course, none of them ever had time. But if they did somehow find that time, they haven't yet said anything to her.

When Uncle Larry is gone, Cammy studies her hands again, checking under her nails and in the creases of her dry skin. No blood. She's been checking for days now. Can't help herself. She sees it on her face in the mirror. That woman she called Helen. Then it was Mandy. Then Norman. Then Dana. Cammy doesn't even want to know who she is now. She just wants to be somebody other than a Hayden for a little longer.

The messy life she has led thus far feels so distant now, if only she could stop seeing this blood or the man it belonged to. Not that she even participated. But she was there in the Junction and saw it all. Will they come after her when they hunt down the other Haydens who were there? Or will the System's failure keep her safe, the way she always wondered how non-Haydens lived? None of that matters if she can't get that awful moment out of her head.

—

When Reuben Mayfield forced his virus on the System, its effects reached everyone in System City at the same time just like any other scheduled update. But because it happened overnight, most people didn't notice until morning that their, or their loved one's, or their coworker's name had changed. Those in relative solitude, working from home or spending most of their time alone, might not have found out for days. For some, it might have at first felt like minor confusion. *I thought that news anchor's name was Max Neuland,* one might think, and then go about their day until running into the reality of the System's failure with somebody in their more immediate social sphere.

For Cammy Hayden, it happened at the very early hours of the morning, while she was still half asleep. Her roommate, Parnell Jones, with whom she shared a tiny studio apartment, was up early as usual to receive shipments at his floral shop in Harlem. Cammy awoke to the sound of Parnell's boots on the other side of the thin curtain that separated their sleeping areas from the rest of the apartment. When she emerged from her side to use the bathroom, Parnell's back was to Cammy and backlit by the open fridge where he stood. She kept her eyes nearly closed, hoping to maintain this half-slumber to the bathroom and back to bed for another few hours of sleep.

Neither said anything, as they were not very close. They had signed a lease together more than three years earlier and kept the arrangement because it worked for both of them. Shared rent without any of the drama. They weren't friends. More like neighbors who occasionally ate from the same takeout but not together. Any time shared in that one-room apartment was usually in their respective sleeping areas, each on their portos with ear pieces.

Cammy closed the door behind her and used the bathroom in the dark. Then she flushed before shuffling past the sink and mirror, using neither as she made her way back out of the bathroom. The apartment wasn't dark enough to impede navigation but enough to help Cammy keep that calm, sleepy fog in her head. As she emerged from the bathroom, she passed the kitchenette where Parnell was glancing at his porto. And in the corner of her eye, Cammy caught a glimpse of Parnell's face lit by his porto. She shuffled a few more steps, practically back to her sleeping area, before her brain told her who she saw. *Theodore Littleton?*

Her body lurched with adrenaline. "Who the hell are you?" she yelled. She grabbed a fake houseplant by its plastic leaves and swung its plastic-potted end at the intruder. The entire tall bamboo palm and its pot, in one unit, slipped from her hand and struck the stranger in his side before thumping against the fridge and sliding somewhere behind Parnell's curtain.

"What the hell, Cam?!" shouted Parnell.

Cammy backed away as far as she could in this tiny apartment, which gave her less than fifteen feet of distance from this man. "Get out," she said. "Parnell, you there?" She called to the other side of their shared curtain. "Parnell, we agreed, no guests!"

"Cam," Parnell said. "It's me." He stepped toward Cammy.

She pawed the top of a nearby shelf for another weapon but could only produce a small fan, which she lifted threateningly above her head, but it was still plugged into the wall. "Get back!" she yelled.

Parnell stepped to the door and turned on the light. "It's me, Cam. Holy crap. What's wrong with you?"

From across the room, Cammy could see Parnell's face. It was him, the same tall and slender and tired-looking man she'd lived with all this time. His hair was the same wild tuft of gray and black. She took him all in as familiar. But her brain still said that this was Theodore Littleton. Simultaneously, his face began to grow confused. His head cocked back and he began to say something but couldn't find the words.

"Who–" they both said at the same time. "You–" Again at the same time.

"No," he said.

"What?" she said.

"No," he said again. "Nope. Hell no."

"Theodore?"

"No!" Parnell barked, poking a finger at her. Flustered, he turned and opened the door, and then looked back at her one more time. His finger extended toward her again like this was somehow her fault, and he gave another stern "No." He left, shaking his head, and slammed the door behind him.

Cammy didn't know what to say and she couldn't bring herself to go after him. It hadn't occurred to her to look in the mirror. After all, this was something wrong with Parnell, not her. She climbed back into bed and glanced at her porto to find an onslaught of messages from Haydens across the city.

Help! Anyone else gone crazy?

So, this happened. I'm not a Hayden anymore.

What the hecks happening, yall?

Headn to Junction. Find out what happened.

Too many more pings to read through, some panicking, some joking and taking it in stride like Haydens often do.

Wide awake now, Cammy threw on pants and a sweatshirt and left for the Junction, where many of the city's Haydens live and hangout. The old abandoned subway junction is near Central Park on the Lower West Side. So, Cammy would have a long train ride from her apartment in Queens. The streets were still empty at 3 a.m. when she left for the train station. She found a car with only a few people sitting quietly. One seemed jittery, shaking his leg nervously as he flicked through his porto. He kept running his hand through his hair like he was high on something. He looked at Cammy and seemed to study her face. She braced for the usual scoff. When she didn't have to go to work, she often didn't care much about what she wore. Between her comfortable, old attire and her name, she was usually met with grimaces by people who see Haydens as lesser, second-class citizens. But this guy didn't make a face of disgust. Instead, his eyes showed sympathy before he looked back at his porto.

The closer she came to Manhattan, the more people boarded the train. As a late-night/early-morning crowd, people tended to keep to themselves. All of them alone. Cammy noted that she could get used to riding the train at this hour if it suited her work schedule.

At 50th, Cammy got off the train and walked the streets for a few more blocks before re-entering the subway tunnels to work her way down to the Junction. Being a Hayden, Cammy quickly got over any fear of walking alone at night or passing any dark alleys or doorways. She was considered one of the original Haydens, having survived by her grit and growing wisdom. Maybe buying into this reputation made her foolish, but she has survived longer than many.

Beneath the surface, her way gets darker but she doesn't yet use her porto for the flashlight until she gets even deeper. Non-Haydens would probably be able to guess their way to the Junction by following graffiti along the way. To gain access, you need to traverse dark and out-of-the-way passages deep under the existing subway line. Most people don't venture this far down, and graffiti is fairly scarce the deeper you go. However, once you reach any of the four known paths to the Junction, tags and symbols begin to appear. These aren't trail blazes as much as they are acts of opportunity for Haydens passing through.

Still at least two hundred feet down the east tunnel, Cammy could hear a crowd down in the Junction. Its domed concrete ceiling seemed to gather all those voices and send them like one big punch down each of the four tunnels. As she approached, and more light came into view, the dome of graffiti flickered dimly above what seemed to be the largest gathering of Haydens that Cammy had ever seen. While she saw this as a place she called home for several years, more and more her feelings toward the Junction and its inhabitants had become distant. Maybe she didn't understand the younger generation of Haydens but she started to question her place in this crowd.

What she walked into wasn't a normal party or hangout. Nobody had music playing. People weren't lounging around and smoking tobacco. Instead, everyone seemed confused, sad, angry, desperate for answers. A few Haydens had already twisted the news into an anarchist agenda, and they laughed from their corner of the group. There was another circle of speculators trying to make sense of what was happening. One Hayden, who used to be named Gwinny, was going on with a conspiracy theory about why so many Haydens were being found dead lately and what this had to do with MIND agents. Another Hayden, formerly named Monique, was explaining to a small gathering how the System works, giving some crude explanation of code and security operations. Everyone seemed to have a take on the matter.

Cammy felt the confusion and chaos right away as faces came into view and she realized their names weren't Hayden. Jerome Beale. Betsy Mathieu. Valerie Zimmerman. She knew these were Haydens. You basically had to be if you were the type to be in the Junction. But the System now said otherwise. As she weaved through the crowd, touching arms of people she was sure she knew, even if their names were completely unfamiliar, there was suddenly an outburst several feet away. Bodies were too close together for her to see what was going on. Then the crowd began to shift, people making room or getting closer. Cammy couldn't tell. But the crowd fell silent, and her friend Nona's voice could be heard shouting, "You can't be serious! Get over here."

Cammy saw Nona working her way over to a man that Cammy had never seen before.

"I can't believe it. You son of a bitch. Mayfield. Reuben goddamned Mayfield!"

Like some other Haydens over the years, Nona's story is tragic. Much of her personality–shyness and apprehension even toward other Haydens–can be traced back to a time in her life when she fell victim to a predator named Reuben Mayfield, a slimy rich guy with a history of luring young women back to his fancy apartment on the Upper East Side. Some of the other Haydens knew of him for the same reason. And somehow, apparently, Nona saw him in the Junction. Cammy wasn't normally quick to discredit Nona's feelings but the System wasn't working anymore. This man Nona was yelling at probably just got the name Reuben Mayfield, and Nona couldn't process the trauma.

"You've come to the wrong place," Nona yelled. "You don't know what you've done."

The man looked confused as he tried to back away from Nona. His eyes kept sweeping the room, looking for somebody to stop her.

Cammy moved closer, hoping to console Nona. It was then that

Cammy realized that the man's name wasn't Reuben Mayfield. His name was Lawrence Pinto. It made no sense at all but she suddenly believed her friend. For as many times as Cammy has seen Nona wake in a sweat and screaming, her friend must have had Reuben Mayfield's face burned into her memory. Given his age and the way he dressed, whoever this was had no place down here in the Junction. Nobody bothered to question that now though. Nona was bearing down on him, and the rest of the Haydens had her back. How he got there was no longer relevant. The only question now was how he was going to leave.

Cammy put her hand on Nona's shoulder, letting her know that everyone had her back. But it didn't seem to matter.

Nona stepped closer to Reuben Mayfield. With a flick of her hand, she snapped open a box cutter and said, "Welcome to the Junction."

She leapt onto her prey and started tearing at his clothes in a flurry of movements like she was some wild animal. Cammy and the others momentarily froze until the first sight of blood. Then several Haydens moved in to seize Reuben Mayfield from wriggling away.

Nona screamed and cried. But when the other Haydens had the man pinned, he gave up fighting. The terror in his face was nothing Cammy had ever seen before. "P-please," he said. "I am sorry."

"No, you're not," Nona growled, and she proceeded to tear open his shirt with her free hand. Others helped to expose his chest.

"We'll never be able to get rid of you," Nona said. Then, with more tedious precision, she brought the box cutter down on him. "And now I'll make sure you never forget us."

Cammy couldn't bear to look. She quickly turned away, like many others, as Reuben Mayfield cried for help. Others looked on, perhaps spellbound or maybe watching for closure. Cammy saw Hadley leaning in, a strange look of sympathy on her face. Empathy often burned Haydens, even if it was their greatest strength. So, it always struck Cammy with a sense of admiration and pity to see a fellow Hayden feel such a way.

Cammy glanced back toward Nona, maybe out of protection for

her friend or out of a need to see justice unfold in their favor for once. But she immediately regretted it, as Nona's blood-drenched hands came into view. The only sounds were Nona's heaving and Reuben Mayfield's sobbing. In a brief flash, she could see the bloody carving on his chest and stomach. It looked something like an old-timey computer or typewriter smeared in blood.

"That's enough," Cammy said. But Nona kept going. She touched a hand to Nona's back, and her friend paused just for a second.

"Nona," Cammy said, trying to sound calm. She placed both of her hands on Nona's shoulders until she stopped attacking. Cammy tried not to look at the blood-soaked pile of a man lying still before her. She already had blood on her arms from embracing Nona. Instead, she whispered, "You're okay," to Nona, and gently led her away through the crowd. "You're okay."

—

You're okay, Cammy thinks to herself. *We'll all be okay.* She's thinking about the other Haydens now as she peers distantly through her iWindow, past her boss's calendar and a spreadsheet of client contacts, to a frosted glass wall across the corridor where Uncle Larry, Edna Boylan, and Ronald Trapper (whatever their names are now) meet in a conference room. Cammy has been back to the Junction since that early morning of confusion and violence, only to find a few Haydens lazing about, ignoring the blood stain by the tracks at the center of the domed room. She wonders how they can just go on like nothing happened. But immediately she pities their need to move on, that Hayden necessity to survive.

Maybe it's a sign that she's become less Hayden-like but Cammy can't get those bloody images from her mind. Red smears appear on her hands and her arms. She's too afraid to ask what they did with Mayfield, if they buried him somewhere deep in the bowels of the subway tunnels or burned his body in a pyre. Is the evidence gone forever or will somebody come looking? If there's anything Cammy knows, it's that society is always looking for a chance to come down on Haydens.

CHAPTER SIX

Music plays an ominous chip tune.

An animated graphic splashes across the screen. The background is of 1s and 0s raining down in blurred green against a black screen. Then comes a crude icon of a computer chip, lines tracing away from it as the chip moves farther into the distance and the outline of a human head comes into view, the chip located roughly behind where the human ear would be. As the human outline and its chip move farther into the background, the lines trace away into all directions, passing through images of faces, some smiling and some serious. The lines continue on through more faces, all of them moving farther into the distance, creating a massive web of interconnected faces until it all dissolves into an aerial shot of System City.

A title fades into view. *The System: Are we really safe?*

A voiceover says, "Since its inception, the System's prime objective has been to keep the citizens of System City safe. But are we any safer now than we were before?"

Cut to raw footage of the first chipped baby. He looks no different than any other sleeping newborn. Hundreds of faces superimposed over the screen flicker faintly like memories.

"In a new report, we look at the history of the System and the heroes of innovation that brought it to life."

Cut to footage of a MIND official, a green screen background of the old MIND logo, before it was all caps. The official says, "We're steps away from a city so safe that we might as well call ourselves family." He smiles into the camera.

The voiceover says, "We'll trace the evolution of ideas…"

Cut to footage of people looking at a diagram on a screen. One person points and says, "Data beyond the edge," while the others nod. Cut to a man at a computer. Over his shoulder is a screen of code. He turns to look at the camera and force a smile. It's a young Reuben Mayfield.

The voiceover says, "…and a tangle of missteps."

Advertisements flicker across the screen. The same MIND official, a bit older and in front of a different version of the MIND logo, says, "Sustaining System infrastructure will continue to be a challenge but, in light of recent events…"

Cut to shots of an ambulance, police tape, a body. Cut to protestors marching with signs that read, *Keep ads out of my head* and *Brains aren't billboards.*

The MIND official's voice continues, "…we're suspending the pushed advertising program. Chips will now be ad free."

The voiceover says, "We will look at how we got to this point…"

Cut to footage from today. A woman looks into a news camera and says, "My own son doesn't even know me."

Screenshots of messages to a MIND emergency account pile up on the screen.

What's happening to my mind?

Please fix the System.

The voiceover says, "…what officials are doing to fix the problem…"

Cut to a different MIND official, in front of the current MIND logo, who says, "Everyone's patience is greatly appreciated as we continue to mitigate disruption as best we can."

The voiceover says, "…and the alternatives we may have to consider."

Cut to an anti-System advocate standing on the street outside of MIND headquarters. He says, "Our ancestors carried a driver's license. They had passports. They had no more problems than we have now."

Cut to a montage of scenes from across System City. Children at play in a park. Commuters filling the sidewalk.

The voiceover says, "And we try to uncover who is behind the System's unfortunate crash."

The 1s and 0s from before cascade down the screen but then melt like plastic in a fire. Images of faces careen across the screen, looking directly into the camera. Most of the images are of Haydens. Their names no longer align but judging by their appearance, most people could guess.

Cut to a man standing at his doorstep, talking to the news. He looks angry as he says, "We all know who did this and we need to do something about it."

More images of faces, mostly of Haydens, flash across the screen, flickering faster until the screen goes black. The man's voice can still be heard. "We need to stop them."

The title appears again. *The System.* And now in red lettering, *Are we really safe?*

The voiceover says, "Streaming on Thursday, only on SON Max. Order your flash load now."

CHAPTER SEVEN

Everything at the colony is as Paul left it. There is no mayhem or chaos anywhere near this small plot of land outside of the tragic mining town of Centralia, Pennsylvania, despite the violent episode that occurred before its founder and leader left with a hostage. But while Weston paces between the kitchen and cafeteria, he can't help but feel that everything is different now. Residents chatter like a cafeteria full of unruly children. Trevor and Renee are trying to explain everything to those who missed what happened outside and, as expected, everyone is confused. Weston knows that this wouldn't happen if Paul was here. He would have them rapt while holding court with some philosophical story that led to a motivational moral that might carry them through the day. And thinking about that now, Weston both misses Paul and feels slightly betrayed. There's no doubt that Paul's absence, and that he chose to leave, has already impacted the group. Now Weston wonders if the residents will look to him to fill those shoes.

Perhaps taking the helm will help with Weston's sudden sense of loss. It's not that he lost a friend or father figure but more that Weston realizes how Paul's departure leaves him without purpose. For nearly three years, Weston has been Paul's chief of staff, his right hand man, his consigliere. Weston executed what Paul asked, when Paul asked, and without question. For most of the residents, Weston was the first to meet them in person. He escorted newly-fried residents to the colony, led all supply runs, and chaperoned the group on excursions into the wild. He was Paul's conduit to the city, even caring for Paul's old apartment. Every few weeks, Weston would discreetly visit Paul's Upper East Side apartment to keep up the appearance that the place was occupied.

Until this day, Weston wondered if Paul was keeping the apartment to eventually return to the city. Paul never let on about his real name, Reuben Mayfield, or a checkered past with MIND agents. Weston figured that Paul had given up on the city for a simpler life in this remote Pennsylvania territory. Paul had the means and was certainly eccentric enough to keep an apartment he would never see again. But Weston realizes that he may not have truly understood his now former boss. And sometimes the distance at which Paul kept Weston was probably unkind. For instance, with all those trips to the city, especially to that apartment, Weston was never allowed to stay there overnight or even rest for a bit. He never kicked his feet up on the couch or had a glass of water. He only ran the taps to make sure the plumbing worked and the utility bill showed some water usage. Weston wonders if he would ever treat these residents the way Paul treated him.

Standing here like a substitute teacher with no control, Weston watches the residents talk over each other, waving their hands, debating why Paul would leave and take Hadley with him, or why there's a MIND agent tied to a chair outside at gunpoint, or who those soldiers are that came out of nowhere.

The door to the outside swings open and cool air rushing in, as the room suddenly goes quiet. The soldiers slowly enter to everyone watching. Across the residents' faces is a mix of wonder and fear.

"Who are they?" asks one of the residents who wasn't outside earlier. "Are these the two, what did you call them... watchers?"

Weston braces for panic and screaming. Instead, the room erupts again with chatter, ignoring the two strangers, as witnesses try to add their bits to what happened. The watchers, as everyone calls them, quickly survey the room and then approach Weston. Without words, the older one gestures for Weston to follow him into the kitchen.

Noise from the cafeteria goes muffled behind the closed kitchen door, and Weston feels pinned between a long steel table and the watchers who now have the doorway blocked.

"What happened out there?" Weston asks. "What did you do with him?"

"Who?" the younger watcher asks.

"Twenty-three eighty-eight," says the older one.

"Right," says the younger one. "He's gone."

Before Weston can say anything about how Agent Stevenson didn't need to die, the older watcher says, "We need to see Mayfield's office. He had some sort of command center, no?"

"I'll handle the residents," the younger one says, stepping to leave.

"Wait!" Weston says, fearful of more carnage. He quickly scans the room for a nearby weapon, maybe a kitchen knife. "There's no need to do that."

"Huh?" says the younger watcher, pausing before going back into the cafeteria.

"No!" Weston says, reaching to stop the younger watcher.

The older watcher steps in front of Weston. "Easy," he says, putting up a hand.

Weston has enough training that he could probably take this old man, but probably not the younger one. He would have to rely on the residents to jump in. He tries to push the old man's hand out of the way. But when that proves to be difficult, Weston gives up and pleads, "You can't just slaughter everyone."

"What?" says the older watcher. "Oh!" He suddenly starts laughing, which seems out of character to Weston. "We're not gonna kill anyone," the watcher says, composing himself. He steps out of Weston's way. "We need to get down to business. We should talk about how we'll run things from here on out."

Still confused, Weston says, "But Agent Stevenson?"

"We let him go," he says. "That's what Mayfield wanted, right?"

Weston remembers that was Paul's request. "But–"

"But what?" says the watcher. "Mayfield is gone. We have a colony to run. And the way we see it, you're the next in command."

A profound sense of importance and anxiety befalls Weston. Everything he has done for the colony and for Paul has brought him to this point, and now it's official–Weston is going to take over. But instead of an assured acceptance of his new duties, the only word Weston can utter is, "Okay." Fear, apprehension, maybe a dizzying mix of fight or flight battle for Weston's mind. As proud as he feels at this moment, all those feelings swirl and swirl, so much that Weston has no other words. "Okay," he mutters again.

"You should address the residents," says the watcher. "I think we should maintain business as usual. Have everyone keep their roles but give them the opportunity to leave."

"Okay," Weston says, still a bit stunned as this new reality has yet to settle in.

"Let's go," says the watcher, opening the door to the cafeteria.

"Okay."

They enter the cafeteria to find everyone surrounding the younger watcher. He doesn't have a gun in hand. While the group seems angered by what they've learned from Renee and Trevor, the watcher shows no fear of harm. "I do apologize, Mister... what was it?"

"Laars," says Laars, sitting with his leg up on another chair, his knee wrapped in pink bandages. "Maybe I had it coming," he grumbles.

"I was just following orders," says the younger watcher.

"Yeah, well," says Renee. "You didn't *have* to shoot him."

"I'm telling you all now," the watcher says, his hands up in surrender. "Our duties to Reuben Mayfield are hereby dissolved."

"I still can't believe you've been up there all this time," Trevor says. "Were you two just hanging out in those hills?"

"That's what Mayfield hired us for," says the watcher. "Again, just following orders."

"Wait, wait, wait," says Pete. "Where'd you sleep?"

"Yeah," says Renee. "Where did you eat? Did you come down here?"

"We did," says the watcher. "Sometimes."

"Folks?" says the older watcher, stepping into the group. "You all know Mr. Weston."

"Sure do," says Renee. "What's going on, Weston?"

"Have you heard from Paul?" asks Pete.

"Yeah," asks Trevor. "Is he coming back?"

The older watcher looks to Weston to address the group.

"People," Weston says, unsure of how to address them. "Thank you for gathering here." This is where Paul would shine. He knew how to grab people's attention. There was never a moment of hesitation with him. "I have some bad news," Weston says. He waits for them to present even a shred of the anticipation that they would normally show to Paul. When Weston realizes that they're more annoyed by his pause than captivated, he says, "Paul isn't coming back."

Residents look at each other in confusion. Renee says, "Yeah. So?"

Then chatter starts to creep across the group.

In a raised voice, Weston quickly says, "I'd like to maintain business as usual," borrowing from the older watcher's advice in the kitchen. The group quiets again. "Let's everyone keep their roles for now," he adds, "if that's okay."

When nobody says anything in response, Weston says, "Anyone looking for the opportunity to leave, please let us know now."

The room quiets again. People look at each other as if reading the room for how to react. Paul leaving the colony was never a thought, and rarely did anyone ever consider leaving themselves. For most, the colony is home. System City gave up on them the moment their chips stopped working. At the colony, the fried find their own. Paul formed a community of people who shared similar struggles. While many arrived with the idea that they would somehow be fixed or adjusted for a society that didn't accommodate them, the idea of actually returning to that society never seemed plausible.

"Go back to the city?" Trevor asks, almost as if testing the idea by saying it aloud. "You mean to say that we can just leave?"

Weston looks to the older watcher who flashes a quick grimace like it's up to Weston.

"Or you can stay and help us keep this place going," Weston says. "It's up to you."

Trevor looks to Renee, who looks to Pete, who looks back to Trevor. Residents nod at the idea of staying put.

"Okay," Trevor says.

"Okay," Weston says. As if it's decided, he gives a subtle fist pump and immediately regrets it. He tucks his hand away and smiles. "Okay," he says. "Okay."

CHAPTER EIGHT

Haddy toys with the flint and steel hanging from a leather cord around her neck. She doesn't hit them together to make a spark. Instead, she has one in each hand, tapping them lightly against the table between her and the MIND agent across from her.

"Planning to set a campfire, kid?" he asks with a tone of lazy condescension.

Haddy keeps tapping to a rhythm in her head. Nothing in particular that she can name but maybe something she heard Step's band once play.

"If we search you," he says, "will we find tobacco on you?"

"If you search me," Haddy says calmly, without looking at the agent, "I'll set *you* on fire."

The agent sits back in his seat. From what Haddy can gather, this guy was just the gofer, and now he's babysitting Haddy in this–she guesses from its blank white walls and hard metal chairs–interrogation room. He hasn't asked any meaningful questions and seems only to be biding his time for another agent, hopefully Agent Stevenson, to arrive. But Haddy knows that Agent Stevenson, dead or alive, is probably still tied up at the colony.

"Any chance I can get my porto back?" she asks, rapping the flint and steel against the table one last time before tucking them back under her sweatshirt.

The agent sighs and says, "Eventually. We're scanning it to see where you've been these last few weeks."

Haddy tries to play it cool but she feels naked without her porto.

More so, she wonders how much on that porto can incriminate her, or how deep these agents are willing to dig. Since the accident that fried her chip–an accident that she now knows MIND agents orchestrated–she's been recording her thoughts and experiences like a diary, perhaps to make sense of what was happening. Up until these MIND agents accosted her in Step's hospital room, Haddy recalled every moment she could remember each day, about how MIND agents were following her, how Reuben Mayfield–whom she knows as Paul–took her under his wing at the colony, and how Agent Stevenson became an unlikely ally. Everything she learned about the System, what MIND was doing to Haydens, and what Reuben Mayfield eventually did to the System, is buried in hours of audio that Haddy pieced together. How any of it will help or hurt her fellow Haydens is unclear. But like everything else in her life as just some subway kid, Haddy can expect that her actions will have little impact or influence on the world around her.

"You're fried," the agent says, a mix of curiosity and accusation in his voice.

Haddy doesn't respond but looks at her hands fidgeting over her lap.

The agent waits for her to say something but then shifts in his seat, glances at the door, and says, "Anyway, you're probably better off right now. I can't keep anyone straight anymore."

The room goes quiet again. The walls are bare and there's no telling what time it is. Haddy wonders why that's something they didn't program into the System. They let you pay to instantly flash load and binge an entire season of *Beirut Billionaire* so you can talk about it with your friends without actually watching it, but they can't program in the stupid time? Then she remembers how Paul explained that the System updates chips four times a day. So, she reasons, maybe the chip doesn't have an internal clock.

"What's on your mind?" asks the agent.

Haddy looks at the patchy growth of hair on his chin. He's maybe in his early thirties. Not that old, but that sort of longevity is a luxury for a Hayden. She thinks that if he's a MIND agent and he's been around long enough, he should know a thing or two about the System. And she's willing to bet he doesn't. "Tell me how they update the System," she asks.

The agent laughs. "What?" he says. "What do you mean?"

"What has to happen for the System to update?" she asks. "How does it update?"

"It just does," the agent says. "That's above my pay grade, kid."

Just then, the door swings open and the other agent who accosted her at the hospital brings back her porto and sets it on the table. He has on yellow-rimmed glasses that make him look almost sporty. The two agents look at each other, and the one standing shakes his head with slight disappointment.

"It's only been a few hours," says the agent sitting down. He reaches over and flips the porto screen up on the table. His hand hovers over it for a second, gesturing either to leave it there or something else that Haddy can't tell.

"We'll survey the locations," says the other agent with the glasses. The agent across from Haddy nods thoughtfully and the other agent leaves.

Haddy looks at her porto without reaching for it and says, "Can I?"

"No," says the agent, matter of fact.

Since she isn't in handcuffs or zip ties, Haddy decides to test her limited freedom and stands up. The agent doesn't stir. She drags her chair loudly away from the table, turns it toward the wall, and sits. She puts both feet on the wall and pushes herself far enough back to still allow her feet to be propped up with her heel against the wall, her chair teetering back just so.

The agent watches her, probably judging her balance, and says, "Wanna tell me where you've been?"

"When?" asks Haddy.

"Let's start with last night," he says.

"So, you're not my babysitter?" she asks, seeing now that he's willing to start prying.

"What's that?" he says.

"Nothing," she says, and she looks at the already chipped nail polish on her fingers. She had gotten gussied up for her dinner with Step but now her fingernails look like trash. "Where's Agent Stevenson?" she asks.

"Who?"

This annoys Haddy but she's not going to bother asking again. There are plenty of agents, and no reason for this one to know all the others.

"Were you with Reuben Mayfield?" asks the agent. He leans over the table and rests his weight on his folded arms in deeper attention. "You know we're looking for him now." He gestures toward the door, as if to the agent who was just here.

What can she tell this agent? That Paul fooled her into false hope of being rehabilitated? That he's a monster that preys on Haydens? The whole drive back to the city from the colony, all she wanted to do was throw the car off a bridge and end him. Even if it meant killing her too. The damage Reuben Mayfield caused can be seen on the faces of so many Haydens. But she can't say any of that now because of what happened early this morning at the Junction. What Nona did to Mayfield in front of everyone. Haddy isn't sure if this agent really knows that they were together. Anything she says now might implicate her in what happened.

But before she can muster any response, the agent gestures to Haddy's porto and says, "Based on your previous conversations, we're fairly certain that Mayfield is going by the name Paul." He lightly pushes the porto with one finger. "You'll see that you've sent some messages to him in the last hour."

"Is that what they were doing back there?"

"He didn't reply," the agent says.

"So, I'm the bait," Haddy says. She wonders if they now suspect that he's not replying because he's dead. Perhaps out of guilt and a need to justify what Nona did, she says, "Do you even know what he's done to us Haydens? The vile things he's inflicted on young, innocent girls?"

"Innocent," the agent chortles.

Haddy kicks her chair back away from her and the metal rattles loudly against the concrete floor. "Damn right, innocent!" she yells. "Chaste as hell compared to that... that predator!"

The agent settles back in his seat, seemingly unfazed.

"And you," she says, standing over the table now, a finger extended at the agent. "All of you. How many Haydens have you killed to... just to, I don't even know?" She's referring to how the System updates itself. As Paul explained it, in order to update the identity recognition program, the database is opened every six hours for a nanosecond to push through new code, including deaths, births, and other information. Only, to keep that pathway secure, the password to open it is randomized and unknowingly entered by some unlucky person. They receive a ping with a seemingly nonsensical message. Subconsciously, they understand whatever it says and reply with something their brain is telling them to say. And that opens the pathway.

Only, to keep it completely secure, at some point MIND decided that the person who unknowingly opened the pathway, which they can't even access themselves, must be eliminated. And it appears that the latest candidates have all been Haydens.

"We're not concerned with you," the agent says.

"Don't I know," says Haddy. "You tried to kill me and now I'm fried."

"Is that what happened?" he says. Haddy doesn't believe that he's so naive.

She walks away again to the wall opposite him, puts her back against the wall, and slides down to sit on the floor. "You've killed so many people for nothing. For some stupid System."

There's something in the agent's face that changes and Haddy can't quite place it. It's not compassion but it's some strange mix of sorrow and maybe obligation. "You know a lot about the System, don't you," he says.

"Maybe," she says, trying to assert her position.

"Okay," he says, nodding with some respect. "So, Reuben Mayfield needed you?"

"I don't know," she says. "He certainly used me."

"Oh?" he says. "Why you?"

Haddy knows that if she wants this agent to believe her, she has to make it clear what she knows about the System. But that also makes her a liability to MIND. "How am I supposed to know? Maybe because I'm a Hayden," she says.

"Maybe," says the agent, nodding like he's following her logic.

"He's a sicko," Haddy says.

"You seem to know him well enough," the agent says. He stands and comes around the table. He half sits on the table and crosses his legs at the ankles. "I'm going to be straight with you, okay?"

"Sure, yeah."

"You know those crime series that are so popular?"

"Yeah," she says. "With stupid scenes like what we're doing here."

"Sure," he says, laughing a little. "Those detectives are always gathering in some room at headquarters, looking at diagrams of perpetrators and victims on some big screen."

"Leaping to conclusions in an instant," she adds. "When we all know that real cops are dumber than a box of hair."

The agent laughs. "Everyone is the smartest person in the room," he says. "They finish each other's sentences. They're talking to each other but they all seem to already know the answer."

"Yeah," Haddy says. "What about them?"

"Well, you see," he says. "Reuben Mayfield *is* the smartest person in the room. Any room."

She knows this firsthand. Never before has she felt so inferior to somebody, even while simultaneously feeling disgusted and enraged.

"What you're describing about your friends," he says. "What we apparently tried to do to you." He points to his head. "He's the architect."

With everything awful about Paul, the man everyone knows as fugitive Reuben Mayfield, Haddy still doesn't believe that he would be capable of architecting somebody's murder. "I don't know," she says. "That doesn't sound like his idea."

"No," says the agent, nodding. "It probably wasn't his idea. That sort of decision is way above any of our pay grades, even for a very well compensated genius like Mayfield. But he certainly made that decision a reality."

The agent steps toward Haddy. "He did awful things to your friends," he says. "I understand that. We've seen his file."

"He's a monster," Haddy says, angrily, disgusted at the thought of what he did to Nona and others. The image of Nona carving Mayfield with a box cutter flashes before her eyes. As much as she doesn't want to, she savors the violence for a moment. She closes her eyes and composes herself. She can't let on that she knows Mayfield is dead. When she opens her eyes again, the agent is crouched down right in front of her.

"I know," he says, softly. "I know. But he's also the only person who can fix the damage he has caused." He extends Haddy's porto to her and says, "And you're the only one who can flush him out of hiding."

She doesn't take her porto right away. "I can't do that" she says, knowing that the only thing she would lead them to is his body, if it still exists.

"We installed a tracker on this," he says, extending her porto to her. "Take it and you're free to go. We'll know everywhere you're going. Just lead us to him."

"Why would I help you?" Haddy takes her porto and turns it over in her hands. It looks the same as before.

The agent stands up and starts toward the door. "You know a lot about the System," he says. He opens the door to leave. "Seems to me you could have done all this on your own."

"I'm not your scapegoat," she says, standing up.

"Then bring us Mayfield," he says, leaving the room and letting the door close behind him.

Haddy goes to the door and tries the nob. The door opens. The hall is empty in both directions. She taps her porto screen to see what's changed. Nothing evident. She goes to her messages with Mayfield and sees her last communication with him before going to the colony. She was offering to bring him Step's porto.

Her heart sinks at the thought of Step in the hospital and what happened to him at the restaurant. She knows this is all her fault and wishes that there was something she could do.

After that message are two more messages from her that Mayfield (or *Paul*, as her screen says) hasn't replied to. They were sent today and written by MIND agents to lure him out. The first one reads, *I need your help.* It may not be something Haddy would write but it sounds enough like her to be convincing.

The second message reads, *57th and 9th. 3:00pm tomorrow.* That's close to the Junction and not somewhere Haddy would ever want to meet him, let alone any non-Hayden. If anything, she would have picked Joseph Brant Circle at 59th and 8th. The only thing she can think is that this is about where her GPS signal cut out, because it's below this spot that Haydens are able to descend deeper into the old subway lines. To MIND agents, her movement must have stopped at this point, a mysterious and abrupt termination in her GPS record.

No matter. Haddy knows that going there is pointless, since Paul isn't alive to even show up. Still, she wonders what might happen to her if she doesn't at least play along. She'll need to buy some time anyway. If MIND finds out that Paul is dead, they'll hunt down Haydens one by one, using justice as their excuse. In either case, Haddy is in the crosshairs.

CHAPTER NINE

News anchor, Max Neuland, looks into the camera and says, "Tonight, you'll notice a new format, one we've only seen in classic footage from long ago. You see my birth name, Max Neuland, at the bottom of the screen." He says this gravely, like it's one of the biggest hurdles of his career. "This is just one of the many changes we have to make in this new world we live in. Please don't let these changes affect you. We're all coping together."

He composes himself and says, "We come to you with breaking news from MIND headquarters. Chelsea O'Brien is on the scene."

Cut to Chelsea O'Brien, her name presented at the bottom of the screen in orange text, standing near the curb outside MIND headquarters.

"Thanks, Max," she says. "I'm outside MIND headquarters where MIND Director Arthur Klopek just addressed a crowd of concerned citizens. Before we roll footage from that speech, it appears that MIND is taking a two-pronged approach. We're told that efforts to restore the System are still underway. Meanwhile, as Director Klopek addresses in his remarks, MIND is ramping up efforts to find those responsible for this attack on the identity recognition program."

Cut to Arthur Klopek, standing at a lectern, his name in orange text at the bottom of the screen. "We have reason to believe that this was an organized attack," he says. "Intelligence suggests that this was done by an organization with the purpose of betraying our sense of security. We have reason to believe that this group has a distinct interest in masking their identities, more than likely to carry out nefarious behaviors under the cloak of anonymity."

Klopek pauses for effect. "I'd like to speak with you candidly. Despite the System's efforts to keep us all safe, we are a city divided." He looks at the crowd before him. "But we don't have to be. We can be great. We can make System City safe again." The crowd cheers in support.

When the noise settles, Klopek continues. "I'm asking you to do your part. Good citizens of System City, I'm asking you to stay vigilant. A party that takes aim at the System is an enemy to us all."

The crowd applauds with more energy.

"Please do your part in making this great city safe again," he says. "If you see something, say something. Thank you." Klopek waves to a cheering crowd as he steps away from the microphone.

Cut back to Max Neuland. "Thank you, Chelsea," he says. "Arthur Klopek is an inspiration." To the camera, Max Neuland says, "Let this bring hope to all of you watching tonight. We're all dealing with this horrific attack in different ways. But we're all in this together. Be on the lookout. As Director Klopek says, 'Do your part.' We'll root out the enemy together and make System City safe. Good night."

CHAPTER TEN

From her sister's apartment in the Bronx, Miss Ula Mae takes a bus to a train to another bus that brings her within a block of Hayden House, where she has a small apartment in the basement. Nearly all her time is spent running Hayden House. But on Tuesday evenings, she visits her sister, Dora June, and nephew, Ronny, with whom she plays Up the River, Down the River and gets to enjoy Dora June's home cooking. This week they talked only of how crazy things have gotten with the System being down. Dora June said everyone at her office is on edge and second guessing each other. Ronny kept repeating, "Thank goodness for my uniform," which he wears every day on his delivery route.

"Can't get by on good looks alone," Dora June said, laughing.

Miss Ula Mae thinks about that comment all the way back to Hayden House. She also thinks about how her girls are fairing under these newest of normals. In a way, she knows that the Hayden name, as proud of it as she is, may often be seen as a uniform. Only, to many, that uniform is more like a prison jumpsuit.

Walking from the second bus, Miss Ula Mae feels the weight of her leftover dessert shifting in a bag as it hits against her leg. A small price to pay for such a delicious treat. Dora June's homemade apple crisp is made from apples that Ronny brings back from the northern territory where he trades with local tribes along his delivery route. He drives for a textile company called Multirobe Technologies. His company has vendors up along the Hudson River, as far as the Catskills, where the land is perfect for farming. Visiting her sister on

Tuesdays is one of the few chances Miss Ula Mae has to access fresh produce that Ronny brings home.

Before she even reaches the brick highrise, Miss Ula Mae can see spray paint across the Hayden House entrance and ground floor windows. She can make out the crude lettering of *Die Haydens* and *Hayden Trash.* Some windows are broken, and Hayden House staff has already patched them up with tarps and duct tape.

"I didn't want to bother you," says Vicky, the night manager. She has doughnuts for the night staff's end of shift. "You'd have come back here in the middle of the night, and for no reason but to get all riled up."

"Are the kids alright?" Miss Ula Mae asks. They go inside and make their way to the staff lounge, which is just Miss Ula Mae's living room.

"They're fine," Vicky says. "A few woke to the glass breaking and we calmed them down before they made trouble."

"Did you see who did this?" Miss Ula Mae puts her dessert in the fridge and drops her night bag in her bedroom. She can see something splattered on the outside of her fogged window. It looks like feces.

"GCs, I'm sure," says Vicky.

"Not so good, these citizens," says a staffer named Ian, as he walks in. He sees the doughnuts and immediately helps himself. "They're getting worse."

Hayden House has always suffered vandalism, and hate groups have long made it their mission to punish Haydens. According to these people, if Haydens are outcasts from their own homes, then they will apparently always be outcasts. Compounded by a lack of social support from the city, Haydens often end up on the street to carve out whatever living they can make and sometimes resort to petty crime.

"This too shall pass," says Miss Ula Mae. She has seen this sort of behavior, maybe even worse, in her decades at Hayden House.

"I don't know," Ian says through a bite of custard-filled doughnut. "Talk to some of these kids who've been out there these past few days. It's heating up."

"These groups are empowered," Vicky says. "Have you seen what that MIND fella is saying?"

"Is anybody coming back hurt?" Miss Ula Mae asks. "Have you heard from any hospitals?"

"Fortunately, no," Vicky says. "Though, with the way things have gone, hospitals aren't able to identify everyone so easily." She glances at the box of doughnuts, ponders which one to take, and then practices restraint. "I'm worried we're only seeing the beginning of it."

Miss Ula Mae steps close to Vicky and puts her hands on Vicky's arms. "One day at a time," she says. "We're going to be okay. Why don't you go home and rest up."

"Sure," Vicky says.

"I'll be here tonight too," Miss Ula Mae says. "If you want, I can find room in the budget to ask others to work overtime the next few days."

"No," Vicky says. "I don't want that."

"We'll board up the windows before I leave," Ian says.

"Thank you, Ian," Miss Ula Mae says. "Have another doughnut." She leaves her two staff members in the lounge and heads upstairs to do some quick rounds before the kids all wake up.

Early morning is one of her favorite times of day because she can go upstairs and catch the babies sleeping. Seeing all those little onesies in cribs and the toddlers tangled up in their blankets just seems to ground Miss Ula Mae and brings her a rare moment of calm. They all look so peaceful and warm. Miss Ula Mae can't help but feel bad for these babies and the future they'll have to endure if they aren't adopted. But so few are.

Back when she started at Hayden House, under the direction of Laura Hayden, it was just an adoption service that housed infants and toddlers. They endured the normal troubles of finding homes for children in a city with increasing population density. For a time, Laura Hayden traveled far outside System City to find them families. With repatriation, tribes were reacquiring massive swaths of land. People who didn't belong to the tribe, as well as several who did, had to choose between allegiance to the tribe's governance or move away, usually to the nearest city. Tribal territories are no less advanced, at least where they've grown around smaller metropolitan settlements. But places like System City benefit from more developed infrastructure from generations past. These large hubs of innovation and employment have lured more and more residents.

Laura Hayden founded Hayden House a few years before the city enforced the Foundational Acceptance of Male Infant Legacy Yield Act, or FAMILY Act—more commonly known as the One Child Rule. Before the One Child Rule, she had the leisure of dedicating personal time to connect infants with families. She would often travel to territories in Upstate New York, New Jersey, or Pennsylvania, and meet with families that struggled to have children of their own. Many of these families had land to maintain or they were part of communes that sought to develop villages into towns or towns into small cities. So, as disingenuous as it was, Laura Hayden centered her appeals around the potential for future labor.

But once the One Child Rule was passed, the Hayden House population exploded, forcing her organization to move into a larger building with a bigger staff. Young Ula Mae began working there in her late teens as a daycare assistant. She was born prior to the rule and raised with her sisters Dora June and brother Augusta July in a loving family. Throughout school, she aspired to be a civil meteorological engineer like her father. It fascinated her to see how buildings were retrofitted to withstand the dynamics of altitude and accelerated climate destabilization.

"My daddy helps pop the tops of buildings," she liked to say as a kid.

Throughout her childhood, she could see buildings around her that had stood the test of time from old New York grow taller and taller. Only once, when she was very young, did her father take her to see a project in action. She doesn't remember now what building that was, only that, when she emerged from the temporary lift at the top, a constant rush of cold wind felt like it would carry her away. Like the workers, she had to be tethered by rope to cables that ran along all the rigging at the top. This brief visit left the lasting impression that her father worked in a different world from that on the street. Up there, buildings didn't shield people from the harsh effects of weather. On the street, it would be hard to tell that climate has changed so drastically from the old days if it weren't for rising shorelines that encroach on subway tunnels and low lying streets.

Ultimately, Young Ula Mae took the job at Hayden House for extra spending credit while she finished up high school. But as she watched Laura Hayden struggle to care for the constant influx of babies, Ula Mae dedicated more and more of her time. She didn't struggle to finish high school but by then her heart was already fully invested in helping the "Hayden Girls," as she liked to call them. Within a few years, she became Director of Early Childhood Education, and would eventually become Assistant Director to Laura. And when Laura passed, Miss Ula Mae took over as Director of the entire organization. By this point, in her early thirties, Miss Ula Mae had raised hundreds of children, dozens of which were now adults.

It was around this time that she started to see some backlash from concerned citizens, or as many liked to call themselves "good citizens." Hayden girls quickly began referring to them as GCs for short. A fear had been stoked by MIND officials who warned of rising criminal behavior. Public announcements from MIND became dog whistles that spoke of those "sirens of unsavory intent," which everyone knew to be those Hayden girls who now roamed the streets. Where a Hayden might have previously been able to find employment like anyone else, or date and marry like anyone else, or just live normally, it now became harder to get beyond the stigma of their last name. Segregation was never made official but it became commonplace to look the other way from discrimination, be it in employment, at school, or at a restaurant. The System helped perpetuate a belief that Haydens were lesser people until it was no longer a backlash but a way things were.

Accordingly, Miss Ula Mae started to prepare her girls for a life under this new normal. Hayden House schooling didn't change. The girls weren't pushed into any form of training to deal with the adversity of life in System City. But when the older kids ran away and eventually returned with stories of violence and hate, Miss Ula Mae didn't stop those stories from spreading to the younger girls. If they were at a park during a day out, she wouldn't shield her girls from witnessing how older Haydens were treated, or how GCs looked at them with pity or disdain in passing. After all, they would have to get used to it.

But as she hears MIND officials like Arthur Klopek echoing the inflammatory rhetoric of the past, stoking fires where embers have never stopped smoldering, she can't help but worry for these peaceful little babies and how unfathomably bad their future might be.

As she scans their beautiful faces, and names come to mind like Kailey Everette, Greta Opinsky, and Frederick Weingartner, she can't help but find a little hope beneath the sadness. If the System never rights itself, she thinks, will these darling little girls grow up to be doctors and civil meteorological engineers? Or will they always be Haydens, no matter their name?

CHAPTER ELEVEN

Preston Blake's swollen red face looks like it's going to pop. When he speaks into the microphone, spit occasionally arcs away from his chapped lips and nearly hits the camera. The fact that he records video of his rants is purely self-serving, since most of his audience either listens to his show or flash loads it for a quick bump of hate in the morning.

"Welcome to *What's the Matter?* I'm your host as always, Preston Blake, and here's what's the matter. Street trash. Gutter punks. Nasty derelicts. That's what's the matter."

He takes a drink from a can of Cougar Drops energy drink. When he sets the can down, he adjusts it so the label is visible to the camera. "You know who's the matter. You know who I'm talking about. It's not *system savvy* to call them by name. I might get in *trouble*. But we all know. We all know."

He adjusts the microphone like a nervous tic.

"Let's do a little thought experiment," he says. "Let's imagine that every single one of them is rounded up tonight and thrown in jail. Sounds good, right? We take every single one of those girls... you know, they say they're kids. You got all these bleeding-heart goodies down there at the Hell House or whatever they call it. They're all crying, 'We're just kids. We're just kids.'"

He makes a crybaby face, pulls the microphone closer.

"We know what they're up to. These aren't kids. They're adults. When you pull the stunts they do–smash and grabs that leave a poor mom-and-pop grocery with a mess to clean up; robbing a family just strolling through Central Park; home invasions. They happen all the time! These are adults. That's what I say. These are nasty gutter punk women. If you want to play tough, beat on some unsuspecting little, old grandma... well, then you'll be treated like an adult. A sick one at that. Lock 'em up!"

He adjusts himself in his seat, sits back, and looks into the camera.

"You know what I'm talking about. What did I read the other day? Forty-three percent of all commuters say that they've had a confrontation with one of these *adult* girls in the last year. I'm sure it's *many* more than that. These things tend to be underreported. We all know that. We all understand."

He sits forward like he has a brilliant point to make, then adjusts the microphone like it will make a difference.

"I'll tell you what I think. I think it's one hundred percent. These girls affect every single one of our lives. Every one of us is robbed by the entitlement of these... these street thugs. Who do you think pays to feed and raise these little monsters in that Hack House? You and me. Credit taxes at their worst. And... and don't get me started on what all these girls are doing to make a living now. We keep subsidizing their lives well into adulthood. But they're out on the street terrorizing good people, good citizens like you and me."

He sits back like he's giving up. Shakes his head.

"Lock 'em up. That's it. That's all we can do. And then–"

He lurches forward again.

"But then we're still paying for their food! We're still footing the bill for their housing and well being. Where does it end?"

He looks into the camera.

"Where does it end, my friends?"

His eyes go wide. "I almost forgot!" He pulls a baseball cap from under the table and puts it on. The cap is white with red lettering that reads *MIND Over Matter.*

"Join my new community of good citizens–MOM," he says, and

points to the cap on his head. "MIND Over Matter is raising credit to fund police and MIND agents who have been hurt in the line of duty. Now that crime is on the rise, we have to look out for our brothers in arms just like mom would. MIND Over Matter is here to help. If you care about what's the matter. If you want to stop these thieves and heathens from ruining our city and taking more lives, then join MOM."

He pulls the hat from his head and positions it for a close up in front of the camera.

"Donations of one hundred credit or more to MOM will get you a free MOM hat like this. Scan the code now at the bottom of the screen or ping PrestonBlakeMatters, all one word, to post your credit where it matters."

CHAPTER TWELVE

Step doesn't understand why Haddy is pacing along the curb at 57th and 9th but she is a welcomed sight. Feeling weak from being at the hospital for days, Step just wants to reach the Junction and hunker down for a while.

"Haddy," Step calls, crossing over to see her.

She seems on edge, pacing and rubbing her hands together. She doesn't hear Step at first. When she does, Step has already reached her.

"What's good?" Step asks.

"Step!" she shouts and throws her arms around him. "I'm so glad you're out."

They give each other a squeeze and Haddy sizes up her friend.

"Hospital food," she says, smiling stupidly. "Good stuff, huh?"

The food wasn't all that good but it was plentiful. Step hasn't felt this full in months.

"You coming down?" Step asks, assuming that Haddy is on her way to the Junction. There aren't a lot of reasons for a Hayden to hang around this area, unless they're slinging tobacco or running some other hustle. And doing it here, so close to a common Junction entry point, is just a bad move.

"I'm good. I'm good," she says, nodding almost without realizing it. Her eyes dart around like she's tweaking on some drug. But Step knows she's not into that stuff.

"Come on," Step says, waving her to follow.

"No," she says quickly. "Stay here. Hang with me."

"Nah," Step says. "I'm just going to crash for like a few weeks."

Haddy laughs but then looks really serious. She glances over her shoulder. They're standing in front of a small grassy area with a name that Step can't remember. But everyone calls it Ballsy Park. The real name is something similar. Haddy sits on a short wall where the grass begins and pats the spot next to her for Step to sit down.

"I'm good," Step says. "For real. I just need to rest."

"Sit," she says, more serious. Then she playfully pats the spot next to her again.

Step sits. The two stay like this for a moment as cars and people go by.

"We good?" Step asks and stands. Haddy yanks his arm to sit down again.

Step watches as Haddy nervously scans the street each way, and looks intently across the intersection in every direction. Then she drops her head and mutters something.

"What's that?"

"I said, don't go down there," she says, but without moving her mouth.

"Why?"

"They're watching us," she says in mostly vowels.

"Who's watching us," Steps says, mimicking her unclear speech.

She shushes Step. They sit in silence for a minute. Haddy looks at her porto for the time. "Maybe we should go," she says.

"Maybe," Step says.

"But not down there," she says.

"Where then?"

"Maybe I can talk to Cammy," Haddy says and stands. She starts walking and Step follows.

After the first block, Haddy seems to relax a bit. She stops looking over her shoulder and slows down to a more casual stroll. Step doesn't understand what's going on but she has been through a lot over the last few weeks, ever since the accident that left her fried. Step tries to remember her accident every time she starts to get annoying or does something to get them in trouble.

"Maybe I should just go straight to Nona," she says to herself.

"What for?" Step asks. "What's going on?"

They reach 57th and take a left to work their way east across town. Haddy has a more determined stride and Step works to keep up.

"What do you need from Nona?" Step asks. "Or from Cammy?"

"I need to find Paul's apartment," Haddy says.

"Paul?"

Haddy stops suddenly and says, "Reuben Mayfield. I need to find his apartment."

The name comes out of nowhere like a sucker punch. "No way, Haddy. No!"

"I have to, Step." Haddy starts walking again.

"You can't just ask Nona about that disgusting prick."

"I know," she says. "But I... I have to do something."

"Why? What's going on?"

Just past Carnegie Hall, Haddy stops and seems to be gathering her thoughts. She pulls out her porto, steps over to a building and leaves the porto on the window sill resting precariously on top of a strip of pigeon deterrent spikes. She walks intently away, grabbing Step's arm. At a decent distance from her porto, she softly says, "I'm being watched."

Cars swiftly pass along the street behind Step. The sidewalks are alive with passersby, their heads down as they march to some destination or another. It's hard to believe that decades ago, these same sidewalks were apparently full of wide-eyed tourists gazing up at all the big, shiny buildings. Those seem like simpler times, Step thinks. It's crossed Step's mind more than once to ask the wizard for some sort of power to travel back in time. Even Step knows that's a silly thing to hope for.

"Is somebody following you?" Step remembers the nurse mentioning something about men taking Haddy away. "Are you in trouble?"

Haddy takes a deep breath and gathers herself. "What's my name?" she asks.

"Uh," Step says. "Haddy. Hadley. Why?"

"What is it right now?"

"I mean, I'm being told it's Winona Hewett. But I know it's–"

"Mayfield did that," she says.

"Did what? Messed up the System?"

"Yes," she says. "Well, he built it, actually. But he also screwed it all up on us."

"Okay." Step says. "Wait, how do you even know that? What have you been up to?" Already, Step realizes that Haddy must have done what she does best, and that's plant her foot in another mess. And Step is done with messes. Being a Hayden is hard enough as it is. "You know what? I don't want to know. Forget it."

"Look," she says. "It's a long story, and I really really *really* want to tell you everything." She gets close to Step like she wants a hug or something. But Step is feeling vulnerable and confused. Something seems really off with Haddy.

"But right now," she says, "MIND is on me because they think I can lead them to Reuben Mayfield."

"Can you?"

"No," she says. In a smaller voice, she says, "That's the thing. I have no idea where he is. And if they don't have him to pin all this craziness on, they're going to put this on me."

"What?" Step asks, shocked by the absurdity of this thought. "They'll say that you took down the System?" It doesn't even make sense as Step asks it.

With deadpan eyes, she says, "Yes. That's what they told me. And they put a tracker on my porto."

Haddy can be dramatic sometimes. She brings a lot of heat on herself, and sometimes she's been known to escalate situations. But Step knows that she never lies about danger. Haydens don't do that as a general code, and Haddy is among the best at treating imminent peril with pragmatism, even if she also brings that danger on herself.

Basically, like Step, she cuts the bull.

"What do you know?" Step asks. "No. Forget it. I don't want to know." Step realizes that knowing what she knows won't get them anywhere but in deeper trouble. Head in hands and unable to make sense of the situation, Step says, "Okay. Fine. What do you need from me?"

"That's what I want to hear," she says. "Thank you."

A lifetime of owing Haddy has led Step into far too many bad situations. But she's Step's best friend.

Step watches as Haddy trots back to her porto, grabs it, and jogs by again saying, "Let's go see Cammy. Come on!"

CHAPTER THIRTEEN

Coming off a seemingly unmaintained country road, main street Hackettstown feels as revitalized as a small town can get. Everything is clean. Trees and shrubs are manicured. No debris or litter like in System City. Buildings range from the late 1800s to today, save for some unaccounted decades when everything built seemed to mimic another time. Newer, larger concrete buildings contrast with the quaint, worn brick of older storefronts. Each facade features a vibrant color, creating a rainbow that leaves Agent Stevenson to wonder if these paint colors serve some symbolic purpose for the Lenape community that lives here.

His zipbike's battery died just off the main route back to System City, and Agent Stevenson has pushed it more than a mile over rolling hills to find this oasis in the countryside. Most territories this distance from System City have modern amenities to charge zipbikes. At least he hopes.

There are cars parked along the street, while others roll past in no hurry. He can't see if they're moving slowly to study him or if this is the casual speed they normally go. *Half-speed*, he thinks. Life seems simpler here. While he doesn't know what their economy is based on or what it is that people here do, he imagines it to be an easier life.

Some people come out of a shop down the way, and Agent Stevenson, with his zipbike alongside him on the sidewalk, doesn't attract their attention. He keeps pushing it until he finds a suitable place to park it. He takes a moment to remove his gloves and catch his breath. The main street stretches a few blocks in each direction with only a few side streets to offer more commerce. He finds this somehow comforting, if not appealing.

Normally he doesn't stop to consider his surroundings so intently when danger isn't present. In fact, Agent Stevenson hasn't casually taken in a setting like this in quite some time. He watches people, maybe the places they go or what they do in those places. But he has never actually admired the architecture or ambience of a given location until now. And it strikes him as a place he hopes to return to one day. He even imagines himself strolling down this sidewalk, giving a friendly nod to people as he passes.

But for now, he has a mission: find Reuben Mayfield. Once that is complete, maybe then Agent Stevenson will consider another path in life. What led him to tracking Mayfield was unexpected at the time. And he knows enough to be open to what might speak to him next. Maybe it's in Hackettstown. Maybe somewhere else.

What he knows above all is that his sense of purpose depends too heavily on the welfare of others. As a MIND agent, it was the safety and security of the citizens of System City. Eventually, with the tangential help of Hadley Hayden, his focus narrowed on the safety of Haydens, who just so happened to be Mayfield's primary prey.

Like many agents-in-training, Agent Stevenson put his all into being the best servant he could be. Finishing 88th in his class may have been slightly disappointing but being among the one hundred newly appointed agents out of 147 classmates was a high point in his life.

Never would he consider himself a great agent compared to some of his colleagues and contemporaries. But he felt competent, if not sometimes essential. Within a year on duty, he was promoted from Agent Constable to Agent Operative within the Department of Investigations. His authority grew along with his responsibility, both of which he accepted with tremendous pride.

If there was one area in which he felt–rather, he was told–he could improve, it was his personality with citizens. Often he was recommended, and eventually assigned, training in interpersonal relations. Many agents required training in de-escalation. That wasn't Agent Stevenson's problem. If anything, he showed such a disconnect with people that he could neither escalate nor de-escalate a situation. He was mostly an observer, and a very good one at that. When he finally engaged a person, he often had them dialed to within a pixel of their character and, often, their motivation or intent. But beyond that, he was no good with people.

When courses in interpersonal relations and communications didn't seem to affect his demeanor, his supervisor recommended he be "promoted" to a new department that had recently been formed–the Department of System Dependencies and Continuity. Little had been said about this new department, and those in the know seemed already assigned to it.

When his supervisor, Agent Lieutenant Saperstein, sat him down with the news, he had only a brief description. "Says here," he said, regarding an iWindow with a short brief on the new department, "Dependencies and Continuity is the latest in MIND operations to ensure that the System is running and relevant to best serve the people of System City."

"So," Agent Stevenson said, "I'm in software operations now?"

"No, no," said Agent Lieutenant Saperstein. "Every department at MIND treads the fine line between IT and civil servitude. This is no different." He regarded the brief again. "Seems to me that this position ensures that the people have the best possible access to the System."

"So, I'm customer service."

"No, no. Not at all."

Agent Lieutenant Saperstein looked away from his iWindow and leaned across his desk toward Agent Stevenson. "Look," he said. "We both know why this transfer is best for you. You won't need to interact directly with... well, anyone." He was clearly flustered both by his lack of information and Agent Stevenson's lack of understanding. "You can be a lone wolf."

"But I'm, how'd you put it, going to ensure that people have the best access to the System," said Agent Stevenson. "Without interacting with those people?"

"Okay, I know," said Agent Lieutenant Saperstein. "I know. You want to know what guys in your new position call themselves? Stagers.'"

"Stagers."

"Yeah, stagers," Agent Lieutenant Saperstein said, as if repetition would bring clarity.

"What am I staging?"

"Hell if I know," Agent Lieutenant Saperstein said with a chuckle. "Our work is as real as it gets."

Less than a week into onboarding, Agent Stevenson would learn exactly what being a "stager" meant. The official training described this duty as an obligation to "follow unconventional missions to completion." But the more informative unofficial training came during a drive-along with Agent Lacey. Agent Lacey, upon first impression, seemed aloof and all too chatty for Agent Stevenson's liking. It worried him that Agent Lacey was the sort of person who would be reassigned to this new department, and that soon he would be surrounded by other rejects like Agent Lacey.

Agent Lacey had been in the position for the better part of a year and was, as he put it, "often pegged to lead ride-alongs for new recruits."

The mission for this ride-along was simple. They were to deliver a meal to an apartment and make sure the recipient had possession of it. The meal was nothing special, just a hamburger and fries from a burger joint Agent Stevenson recognized. Only, they weren't getting the meal from the restaurant. Instead, they were picking it up from a delivery guy en route.

"We're delivering a meal," Agent Stevenson said, reading the mission on his porto more closely for details.

"Just delivering a meal," Agent Lacey said, and nodded to the delivery driver who didn't seem in a rush to get to his next delivery. The driver wore a rain jacket and baseball cap with a hamburger on it. It wasn't a logo Agent Stevenson recognized but he also didn't keep up with that sort of thing.

They got back into their car, and Agent Lacey handed him the meal. He half expected it to be a decoy with some sort of contraband or covert material. But when Agent Stevenson opened the bag on his lap, he saw a tuft of fries pinned to the side by a large hamburger wrapped in greasy foil.

"Don't steal any of those fries," Agent Lacey said. "Really."

They drove for a couple of minutes in silence before Agent Stevenson said, "Is this some kind of joke? Are we bringing Captain his dinner?"

"Nope," Agent Lacey said. "Order says to bring the meal to... what's the address?"

Agent Stevenson was about to read him the address when he remembered it was already on the car's GPS. "Do you know what to do after that?"

"Head back to HQ," Agent Lacey said. "File the report."

"What do we report? That we delivered the meal?"

"Yes," Agent Lacey said, quickly and definitively. "The time and location. Confirm that it was received."

Just as Agent Lacey would later describe, they arrived at 317 West 30th Street at 7:42 pm. Eugene Dietrich came out to receive the meal. Upon quick inspection, Dietrich complained about the volume of fries but apologized because they were obviously just delivery drivers and not at fault. But Dietrick promised to leave a strongly worded review. Dietrich then took his meal inside the building.

"That's it," said Agent Lacey.

"That's it?"

"That's it," Agent Lacey said again. "All done. Mission complete."

They got back in the car and Agent Lacey started humming a song.

"We don't wait for whatever is supposed to happen... to

happen?" Agent Stevenson said.

"It'll happen," Agent Lacey said. "That's the best part. I was in the Department of Counter-terrorism for four years. So much stress. But this is as easy as can be."

Agent Stevenson cringed at the thought of Agent Lacey holding a position in counter-terrorism.

"It might change," Agent Lacey said. "You know, because it's all so new. But right now there isn't much accountability. We're sort of spearheading the initiative. So, a mission either passes or fails. And, frankly, it always passes."

"On what criteria?"

"What's that?"

"On what basis do we measure pass or fail?"

"Well, uh," he said. He gave a nervous chuckle. "You know."

"I don't."

"It's been a while since I was onboarded but I thought they covered that."

"No," Agent Stevenson said, recalling the most vague and uninformative onboarding he had ever experienced. "Nothing about actual missions."

"Well," Agent Lacey said. "They're all sort of the same. At least the outcome."

"That is?"

Agent Lacey looked at him a few times to see if he was kidding. Then he said, "Death."

"Whose death?"

"The subject."

"Do you mean Eugene Dietrich?"

"In this case, yes," Agent Lacey said with some hesitation.

"Are you sure?" Agent Stevenson asked, thinking about how unthreatening Dietrich seemed. If he was the subject of an assassination, wouldn't the agents executing the mission be briefed? "So, wait. We killed him."

Agent Lacey, keeping his mouth closed tightly, nodded *yes*. But then he shook his head *no*, and said, "No. No. Not really. We make sure they die." After a moment, he added, "You should know this already."

"And what does the subject do to deserve death?" Agent Stevenson asked.

"Hell, Stevenson!" Agent Lacey yelled, clearly uncomfortable with the conversation. He took a deep breath, exhaled slowly, and said, "What does any of that matter? Orders are orders."

Agent Stevenson would go on to learn that the job of a stager was to create the scenario for somebody's death. At the time, he didn't know why the subject needed to die. Neither did Agent Lacey or any of the other stagers, as far as he could tell. It wouldn't be until he eventually defected from the Department of System Dependencies and Continuity that he would learn what really happened. Subjects were drawn at random to somehow open access to the System for data updates. It was the stager's job to ensure that the subject did not remember creating that access. This usually meant death. But in some cases–like with Hadley Hayden, who was unfortunate enough to drive a car with faulty brakes and disengaged safety foam over the Bloomburg Skyway and end up crashing onto the roof of an apartment building–the subject lived. And in her case, her chip was fried, which would eventually be considered an "acceptable outcome."

Over the course of the next few weeks, Agent Stevenson would perform another dozen stagings, while devoting the duration of his time to investigating the origins of the Department of System Dependencies and Continuity. It seemed antithetical to the System's mission of safety and security to systematically kill citizens at random. He wanted to get to the root of this awful program.

According to his research, the basis for the department revolved around a software developer by the name of Reuben Mayfield, who had developed the data update protocol, as well as architected much of the System's more robust backend functions. Agent Stevenson would learn that Mayfield was revered in the software development community and awarded handsomely by MIND. But it was another part of Mayfield's file that made Agent Stevenson view him as an extreme danger to society. A trove of buried files indicated Mayfield's repeated assaults on female victims. From the sparse notes he could find, Agent Stevenson deduced that these charges were overlooked because nearly all of the assault victims were Haydens.

He took this information to his former lieutenant in the Department of Investigations, who agreed to look into it. But Agent Stevenson decided to continue his investigation by tailing Reuben Mayfield. Over the course of a few days, Agent Stevenson followed him around the city. Mayfield provided no evidence of sinister behavior and, in less than a week, would ultimately disappear. Agent Stevenson reported back to Agent Lieutenant Saperstein his findings and that Mayfield was on the lam.

"I looked into him for you," Agent Lieutenant Saperstein said. "And there's nothing there for us to go on."

"What do you mean?" Agent Stevenson said. "You have the file."

"We do," Agent Lieutenant Saperstein said. "But it seems to be handled."

Coming to the only conclusion a stager could possibly come to, Agent Stevenson said, "Has he been killed?"

"I can't say," said Agent Lieutenant Saperstein. "Only that I've been told that he was *handled*."

That evening, Agent Stevenson took one last look at Mayfield's file before he would delete it. He knew that there wasn't always a sense of closure to investigations but this felt different. When he came across the picture of Reuben Mayfield, something didn't happen. The System is supposed to indicate that somebody is deceased, a feature that Mayfield himself might have coded. Agent Stevenson knew that, when the System updated, Mayfield's death should have been recorded. But, according to the System, Mayfield was not deceased.

Instead of confronting Agent Lieutenant Saperstein, Agent Stevenson decided that finding Mayfield would be his main mission. The next time his turn came around to conduct a staging mission, he ignored the order and braced for reprimand. Only, it never came.

Over the next few years, Agent Stevenson would come to realize how MIND works. They use him to keep Mayfield at bay. Whether they have tabs on Mayfield already or if they're using this ongoing manhunt to do so, they've been tracking Agent Stevenson all this time, probably since he started meddling in the Mayfield file.

As he sees it, MIND either knows where Mayfield is but worries that Agent Stevenson knows too much about the protection this monster has enjoyed, or MIND doesn't know where Mayfield is and needs Agent Stevenson to find him. Either way, Agent Stevenson is neither fired nor has he quit. He just operates on his own. He has MIND resources at his disposal, but will never be able to report his findings or recruit others to his mission. What happens when he finally gets Mayfield, he doesn't know. He may always have to look over his shoulder for a stager.

"Hey there, friend," says a voice.

Startled, Agent Stevenson turns to find an elderly woman at his side. A welcoming smile looks up at him.

"Sorry," she says. "You look lost."

Agent Stevenson thinks about how maybe he's found exactly what he's always been looking for, a place that doesn't need him.

"No, ma'am," he says. "I'm alright. But is there someplace I can charge my bike? Then I'll be on my way."

"No worries, friend," she says. "Of course we can charge you up. But stay as long as you like. Have you been here before?"

"No, ma'am," he says.

"Well, now you'll have to come back through," she says, giving his arm a squeeze. "Follow me."

He grabs his zipbike and pushes it slowly beside him, keeping pace with this lovely woman to his other side, while she gives him a brief history of her town. All the while, he thinks about what it might be like to make this place his home. He doesn't know her from the System, and he wonders what it would be like to recognize somebody from memory. After all this Mayfield business is behind him, he thinks, maybe this is just the place to learn how.

PART TWO

People take the law into their own hands, maybe because they think they know us just because they know our names, like they own us. You probably don't know any of this or care if you're not a Hayden. But to us it matters a whole lot. It becomes an issue of life and death when you got half a dozen GCs coming at you. They're always juiced-up young guys looking for a fight, acting like they're just trying to clean up their neighborhood, even when they're a long way from home. Maybe that's why they come after us, because they're scared.

CHAPTER FOURTEEN

A familiar stripped-down jingle as if played on a kid's toy instrument. Along with it comes sophomoric lyrics sung by two untalented vocalists who also happen to be the portocast's hosts, brothers Tony and Johnny Stanforth. "Dude man bros. Dude man bros. Bruh man, who man, dude man bros."

They started when they were kids and their listenership joined out of curiosity. Siblings are rare in System City. Tony and Johnny are twins. And that's the entirety of their premise–brothers talking.

Johnny: "Welcome to another episode of *Dude Man Bros*. We're your hosts, Johnny."

Tony: "And Tony."

Though it doesn't matter who is whom. Nobody cares. They could basically be the same person.

"Johnny. That's funny. Look at you. You're not even Johnny anymore."

"What a week. Right? Who am I?"

They laugh.

"Dude, you're Erika."

"No, I'm not."

"You are. You're a girl!"

They laugh even harder.

"Crazy, crazy times, man."

"Crazy, crazy times. Man, I was thinking about it."

"Yeah?"

"Dude, I was thinking how crazy this all is."

"Yeah, totally."

"No, no, no. I looked it up. It's super wild. Think about what we're experiencing."

"Dude, I know. I'm here, living it."

"No, really. Like, I looked it up. The System is wild."

"Yeah? I think it's kind of dumb."

They laugh.

"Sure, yeah. I mean, it sucks that we have to deal. Like we have to put up with whatever the hell is going on. But, dude, the System is a wild west of innovation, man. Like the stuff I read is crazy."

"Sounds provocative. Tell me more."

"Shut up, bro. For real."

"Alright, alright. Tell me."

"Dude, the stuff they tried with this thing. Like, we know it's all about names and stuff."

"Sure, for safety and whatnot."

"Right. And, like, you know we can get flash loads."

"Dude, totally. I just flash loaded season seven of *That Jealous Janie*."

"Great show, dude."

"Great show."

"Tell me later how it is."

"So good, dude. You should flash that biz."

"Dude."

"Do it."

"Will do, dude. But, like, think about that. Pay sixty cred—"

"It was fifty-five."

"Whatever, dude. Fifty-five, sixty. You pay that cred. Within six hours, you got a whole season in your head. Crazy!"

"Crazy. But *you* can do it too, listener. Flash load this and every episode of *Dude Man Bros* right to your noggin."

"Easy as can be."

"No, you have to say it faster."

"What? Oh, because it's flash loading."

They laugh.

"Easy as can be. Easyascanbe. Easycubee."

So much laughter.

"So fast."

"For real. Think about that. Like, how does that work? You know? You didn't watch *That Jealous Janie.* You didn't experience the story beats. Or feel that tension, the highs and lows of a character arc."

"Look at you with the cinema lingo."

"You know what I mean."

"I do, bro."

"But when you think about it, it's like you *did* watch it. Right? Because you recall it."

"Exactly, my broster. I mean, it's like I totally know what happened in each episode. Like how, in the third episode of season seven, Lester ends up falling in a—"

"Bro! Stop it! Quit spoilin'!"

"Right, right. Sorry, dude."

"So, like, I wonder what people experience when they flash load us."

"Look at me, bro. I've been flash loaded."

They laugh.

"But like. Are they laughing with us? Or do they just remember us being funny?"

Silence.

"Weird, man. I don't know."

"And, like, if they don't think about us. Like if nobody asks them how this week's totally rad episode popped, then will they even know they know?"

"I mean, they know."

"Do they?"

"Sure. But I guess they don't know they know until... they know. You know?"

"Bro."

"Perplexing, my dude bro."

"So, I'm thinking about that, and I'm like, man, what else?"

"Yeah?"

"Like, what else did they do with the System?"

"Sure, man. So, we can flash load songs and portocasts—"

"*Dude Man Bros!*"

"And, like, movies. But, actually, that's a really interesting one."

"Yeah?"

"Dude, totally. Super crazy."

"I'm seduced, bro. Lay it on me."

"So, like, way way back when. Like, when all this started."

"Ages ago. Stone age."

"Crazy forever. So, everyone's chipped and loaded. They're doing their thing. Mom and dad are there on the couch scoping a movie. But, like, you know, a fictional movie."

"Unreal, man."

"Totally."

"And boop! Like that..." Finger snap! "...Dom is now Vin Diesel."

"Dude, great pull. *Fast and Furious!* A classic."

"Grandfathers of cinema, my guy."

"Totally."

"So, like all of a sudden, you'd be watching some show or movie and you can't see the character. Like, you just can't suspend disbelief."

"Such a nerd."

"Bro, it's a thing. You can't not see the actor or actress. Like, people used to watch movies and think, *That's not Harrison Ford, that's Indiana Jones, and for now Indiana Jones is a real person doing real things in a real alternate universe.*"

"Mind blown, dude."

"So, like, you wouldn't believe what they did. They went into the System and scrubbed... that's the term they used, *scrubbed*. They scrubbed out famous people like that."

"That must have taken forever."

"Imagine, dude. So, then Indiana can be Indiana. Or Han Solo."
"Super smart, dude."

"But then–"

"There's more?!"

"Always, my guy. So, like, remember when Vader force chokes that guy?"

"In the first one?"

"The real first one. The first one they ever made."

"Oh, when Vader chokes his lieutenant?"

"He was an admiral. Well, Admiral Motti to be exact."

"I didn't know he had a name."

"Nobody does."

"Why do you?"

"Because I grew up watching those movies."

"Dude... bro, I grew up with you!"

"Brother?"

"Bro?"

More laughter.

"But, yeah, to your point, most people saw him as just some dude. They don't even care. He's practically an extra. Nameless."

"I believe they call that *uncredited*."

"Look who has the big brain now! But, no, he wasn't an extra. Just not a big actor."

"Okay, fine. You're so smart."

"I am. But I'm getting this example from what I read. I'd have picked somebody more obscure. Like that dude who puts the medals around their necks at the end ceremony."

"Oh! Totally. Who was that?"

"No clue. Anyway, back to what I read. So, you don't even know this admiral guy. He's just some admiral dude getting force choked by Darth Vader, when..."

"The System goes live..."

"...and, boop! He's Richard LeParmentier!"

"Richard Le-who?"

"The admiral dude, dude! But like he wasn't anybody until the System said who he was. Like, you wouldn't look at him and have any name in your head. Until suddenly you did."

"So, then–"

"Then he's Richard LeParmentier. A French actor, I guess. But not some admiral."

"So, why didn't they scrub him?"

"Because he's Richard LeParmentier!"

"Is he anybody?"

"No. He's a nobody, I guess. Enough of a nobody to not be scrubbed."

"Dude, I'd so hate to be Richard Le-Parm-something."

"Totally. Though, I don't know. I mean, he probably lived a fine life."

"You're right. You're right. Man, that's wild stuff."

"But here's some other weird stuff."

"Dude, I'm exhausted with your stuff."

"Did you know they tried to push a calendar?"

"Like, so we would always know what day it is?"

"Turns out it was a bad idea. Like, they wanted you to be able to set appointments. But then you might not get the notification in time because the System didn't update until later."

"Dude, that's what *this* thing is for."

"Right? Portos are lame to carry all the time but we got our calendar right here."

"Got your favorite portocast right here too. *Dude Man Bros* is brought to you by Upperdecker Prank Emporium. All your finest gag gifts and prankster paraphernalia all in one easy location. Upperdecker Prank Emporium has it all. 81 Madison Street. Between Catherine and Market. Enter at your own risk, dude."

"So, like, I'm reading up on this stuff. I'm researching like a pro."

"Like a bro."

"Like a bro!"

"Like a brofessional bre-bresearch... you get it."

"I get it, bro. And I'm here for it. So, I'm reading about how they used to push ads on us. Like subliminal stuff."

"It's all subliminal, dude. Like, it's all under liminal."

"So under liminal, dude."

"Way down there."

"Way way down there. And we know how those ads went."

"Rip. Not good."

"People can be lame, dude. But I totally get this. I don't want to have some lame car commercial in my head."

"This is an ad-free zone, my guy."

"So, apparently some company also let you flash load languages."

"Like, for what?"

"Right?"

"So, you'd know how to speak French or something?"

"I guess."

"Weird. Not sure how that worked. Like, you could answer somebody if they asked you a question in French?"

"Who's going to ask you a question in French, dude?"

"I don't know, bro. But I'd be able to answer it."

"Yeah? What's 'Dude Man Bro' in French?"

"Do Me Bruh."

They laugh.

"That's such a Richard LeParmentier thing to say, and I'm here for it. Good talk, my bro."

"Good talk, bro."

CHAPTER FIFTEEN

Cammy is deep in a query for client data when her iWindow suddenly turns charcoal gray with a teal stripe running most of the way down the middle. Above the iWindow appears Ronald Trapper's face.

"Got a minute, kid?" he says. Ronald Trapper is soft spoken and kind. He has always referred to Cammy as "kid," despite her being nearly forty. But when she thinks about it, he is sort of a father figure. Of the partners, he's the one she would most identify as "family." While Frances Boylan has given her a chance as an assistant, she's not a full partner yet, and the Boylans generally take a cold stance with Cammy. She might argue that they do that with anyone that's not a Boylan or Trapper, but there's no proof to that claim.

"Sure," Cammy says. "What's up?"

"Great. Can you come with me?" He waves her to follow.

Cammy drags a finger diagonally across the iWindow to lock it. She knows that it would automatically do that once she and her porto left a certain radius from her desk. But she remembers from the employee handbook that it was company policy to lock iWindows before leaving them unattended.

Ronald Trapper has already started down the hall, and Cammy rushes to catch up. He's been talking to her like she's right beside him, and she thinks he says, "How was your weekend?"

"Fine," she says out of habit. She doesn't normally like to talk about her personal life because, as a Hayden, it's usually so different from everyone else's in the office. But she spent most of this past weekend crying in bed with images of Reuben Mayfield flashing in her mind. "How about you?" she asks.

"As good as any," he says. She knows that he works most weekends. If he does anything special, he generally makes it a long weekend and takes his family to the northern territories to see waterfalls or to take a boat along the Hudson.

They reach the elevator and he lets her get on first. Are they heading out for coffee or a bite to eat? It's not lunchtime. There are two other people on the elevator and, appropriately, their conversation pauses. Cammy doesn't understand this decorum in public. Let people hear whatever. It's their fault for listening. But company policy is to make sure that case-related conversations are kept private. So, most people take this to mean all conversations. Abstinence reduces risk, apparently.

The starred ground floor button is lit but Ronald Trapper presses 3. Quietly and slowly, the elevator descends with no new passengers, and everyone dutifully looks at their feet or watches the numbers change on the floor indicator above.

When they reach the third floor, Ronald Trapper steps aside to let Cammy out first. Once the doors close behind them, Cammy can hear the other two passengers talk again.

Cammy has barely ever come to this floor but she knows that the attorneys here are all dedicated to Mattrest, Inc., a mattress company that has systematically swallowed up any competitor in town, to the point that they are among the top 100 employers in System City. As they move through a sea of cubicles and enter another hallway, Cammy remembers hearing that there are two sleeping rooms on this floor, where Mattrest has provided beds for attorneys and paralegals pulling all-nighters. People jokingly refer to them as the "Third-floor Bedrooms."

"I think you're going to like having your own door," Ronald Trapper says.

"I'm sorry?" Cammy says, afraid she missed something he said.

"It's ok," Ronald Trapper says. "It's really only temporary. Until this all blows over."

"What?" Cammy asks. "Until what blows over?"

They reach a door on the other side of a small cluster of cubicles. Ronald Trapper opens the door to a bare office with a desk, a chair, and a small window at the upper-right corner of the wall where dim light comes in. Cammy sees only the gray facade of a skyscraper through the window.

"We'll have your iWindow brought down," he says. "Frances will be able to ping you from her office. It really shouldn't be too bad."

"Ronald," Cammy says. "Are you moving me here?"

"You don't know?" He looks genuinely curious. "I thought Frances talked to you already." He sighs. "Your friends came by earlier. Security stopped them."

"Yeah?" Cammy says, suddenly worried who it was or what they might have done. "How come nobody called for me?" A flurry of anger overcomes Cammy, not just because security didn't tell her but because her visitors were obviously Haydens, and she has to wonder whether they did something stupid. But then she's also mad at herself for even thinking this.

"Look," Ronald Trapper says. "With everything that's going on, we can't have–" He stops himself to choose his words. "It's a matter of appearance."

"Appearance? To who?" Cammy asks.

"Our clients," he says. "The only people that matter."

"Look at me, Ron! Who do you think they see?" she says, knowing he'll have a different name in his head than even this morning. She almost tugs at the lapel of her suit jacket to emphasize how she's conformed. "Nobody knows!"

"Our clients know," he says, clearly trying to be tactful. But he's failing. "People just know."

"So, you're tucking me away," she says, forgetting that it could be worse. They probably could simply fire her.

"Just for a bit. Until this blows over," he says. "You know we were always taking a gamble with..." He smooths his hands down the door as if inspecting its quality. "You have your own door now."

They sent Ronald Trapper, the kind partner and father figure, to do their dirty work. In another life, Cammy would have chewed him to bits, maybe even marched back upstairs and gave Frances a verbal beating. But that would just be playing into their hands. Another Hayden goes off the rails, just as expected. Serves them right for putting a Hayden in a client-facing position.

"I can't believe this," she says. "What more do I have to do?" The thought of taking legal action occurs to her. Only, she's a Hayden, and no court would even consider her case, let alone show her a fair trial against one of the more prestigious law firms in the city. "This is absolute cowardice," she says. "You're all cowards."

Ronald Trapper's face goes slack the way a father's might when his daughter lashes out at him. Only, he must know that he and the family have betrayed her. His eyes twitch in every direction but not directly at her eyes. Then, as if whatever emotions he had behind those sad eyes has suddenly dissipated, he says, "Ok, then." And like a lawyer that can take one on the chin without flinching, he leaves Cammy to make a home of her new, secluded office, and says, "It's only until this blows over, kid."

CHAPTER SIXTEEN

Paul hasn't been gone long but Weston already feels like it has been months. Paul never left the colony before this, and so much of that time was spent in this office. Now it feels so empty. Weston sits in Paul's black leather chair, staring through the large iWindow at the older of the two watchers sitting in a chair by the door. The System has provided a spectrum of names for this man, and Weston would be happy to call him by his birth name, if he would just reveal it. Instead, the watcher insists he be called 1052, and his partner be called 2701. Weston sees this as a sign of distrust but, with no alternative, he complies.

With residents' duties continuing as before, their biggest concern now is maintaining supplies. Typically, Paul would approve of large expenses and provide the appropriate credit to Weston's account. He also gave Weston a meager bi-weekly operational budget to use at his discretion. Meanwhile, residents were given a small amount of credit as compensation while they lived cost-free at the colony. This was intended to provide residents with a small budget while they reacclimated into System City once the time came for their return. For the sake of the colony, each resident has agreed to pool their credit for the greater colony budget.

Since Paul left, Weston has been hoping that funds will keep coming. He can think of four possible scenarios that might dictate their budget's future. Paul might stop credit flow to the colony now that he is no longer there. Paul might be captured or killed and his accounts frozen upon capture or death being reported, thereby ceasing payment. Paul might keep credit flowing to the colony. Or Paul might be killed but his death not reported, and credit might still flow.

Payment should be due any minute now. So, with Weston's porto sitting out on Paul's desk, the two wait for a payment notification to chime. Weston continues to rummage through Paul's iWindow, searching for anything important to the colony's daily operation. He's afraid to mess around too much because much of what he sees is so foreign to him. This must show on his face, because 1052 asks, "Are you any good with that thing?"

"Computers?" Weston says. "No. Not really. I was just Paul's runner."

"Mayfield," 1052 says. "Let's stop calling him Paul, okay?"

"That's all these people know," Weston says.

"And they revere him," says 1052. "If you want them to move on, this will help."

Weston thinks that 1052 is including him in that group. "They might feel betrayed," he says. "I don't know if that will go over well."

"He betrayed all of us," says 1052.

Weston understands. Anything that can unify the group will help. But it feels wrong. As he sits here before this iWindow looking at what he imagines to be the inner workings of Paul's genius, Weston doesn't know if he can accept the Mayfield side of Paul.

"Anyway, be careful with that thing," 1052 says, gesturing to the iWindow. "I don't think you should touch it."

"Oh," Weston says, pulling his hands away from the screen. "Did I mess something up?"

"I have no idea," says 1052. "And you never know if he has remote access. He might not want us poking around."

Suddenly, Weston's porto chimes. New credit has hit his account. Whichever of Weston's scenarios is true, he doesn't know. But he chooses to believe that Paul–rather, Mayfield–is alive and thinking about the colony.

"All good?" 1052 asks.

"We're good," Weston says.

"Okay," says 1052. He stops leaning against the wall and steps closer to Weston. "Now, if you can create an inventory of known expenses, I can work on culling it down to essentials for a leaner budget."

"I'll have to do it by memory," Weston says, looking at the iWindow. "I can't find anything here. I thought maybe he had a spreadsheet or something."

Weston can hear 1052 sigh. But against his warnings, Weston keeps snooping around the iWindow and comes across a folder labeled, *Resident Records.* In it he finds more folders, each with a name of a different resident at the colony. He randomly taps Pete's folder to find photos taken in the forest and little abandoned towns that the group has visited with Mayfield. Nothing stands out as exceptional. There are hundreds of images, and Weston quickly gets bored looking through them. There are a couple of audio files, but Weston ignores those. The same goes for Renee's and Trevor's and other folders he taps. Hundreds of images and a few audio files. Still, he keeps searching because Mayfield must have found some significance in these files, and it intrigues Weston.

Then, in Hadley's folder, he finds something different. Beside hundreds of images, many of them from around System City, there's another folder labeled, *Diary.* Weston knew that Mayfield thought Hadley was important but never knew why. He seemed to treat Hadley differently from the very beginning. Weston was told to protect her in System City. That's why he fought off those MIND Academy cadets that night in Madison Square Park. Sure, she was clever and maybe even resourceful, but as far as Weston saw she was just another Hayden.

In the *Diary* folder, Weston finds more than a dozen audio files. It's not clear what they are. The labels are strings of numbers likely generated from her porto and probably indicate the time and date of their recording. He chooses a random file and taps it. An audio player opens on the screen. From the iWindow's tiny speakers comes Hadley's voice:

A lack of a clock, porto, or window in my room makes it difficult to know how long I've been asleep. My head is heavy when I lift it. My mind is foggy...

"What's that?" 1052 asks.

Weston doesn't respond, and 1052 doesn't ask again. They both keep listening.

It's dry in this tiny room, the concrete walls almost chalky. People shuffle by in the hallway, whispering. When I roll out of bed, I feel where my head hit the ground last night in the park. That was last night. It feels so long ago, so far away...

Weston taps the pause button. Listening to this feels like he's violating her privacy. He remembers on occasion finding Hadley recording herself into her porto. Mayfield often asked the residents to do this during their memory exercises. But Hadley seemed to do it for pleasure, as well. The fact that Mayfield kept these is odd. But that was Mayfield.

"Do you know that voice?" 1052 asks.

"I do," Weston says, not sure how much he should give away. He still doesn't know how far he can trust these two former MIND agents.

"Does it seem like anything important to you?"

"No," Weston says. "Not that I can tell."

2701 barges in, nearly bumping into 1052, and says, "We have visitors. MIND agents."

"How many?" Weston asks.

"Looks like two," he says. "Parked their car up by the head of the path."

"We might have one or two flanking," 1052 says.

The two former MIND agents start to leave when Weston says, "No, no. Wait." Weston can tell that, at least in their heads, 1052 and 2701 are still up in those hills reacting like watchers. "Let me handle this."

1052 seems to understand Weston, or maybe he already sees Weston as their leader. Either way, he stands down.

"We'll be right behind you," says 2701.

"Just... wait," Weston says. "Thank you. Really. But please wait inside."

"Do you think twenty-three eighty-eight gave us up?" asks 2701.

"Or Mayfield sent them," 1052 says.

"Let's not jump to conclusions," Weston says.

As Weston squeezes past the men, 1052 mutters to 2701, "We need to install cameras."

Outside, Weston sees two MIND agents walking roughly side-by-side, studying the colony as they follow the gravel path in. A few of the residents are tending to the garden at a safe distance. They pause to watch the agents encroach on the colony. Weston opts to leave his rifle by the door. This is the first time the colony has unexpected guests, aside from Agent Stevenson or wildlife.

Weston walks slowly toward the agents, displaying a mix of curiosity, welcome, and authority. *Is this what Paul would do?* he thinks. He lets the agents speak first.

"Very interesting compound," the agent with yellow-rimmed glasses says. For now, his name appears to be Ingred Lewis. Based on this initial comment, Weston can't yet tell if they know about the colony and are just impressed to see it in person.

The other agent, whose name is Howard Duchamp, nods to the residents in the garden. Renee doesn't return a greeting, only stands up to be a witness.

The agents stop about eight feet from Weston, at the edge of the gravel parking pad.

"Pardon us," says the agent with yellow-rimmed glasses. "We've come a long way to see about a girl."

"You'll have to pardon me," Weston says. "Can I get your names?"

"Sure thing," says the agent. "Agent Wilcox. And this is Agent Morelli."

"MIND," Weston says. "You *have* come a long way." Of course, at this point, Weston doesn't think the trip is all that far. To people from the city, though, this is another world.

"And if you don't mind," Agent Wilcox says.

"Right," Weston says. "Weston Reed. I run things here."

Agent Wilcox adjusts his yellow-rimmed glasses as he glances over Weston's shoulder. 1052 approaches the group. He's wearing an apron with food stains on it. Weston is worried that a gun is likely concealed under that apron.

"Mr. Daniel," Weston says to 1052. "I don't think they'll be staying for dinner, if that's what you're wondering." To the agents, "Sorry, hunting has been light lately."

"No worries," Agent Wilcox says. "We're just here to follow up on a lead." Looking up at the hills, he says, "There can't be a lot of settlements like yours out here."

"No," Weston says. "At least not that we know of. We're lucky to borrow what land we have here."

"This gas you're breathing is probably factored into your rent," Agent Morelli says, grimacing.

"Yeah," Weston says, and laughs. "Apparently those mines have been burning for generations."

"You mentioned a girl?" asks 1052.

Weston looks at him, hoping he doesn't continue to act like a former MIND agent. *Play dumb*, Weston wants to tell him.

"We have a Hayden girl detained," Agent Morellis says. "We're checking on her previous whereabouts."

Weston has followed the media enough to know that the System failure is being pinned on Haydens. "I assume you're talking about Miss Hadley," Weston says. "She's the only Hayden who's stayed here." Weston sees no reason in denying knowledge of her. They must already know quite a bit to justify coming all this way.

"Hadley was a hard worker," 1052 says.

"Was she?" Agent Wilcox says, showing muted surprise.

"She's a character," Weston adds. He rolls his eyes to say, *you know what I mean.* "Haydens."

"Sure, sure, sure," Agent Morelli says passively, as he looks around him. Where he stands, he's only a few feet from where Agent Stevenson was tied to a chair. Weston wonders if trained agents like them can read scuffs in the gravel and dirt to sense what might have gone down just days ago. "Seems like a nice little community you have," he says.

"It's really great," 1052 adds, taking on a strange tone of innocence. "Can't say there's any place like this for us fried folks back in the city." He taps a finger to his head about where the chip should be located.

The agents look at each other curiously. Weston is trying to read whether this is news to them or if they're sharing a look of speculation, like they somehow know different. It's still unclear if the agents have a report on the colony or if this is their first bit of intelligence gathering.

"We do what we can," Weston says, taking a humble tone and harnessing his best impression of Paul. "This colony would be nothing without them." He watches 1052 playact bowing.

"So, this is rehab?" Agent Wilcox asks. "Do you—"

"Oh, gosh, no," Weston says. "What's there to rehabilitate?" He turns to 1052 and says, "And we don't like to use the f-word here."

"I know," 1052 says. "I'm sorry. Us *untethered* folks."

"We're talking about fully capable people, Agent Wilcox," Weston says. "Instead of a handicap on their part, I might say that we are burdened with the unnecessary crutch."

"I'm sorry," says Agent Wilcox, and he looks to his partner. "We're very curious about all this. In fact, I don't think MIND knows anything about your... what did you call it? Colony?"

"We would love to have a look around," Agent Morelli says.

Weston's pause in responding may feel longer to him than to the others. But in that moment, 1052 reaches beneath his apron, and Weston braces for the worst. Instead of pulling out a gun, 1052 pulls a dirty kitchen towel from his waistband and wipes his hands.

"I should really get back to prepping dinner," he says, and he waves his dirty towel as he walks away. "My apologies."

"I can answer any questions you might have about Hadley Hayden," Weston says. "But I don't know how residents will take two MIND agents snooping around."

"I wouldn't call it snooping," Agent Morelli says.

"Yes, I'm sorry." Weston leans in close to softly say, "Their view on MIND and the System is a little... woke." He looks around, almost pantomiming it. Renee is still looking on and the other gardeners have gathered around her. "We have a very peaceful existence out here and, frankly, you're probably our first unannounced guests." He says this not only to quell their intrusion but to also test if they know about Agent Stevenson.

"Understood," Agent Wilcox says, looking back at Renee and giving a subtle wave.

"About Miss Hadley," Weston says. "She was a colorful addition, if only for a brief time."

The agents look at each other and then toward one of the concrete buildings where some other residents have emerged. They look to be in transit from a dormitory to the cafeteria but have stopped to see what is happening. Weston thinks for a moment that they were instructed to come outside and show some life at the colony.

Agent Wilcox smirks and nods. "Did Hadley..." he says, and then corrects himself. "Does anyone here have access to computer equipment?"

"Beyond their portos?" Weston asks.

"Sure," Agent Wilcox says. "Anything sophisticated or not."

"No," Weston says. "And their portos are their only links to their families back in System City. We're not trying to go rogue out here. It's simply a place where people offline can come to find their own."

"Of course," Agent Wilcox says. "And how does somebody like Hadley Hayden find out about a place like this?"

"Word of mouth," Weston says, almost surprising himself with how quickly he says it. Somehow Mayfield always knew who was recently fried and was already reaching out or sending Weston to gather them. But to explain his lie, Weston continues, "We have folks coming and going. Not a lot. But I always tell residents who choose to return to the city that they're welcome back, and to spread the word while they're away."

"Can't say I've heard a peep about this place," Agent Morelli says.

"And why would you?" Agent Wilcox says. If Weston thought this was in defense of the colony, the agent goes on to say, "Seems to me like they have a tight-knit community here. I'm sure that there's plenty we don't know about them."

"And if I'm guessing right about Miss Hadley," Weston says, playing into their suspicions, "there's plenty we don't know about what those Haydens are up to."

The agents nod in agreement. Though, Weston isn't yet convinced that they're all on the same page. Still, it seems they've found enough common ground to appease the agents for now.

"I'd like for us to stay in touch," Agent Wilcox says, and produces his porto to share contact information with Weston's. "If that's alright with you."

Weston doesn't have his porto on him and gestures as much. "I'm sorry," he says. "But you know where to find us."

"We sure do," Agent Morelli says, casting a suspicious eye before nodding casually to the onlooking residents.

The agents take their time heading back up the gravel path, getting one last look back at the colony. Weston looks approvingly to the onlookers as he slowly heads back toward Mayfield's office. Inside, he finds 1052 still in his kitchen apron and 2701 tucking a pistol back into his pants.

"They'll be back," 2701 says. "Not sure how soon. When it's clear, we'll sweep the hills for any surveillance equipment they left behind."

"That Agent Morelli was eyeballing for security," 1052 says. "Too bad we'll have cameras set up by the time they return."

Even if nothing comes from this MIND agent visit, the colony has been breached, and news has likely reached all corners of the colony. It took him a few days to convince the residents that they could keep the colony going. Weston worries it might take longer for them to let down their guard.

CHAPTER SEVENTEEN

"Screw Boylan, Boyland, and Toyland, or whatever it is," Step growls and kicks a trashcan outside the law firm's building. "We have enough to find Paul's apartment, anyway."

Feeling dejected, as if Cammy had made the call to remove her and Step from the premises, Haddy starts back toward the Junction.

"No," Step says. "Don't do that. Don't be like that."

Haddy stops but doesn't turn around. This mission is already a long shot. What does she expect to find at Paul's apartment that would appease MIND anyway? Maybe it makes more sense to lead them out to the colony. At least then they'll find the actual computer where he released the stupid virus. Haddy feels like she's out of options, and it isn't like MIND will give her a pass just for trying.

"Nona said that Reuben Mayfield took her to an Upper East Side apartment, right?" Step asks.

Haddy can see the look in his eyes now. It's no mystery that Step is the more cautious of the two. She often has to coax him into her schemes. And lately, perhaps since her accident, his patience has been wearing. But the look he has now–that glint of intrigue or contentment–lets her know that he's on board.

"I think so," Haddy says. "A few of the girls have said that."

"I'm pretty sure she said he treated her to dinner from a nearby Italian joint," Step adds. "Something about getting takeout. They walked right over to his apartment, I think. Is that right?"

Haddy remembers that too and says, "She said it was across the street."

"The name started with an F," Step says. "Fratelli's?"

"No."

"Fantoni's"

"Nah."

Step pulls up a map on his porto and searches for Italian food. "Fellini's! Boom! Lexington and 73rd."

If they speedwalk, it will take more than half an hour, and neither wants to mess with trains right now. It's a fine day for a stroll, she thinks, and it feels like the good old days when the two of them would kick around without a care in the world. Step looks okay, maybe a little tired. But she can tell that he'll be okay. Maybe he's been reinvigorated by this mission. After all, Step loves a good caper.

"So," Step says, walking faster now. "Tell me about Paul. I need the details. What do you know? What else has Nona talked about?"

"She called it a 'fancy' apartment," Haddy recalls.

"Right. He's rich or something."

"He's sort of a dandy," Haddy says.

"What's that supposed to mean?" Step asks, almost curt.

"I don't know," Haddy says, defensive. "Like he's particular."

"How so?" Step starts to lose his breath. He's still out of shape from his allergic episode, and Haddy worries he might be getting worked up. His face is red.

"I don't know," Haddy says. "He liked things the way he liked them."

"Seems like anyone," Step shoots back.

"Sure. Okay. Fine," Haddy says. "Yeah, that's anyone, Step. Except maybe a Hayden or pretty much anyone who doesn't have wealth or power."

Step stops, catches his breath.

"Chill," she says. "Alright? He's a damn control freak. Okay?"

"Okay," Step says. "Okay. Sorry."

They walk for a few blocks in silence. Haddy doesn't want to talk now, not so much because she's afraid of what Step is thinking but because she's afraid of unloading on him while he's still fragile.

They've always had a strange dynamic, going way back to Hayden House. She remembers Step having it rough because he was the only boy for a long time. He seemed to always retreat into his own head, especially when the other girls ganged up on him. That's when Haddy felt like she had to stick up for him. She lost a lot of friends that way, but she couldn't stand seeing anyone get trampled the way Step did.

Maybe she also had something to prove to him. In a way, she felt threatened by Step. In a city where boys are treated as heirs to the thrones of safe, simple, domestic life, while girls are cast out like diseased dogs, Haddy felt like maybe Step would eventually rise to power in Hayden House through some sort of patriarchal osmosis. She didn't resent him. She just felt like she had to prove herself to him. Or prove herself to be stronger than the others.

Before long, they reach Fellini's Italian Bistro, which takes up the first two floors of a four-story walkup. From outside the restaurant door, Step surveys the block. There's an eight-story apartment building and the rest are smaller walk-ups.

"This is good," Step says.

"How so?" Haddy says, not seeing what he sees.

Step points to a doorman standing outside the big apartment building and says, "Paul lives there." Step squints to see up past the apartment building. "Judging by that highrise hospital behind it, Paul's apartment is on this side of the building for a better view. I'll say a corner unit."

This is Step at his finest, Haddy thinks. And she suddenly feels that unstoppable strength that gave her courage whenever they hung out as kids. Step's wit and Haddy's no-bull attitude have gotten them out of more jams than she can count. It also got them into many scraps, as well. But she always felt a rush by what it seemed they could accomplish together. Here, Step is fired up and back to his old ways.

"First, I would consider the fire escapes," Step says. "Unless you think Paul would find those too risky."

"I don't know," Haddy says. "Maybe?"

Haddy admires Step as he studies the building. It's not often that he seems so engaged. Even when he plays in his band, he's always in his own little pocket on the stage, performing in a bubble, it seems, like just for himself. But now he's energetic and curious. Sometimes she worries about him, if he's okay emotionally. She has always felt that way with him though, going all the way back.

"Do you think he'll be there?" Step asks.

"He might not be in," she says, knowing he won't. After all, Paul's dead. "But he might be back by nightfall," she lies.

"Okay," Step says, rubbing whiskers on his chin as he studies the building. Suddenly, with determination, Step strides down the block to get a better view of the building's left side. "Yes. Okay. There." He points up toward a unit. "That's it."

"Should I even bother asking how you know that?" she asks, knowing he'll want to share anyway. He has always been proud of his attention to details.

"The blinds," Step says. "You said he was with you at that commune or whatever."

"Colony."

"Right. Well, anybody who leaves their apartment with crooked or uneven blinds is just a slob." Step looks for oncoming traffic before darting across the street. "And no *particular* person would ever do that."

Haddy looks up to find four apartment windows with blinds at the exact same level. No other corner unit, let alone any other unit facing the street, has all its blinds at the exact same level. No time to feel proud of her best friend. She quickly follows after Step. When she reaches the building entrance, Step is already engaging with the doorman.

"Look," Step says. "You can't prove that I'm a Hayden just as much as you can't prove that I don't live here."

"I know everyone who lives here," the doorman says. "And *you* do not live here."

"Is that what he told you?" Haddy says to the doorman. "Don't listen to him. He's always messing around. That's why Mayfield likes him so much."

"I don't think it's funny at all, whoever you are," the doorman says. "This is my job, and I don't let anyone in who isn't a tenant or cleared by a tenant."

Haddy takes Step's arm and says, "Come on, now. We'll send Weston by later. Reuben will be annoyed but that's nothing new."

The doorman's face changes to curiosity. "Wait a minute, ma'am," he says.

"No, no," she says. "It's okay. My friend here can be a real pissant."

"Please, ma'am," the doorman says. He gestures for them to come inside. "I'm sorry. It's just been so difficult lately to keep track of everyone, what with my brain contradicting my eyes."

"I understand," she says. "I won't tell Reuben. You're just doing your job."

"Thank you, ma'am."

The rush of being in this duo, Step and Haddy all over again, sends chills up her spine. Step looks annoyed but Haddy knows that's just Step being Step. They walk swiftly to the elevator, and Step hits a button. "I counted the floors," he says. *Of course he did*, she thinks.

At their floor, it's as if Step already knows where to go. He's already oriented himself based on the street view, and he's aiming for the door at the end of the hall. When they reach it, they quickly stop. The door is ajar.

Haddy signals for Step to be quiet. Her eyes tell him that this is serious. She slowly opens the door, trying to keep quiet herself. From somewhere within, she can hear a cabinet closing. Somebody's there, but it can't be Paul. Can it? It occurs to her then that maybe she didn't see Paul die. It seems completely impossible. Everyone in the Junction saw the same thing. But now Haddy doesn't know.

As they creep into the entryway, Haddy calls, "Paul? You there?" As she says this, she thinks how it can't possibly be him. MIND would have already looked for him here.

She hears a drawer open and what sounds like a kitchen utensil being removed. The drawer closes. All of this sounds calm. Panic in his eyes, Step grabs a long wooden bowl, probably meant for keys and a wallet, from the entryway table. He holds it up like an awkward weapon.

The entryway opens into a living room with a blind corner, and Haddy slowly approaches. Clearly, whoever it is knows that she's there. "Hello?" she calls. When there's no reply, she says, "Paul? Reuben?"

When she rounds the corner, she screams at the sight of a man across the room with a large chef's knife. She jumps back, just as Step sees the man. Step screams and throws the wooden bowl across the room, missing the man completely. The man doesn't move but the two Haydens scamper down the entryway tripping over each other.

"Hadley," the man says from the other room.

Step is out of the apartment, urging her to run. But Haddy stops. When she turns around, Agent Stevenson is standing in the living room at the entryway and holding a knife. Somehow, she is filled with relief at the sight of him still alive.

"Come on, Haddy!" Step yells. To Agent Stevenson, he shouts, "Get the hell back!"

"Haddy," Agent Stevenson says, "What are you doing here?"

She gets up and stays halfway between Step and Agent Stevenson.

"Who is this guy?" Step asks.

"You're Step," Agent Stevenson says.

Step apparently doesn't think to ask how Agent Stevenson knows who he is, or that he knows Step's informal name and not just Stephon.

"Who the hell are you?" Step asks.

"It's okay. It's fine," he says. "I'm a friend of Haddy's." He puts the knife on the entryway table and backs into the living room.

Haddy walks back into the apartment against Step's plea to leave. By the time she reaches the living room, Agent Stevenson is in the bathroom doorway with his back to her. The living room is enormous and well lit from all the windows facing the street. The furniture is clean and modern looking. Agent Stevenson waves her over to the bathroom. Before she reaches the room, she can see through the doorway that blood is smeared on the wall. There are streaks of blood on the sink and what looks like stains from watered-down blood near the tub drain.

Was Paul here? Haddy wonders. She tries to remember what she saw in the Junction. Nona had gone wild. All Haddy remembers of Paul is the blood. He was covered. Nona was covered. People who held Paul down had it on them, as well. There's no way he could have lived.

"What do you know?" Agent Stevenson asks. Apparently, Haddy doesn't have the best poker face.

Haddy doesn't know what she should tell either of them. How long can she even keep this a secret? It was just so horrific. But when she thinks about Paul and the awful things he did, Haddy is glad he's gone.

"I—" she starts to say.

"What the—" Step comes up from behind and looks between Agent Stevenson and Haddy at what appears to be a crime scene. "Haddy, what the hell is going on here?"

Step and Agent Stevenson are each making the same face, and it says, "You know something, Haddy. Now talk."

CHAPTER EIGHTEEN

Donning a crisp MIND Over Matter cap, Preston Blake shakes his bowed head in feigned disgust. His face is as red as ever, like he's eaten fifty strips of bacon while holding his breath for the last hour. "We need to talk, my good citizens," he says. "My fellow MOMs."

He adjusts his hat, then decides to take it off and position it beside a can of Lion Stream energy drink, also positioned for the camera.

"We need answers," he says. "*I* don't have the answers. *You* don't have the answers."

He adjusts his microphone back toward his mouth, as if it keeps moving away out of disgust.

"Our young boys don't have the answers," he says. "MIND willing and the creek don't rise, we will have answers soon enough. But for now, we only have questions."

"Like who did this to our System? Who violated the sanctity of our brains and the safety of our city?" He slaps an open palm on his glass-topped desk. It doesn't make the sound he prefers. It's more of a fleshy slap than a rattling crash of indignation.

"Let me ask you. Who has reason to do this? Who has... who has the motive? If you will."

He adjusts the microphone again and sits more upright.

"If this is about safety... your safety... my safety, who is it that you feel least safe around? Let me ask you this. Pardon my inquiry. But let's imagine you and your family are on your way to the theater or to dinner. It's early evening. Those beautiful System City lights aglow around you. Who is it you fear might be lurking in the shadows?"

He leans forward, practically biting the microphone, looking directly into the camera.

"Who is it that you expect to come from those shadows? What does she look like?"

He sits back.

"You know... you know, there was a time as recently as last week. You'd know exactly who she was. Sure, she might sucker you into handing over some cred. There might be a gang of them waiting to intimidate you or, worse, harm you for your pearls, your diamonds, your jacket."

Again with the palm against the glass-topped desk.

"But you'd have every last one of their names... not that it was hard to guess. They all have that look... that nasty, gutter-crawling look. And while you'd live through that trauma, while your young, vulnerable son had to witness those repulsive acts... had to succumb to the will of such lowly monsters waiting in the darkest cesspools of System City, at least you'd get justice."

He adjusts the microphone, looks into the camera and says, "We deserve answers. We deserve justice. Don't let them take that away from you."

CHAPTER NINETEEN

With each passing day, lights out gets harder and harder for Thomas as he lies awake, stewing about the helplessness and inability of his and his cohort's during these trying times. He hates looking in the mirror at a stranger or having his name written on his uniform shirt. During his argument and inquiry class today, Thomas tried to make a case for mandatory lockdown, citing the city's apathy toward the current crisis. If nobody cares, they should be made to care, he argued. He stopped short of revealing his lack of faith in MIND but he wanted to know why they hadn't done anything. Drastic times call for drastic measures. Surely there was something he and his class could do.

From his limited exposure to media, Thomas has gleaned that the Haydens likely have something to do with this. And while he wouldn't put it past his sister to do something awful, he can't quite imagine a group of downtrodden subway girls pulling off such massive calamity. And still, his mind keeps coming back to her and to that night in the park.

By morning, Thomas is back to his usual self. Showered and ready before everyone else, he lines up at morning drills and waits on commanding prefect Douglas to arrive. That's when he has a thought. Since that night in the park, nobody has spoken to Thomas about their mission. There has been no mention of the missing cadet. His friends have been too afraid to ask, since they failed to find the boy. And why hasn't Douglas thanked them for even trying? After all, it was his command.

With minutes to spare as he waits for the others to join him for drills, Thomas finds Douglas's message from weeks ago on his porto. He wants to confront Douglas about that night. Thomas has always thought he should be commanding prefect, but he reasoned that doing so would take him away from outshining the others in class and training. No prefect in the history of MIND Academy has ever been first in class. The demands of that role often detract from excelling in academics. But Douglas doesn't seem to care about that, perhaps because his father is a MIND agent. Douglas's future is all but sealed.

For that reason, Thomas sometimes wonders if he could carve a future for himself if he aligns with Douglas. Keep his enemy close. Perhaps the two of them can lead some sort of extra credit mission to help MIND capture the real culprit of the System's outage. Surely there is some use for eager sixth-year cadets in all this chaos. In the end, Douglas will be seen as doing what is expected of a legacy cadet, while Thomas will shine among his peers, securing his place in academy history.

That's it, he thinks. He'll write Douglas back and formulate a plan from there. Standing outside the cafeteria, Thomas decides to write his own future, and that starts with a ping.

Meet me at...

He can't meet Douglas about this on academy grounds. There's no circumstance in which Douglas and Thomas would ever be talking to each other alone. So, their meeting would raise too much suspicion.

He almost writes, *Madison Square Park,* but knows better than to bring himself back to that place again. It has to be somewhere secluded from MIND Academy staff and cadets. Maybe the Museum of Natural History. It's not close to the academy but Thomas has fond memories of that place. His parents took him there when he was young. It was his first trip into Manhattan, and going back might help erase some of the awful memories he's had since then. But if he's going to use his two-hour pass on this, he doesn't want to spend all that time commuting. In the end, he decides to write, *Meet me at Hudson River Park.* Just a short walk west, he'll be able to make it there quickly, maybe even before Douglas.

Thomas watches his porto for a reply but nothing comes. Eventually, cadets start to arrive, tucking in their uniforms and smoothing their hair. Still, Thomas keeps his porto in hand, hoping for a glimmer of hope that will get him through the day.

When he sees Douglas come around the corner, he goes to put away his porto. But then he sees those tell-tale three dots on the screen. Douglas is writing back. But Thomas can see Douglas from here and he doesn't have a porto in his hand.

The other cadets start to line up on either side of Thomas. Douglas is almost there to call roll. The three dots keep scrolling, a message en route. Douglas is now before them and Thomas can't make sense of how Douglas is writing back but also right here in front of him.

"Portos away," Douglas says to those, including Thomas, who still have theirs out.

That's when the ping appears. *6:30pm. 12th and 22nd.*

Thomas's heart is pounding. He looks at Douglas, hoping to get a knowing glance. Maybe the academy network is lagging and the ping was delayed. Douglas looks across the line of cadets, checking for uniform tidiness. No acknowledgement of their upcoming rendezvous.

"Karp," he says, locking eyes on Thomas. No shared understanding between them. Douglas has only his commanding prefect face.

Paralyzed by not knowing, Thomas tries to will Douglas to respond at the very least with his eyes. Does Douglas have that much of a poker face? Thomas wants so badly to connect with him, to quickly share that covert knowledge. Has he already compartmentalized? Pinging as a fellow cadet, appearing now as a prefect. A nod, a wink. Thomas just wants some indication of what Douglas is thinking.

He gets his wish when Douglas points to Thomas's porto and says, "Will this be your first demerit?"

—

With Douglas still eating across the cafeteria, Thomas devours his dinner and is out the door at 6pm on the nose, when his two-hour pass begins. This gives him enough time to walk those four long blocks and establish a decent position at the meeting point.

The spot Douglas picked is at a convergence of paths that run along 12th near the old Chelsea Piers, where the river has crept up and sometimes breaches a small barrier that leads along the path. The tops of Chelsea Piers peek from the water like long, linear islands. To the north of those, Thomas can make out the roof of an old carousel that he's heard used to be part of Hudson River Park, now mostly swallowed by the river.

With time to spare, Thomas tries to burn some nervous energy by walking up the path along 12th, going deeper into the park. Some people are walking dogs or running. A few retro scooters zip by. Thomas wonders how many of these people are already okay with the way things are now. Have they moved on from their birth names, willing to be whoever the System makes them every few hours?

The breeze off the river is chilly, and Thomas wishes he brought a jacket. He could warm up now with a short jog, but he doesn't want Douglas seeing him that way. This is serious business. On his walk back to the meeting spot, Thomas notices a man watching him from a nearby bench. Perhaps resting from a workout, the man sits stiffly in a tracksuit. His thinning hair raises and lowers with the breeze off the river. Thin metal glasses amplify the man's prying eyes, as Thomas passes. His name is Horace Carmichael. For now, that is. This is just the situation that makes Thomas nervous about the future. How can anyone feel safe when they don't know who they're looking at?

Thomas moves on, out of sight of the man, and leans against a barrier post near the rendezvous point. 6:31, and Thomas doesn't see Douglas coming down 22nd from the academy. How can somebody like that become commanding prefect, Thomas thinks. This is all a bad idea. How can he rely on Douglas for anything?

"Thomas Karp," a voice says from behind.

Thomas turns to find the man from the park bench. He doesn't look like a threat of any kind but Thomas is still on edge as the man comes closer. As the man draws near, Thomas can see stains on the front of his white tracksuit jacket. A diagonal blue line cuts across the zipper, and faint dots of brown or red seem to show through the material.

"Do I know you?" Thomas asks. He can't place the man's face.

It occurs to Thomas that the man has used his birth name, when just this afternoon, Thomas saw in the mirror that he was Gertrude Van Remmen, which gave classmates the opportunity to briefly call him Gerty.

"You contacted me," the man says. "You wanted to meet with me."

Thomas can't make sense of what the man is saying. Douglas is supposed to meet him. Then again, Douglas never acknowledged their communication outwardly. So, who is this man?

The man smiles and, as if following Thomas's train of thought, says, "I sent you on a mission a few weeks ago."

"That was Douglas," Thomas mutters, realizing now that Douglas's message must have been spoofed. He learned about this and other petty pranks in their cyber crimes class.

"It was me," the man says.

"You're Horace—"

"I am me," says the man, cutting him off. A smile creeps across his face, seemingly delighted by what Thomas is trying to say. "Never mind what the System tells you. Please, for the sake of continuity, as they say, call me Paul."

"Paul?" Thomas says. "I don't understand."

"I believe you can use my help," Paul says. "Can we take this meeting somewhere less breezy?"

Despite his soft voice and non-threatening demeanor, something about this man seems off to Thomas. He could easily overcome Paul physically if he had to, but the comfort with which Paul addresses Thomas makes him feel uneasy, as if this man knows far too much about him.

"I think you have the wrong guy," Thomas says. He moves to leave, but Paul steps in his way and puts up a hand.

"You helped me gather Hadley Hayden," Paul says. "Your sister."

Hearing Paul refer to Hadley as Thomas's sister, the mere mention of her name, sets Thomas off. He slaps Paul's hand away and shoves him in the chest. "Back off, creep!"

Paul winces in pain, holding his chest. He quickly composes himself, tugging lightly at the front of his jacket where, it seems, those faint stains have gotten darker.

"Leave me alone," Thomas says, and starts to walk away.

"I can help you find her again," Paul says. "You can get your revenge."

Thomas stops and looks back to find the man hasn't moved. He stands stock still in the middle of the path, somehow surefooted yet pathetic-looking at the same time.

Thomas doesn't speak. He's not sure what to say or whether he can trust this man. But what he's saying sounds very tempting.

"She lives down in the subway," Paul says.

"What's in it for you?" Thomas asks.

"Maybe revenge of my own," Paul says.

"Why should I listen to you?" Thomas asks. "What good is some Hayden to me?" Thomas knows that trying to distance himself from Hadley is a weak move but he says it anyway.

"Do you know why I sent you to find Hadley in the first place?" Paul slowly steps toward Thomas. "I needed her help."

"What's that have to do with me?"

"It has to do with everybody," Paul says, snickering and stepping closer. Now within reach, one quick punch could knock him to the ground. But Thomas can't bring himself to do it. It isn't that Thomas trusts this man, but something about the way he speaks seems so sure, like everything he says is fact.

"Hadley," Paul says. "Your sister..." Paul steps so close, it's as if he's challenging Thomas to punch him. Still, Thomas can't. "...she helped me bring down the System."

CHAPTER TWENTY

In the old days, if one wanted to threaten somebody, they could send a letter with no return address. To hide their handwriting, they might cut letters of different shapes and sizes from magazines, glue them to paper, and then they would sign the whole thing with some cryptic name like "The One Who Waits." This might have worked nowadays, if there were still magazines, mailed letters, or paper.

For immediate gratification, they might call their victim on the telephone, give a sinister laugh. Should they be close to their victim, they might mask their voice through some voice-altering device, maybe add distortion and raise it an octave so the sound of their voice cuts like the knife they promise to use on their victim's throat. But with telephones being replaced by cellular phones, then replaced by portos, identifying a caller or messenger has become part of the service. Spoofing exists, but not everyone has the capability.

Now, with the System acting as it does, coupled with conspiracy theorists and city officials speaking as they are in violent, hateful rhetoric, people are able to cast their threats in person, emboldened by their leaders and under a shroud of chaotic anonymity.

That's how the officer explains it to Miss Ula Mae as she tries to report what occurred just this afternoon.

The name she gives, Ivan Laurel VI, has already been reassigned to another person who doesn't fit the description of caucasian male, medium height, mid-30s, and dirty blond hair. The System has no record of who last held the name Ivan Laurel VI because there was never before a need to keep that history. People lived full lives with only one name. The very few traditionalists who have changed their names for marriage, do so through an official, exhaustive, and, albeit, discouraging process that becomes part of their biographical data history, not unlike their birth and death statuses.

Recounting the brazen terrorist confrontation, Miss Ula Mae is reminded of just how necessary the System has become.

That afternoon, Ivan Laurel VI came to the entrance of Hayden House, claiming interest in fostering a child. Age and wisdom have helped Miss Ula Mae become a strong judge of character upon first impressions, but experience has taught her to reserve judgment. So, while red flags may have flown at that moment of first contact, she did her due diligence.

"After all," she says, "No child ever found a home by me shutting out the ones who'll learn to love them most."

Despite his eagerness, Ivan smiled when Miss Ula Mae greeted him, and was more than happy to come inside to chat.

"He made good small talk," Miss Ula Mae explains. "But I see why I thought that then. He asked a lot of questions. I generally like curious people."

Ivan asked many questions like: Are the girls creative? Do they get to express themselves a lot? Are they taught to appreciate what they have? How are they socialized?

"Some of his questions felt a little like he was talking about puppies," she says to the police. "Do we socialize the girls? Do they get time to run around at the park?" She laughs just thinking about those silly questions, giving her a moment of reprieve from the memory of what would follow. "I suppose I just thought he was naive about parenting. He kept apologizing for having so many questions."

There are no residences on the first floor, not even Miss Ula Mae's apartment. As a matter of caution, the first floor is a place for prospective parents and other visitors to meet with Hayden House staff. Nobody outside of Hayden House residents and staff are allowed beyond the locked doors that lead to the stairwell and elevators. Miss Ula Mae recalls that when she stopped to take Ivan into her office, he kept walking a few more steps toward those doors and even tried the handle. Realizing his mistake, he showed disappointment before circling back to her office.

"On second thought, he might have been disappointed that he could go no further," she says. "I hate to think of what he might have done if he had reached those children." She chokes up, thinking about it. "Or what he might try to do if he comes back."

He sat down across from Miss Ula Mae's desk and declined her offer of water or coffee. He didn't have long to stay, explaining that he would be back with his wife another day. He was just "popping in."

At the time, Miss Ula Mae enjoyed the conversation. Most prospective parents initiate contact through the Hayden House foster and adoption portal. This allows staff to pre-screen the information that parents provide and prepare relevant matches for parents to review at their first meeting. While it was unusual for an interested foster parent to come off the street, he had caught Miss Ula Mae at a good time. The infants and toddlers were down for a nap. Some of the older teens were in a job training class across town. The grade schoolers and middle graders were in lessons. Miss Ula Mae considers that time of the afternoon to be the calm before the storm of pre-dinner, post-school energy bursts.

"All the girls want to play or take their chemically imbalanced emotions out on each other all at once," she says. "*That's* not a good time to be at Hayden House. Four to six p.m. are–" She sighs heavily. "Well, just don't get me started."

When Miss Ula Mae asked Ivan about his home, about what he and his wife did for a living, and why, if she might ask, were they looking to adopt, Ivan gave little-to-no information about himself or his wife. He claimed to have a job in finance.

"That's right. He said he was a domestic currency trader," Miss Ula Mae reports. "I asked him what that is. He said his firm buys and sells credit and currencies from across the old states, I guess following dips and booms in value." She shakes her head like it's all too complicated for her. "What a crock."

Looking back, she doesn't think a domestic currency trader would have worn a brown canvas jacket and faded t-shirt if he was "just popping in after lunch."

But the credibility of his intent seemed less questionable when he started talking about the daughter he and his wife imagined they would have.

"That's how they sometimes put it," she tells the police. "You have to remember the emotional toll these foster parents have endured. They've always dreamed of having a child but couldn't. The moms are particularly sensitive, which manifests in the strangest peculiarities. For instance, you'll find that it's common for foster parents to have specific requests or specifications, like they're shopping for a car. Mom might want a child between the ages four and ten. They would like the child to have red hair like mommy or be tall or strong. They might want the child to have a prominent chin or chubby cheeks like a doll."

Miss Ula Mae was happy to allow Ivan a moment to express his and his wife's desire to raise a child. While he wasn't forthcoming about their home life, she knew that a full interview, screening, and home visit would take care of those formalities when they finally got to that point. It was around the time that she suggested how he could formally "get the ball rolling" through the foster and adoption portal, he very suddenly dropped the act.

"It was so sudden," she says. "I said I looked forward to having his wife come in with him next time. I stood to see him out and came around the desk to shake his hand. He got up so quickly and said, 'Sure, sure. We'll be back.' He took my forearm, not my hand. He grabbed me so tightly. Squeezed my arm like he wanted to break it." Miss Ula Mae shows the officers the bruising in the shape of fingers wrapped around her skin. "He said, 'We'll be back to kill you and all your nasty little girls.' Right to my face." Her heart begins racing like it did in the moment of that assault, and she begins to cry again.

Ivan may have only accosted her for a few seconds, but it felt like the rest of her life. He finally let go and spit on the floor before storming out of her office. "We'll be back," he shouted from the hallway. "You're all going to pay!"

"He must have known that we don't have cameras," she says. "We don't want to violate the girls' privacy. We have locks and alarms."

Miss Ula Mae looks across to the officer taking her report. The officer is tired, maybe at the end of his shift. He has a department-issued porto and a small ball-shaped microphone sitting on the table between them. For most of this interview, he's been scratching dry spots on his scalp and using the corner of a rectangular uniform chest pin to dig the collected scalp from under his finger nails.

"Anything more to add?" he asks.

"No," Miss Ula Mae says, coming down from reliving the incident. "No, that's it."

Without moving the rest of his body, the officer reaches over and taps the screen of the porto, stopping the recording. Though, as casual as this motion was, Miss Ula Mae would not be surprised if he hadn't recorded any of her report, and instead was acting as though he had.

"So, do you think you can place an officer outside Hayden House?" she asks. "Just in case. I'm worried they might come back."

The officer leans forward and, without looking at Miss Ula Mae, says, "We're stretched pretty thin, what with all that's happening." He stands up. "We'll look into it. But without a name, there's not much we can do."

"That's all?" she says, choking back any thought of yelling. "You can't help?"

She knew it was a gamble to bring this to the police. They haven't been very sympathetic to Haydens. But she thought that they might act differently under current circumstances, especially since there was no ambiguity about this threat. Not to mention that she had been assaulted.

"Lock that front door," says the officer. He steps from the interview room, which looks out to a small gathering of cubicles. The porto is still sitting on the table in front of Miss Ula Mae. "Let us know if you need anything else, okay?" he says.

CHAPTER TWENTY-ONE

An exploded diagram of an old Harley Davidson motorcycle greets Agent Stevenson every time he enters his 130-square-foot apartment. Stretched across the only wall not occupied by desperate storage solutions, the diagram features an array of parts, ranging from simple components like handlebars, crash bar, gear box, and fuel tank, to the many smaller pieces of the bike's complicated combustion engine. Agent Stevenson never tires of looking at this beautiful piece of machinery, often wishing he could live in a time when those two-wheeled beasts roared across the countryside. But on this night, he is too exhausted to even turn on the lights and see that wall art. Under the glow of neon through the tiny twelve-by-sixteen-inch window, the only window in his apartment, Agent Stevenson slumps onto the futon and loosens his belt. Next, he grunts to bend one leg so that he can remove a boot, and gives up when the angle of his futon proves to restrict this task.

He closes his eyes and thinks back to that town in old Pennsylvania where his zipbike broke down. He remembers the breeze on his face, the quiet of the streets in the middle of the day, and the almost eerie calm that came over him the moment he stopped to take it all in.

Fast forward a couple of days, and Agent Stevenson found himself searching the apartment of a fugitive in the middle of an unforgiving, ever-growing metropolis with more people than it can hold and who are clinging to sanity amid the greatest crisis this city has seen in decades, with media highlighting, if not provoking, a near-eminent boiling point.

The fruitless search served only to complicate his hunt for Reuben Mayfield, forcing Agent Stevenson to now piece together what could have possibly happened in the brief time the fugitive was back in System City. Bloodstains in the apartment indicate a crime either committed onsite or elsewhere and, possibly, the assailant's attempt to clean up afterward. Before Agent Stevenson could assume the worst–that the fugitive had murdered his hostage, Hadley Hayden —she and a friend arrived on the scene and offered no sign of distress. And then Hadley informed him that Reuben Mayfield was dead but couldn't–or wouldn't–explain how.

It's possible that Hadley and her friend Step killed Reuben Mayfield and disposed of his body. When asked, Hadley provided no explanation for his disappearance, only that efforts to contact him have failed. Step's confusion seemed convincing, as was his fear of Agent Stevenson and rage over the situation. But something about Hadley's demeanor felt suspicious, like the way she had no story for when she and Mayfield apparently parted ways or her lack of curiosity about what happened in that apartment.

Though not yet confirmed, to further muddle his investigation, Hadley claims that she was arrested by MIND agents who are now tracking her. If she doesn't provide Reuben Mayfield to them, she is going to take the fall for whatever Mayfield did to the System. So, Mayfield's death poses a big problem for Hadley.

Outside Agent Stevenson's window comes a swell of noise. Chants from an anti-Hayden protest group grow louder as they pass. They've been marching through the city, and this is Agent Stevenson's first time hearing them. He doesn't have the energy to get up and look outside but just waits for them to pass. Once the usual murmur of street noise and car horns returns, he goes back to deliberating his next move.

Finding Reuben Mayfield was no easy task before but now it's going to be nearly impossible to find his body. To think that he was hiding in plain sight that whole time in a secluded colony fills Agent

Stevenson with dizzying exhaustion. And now he doesn't know if it's even worth tracking down the corpse for anything more than his own closure.

Unfortunately, Agent Stevenson can relate to Hadley's situation. Given his current status with MIND and their likely displeasure with him going rogue, Mayfield was going to be his one bargaining chip. If he can't save himself, he can at least help her. He doesn't believe that Hadley killed Mayfield but he suspects that she knows how he died. And the last thing she needs is for MIND using her and the Haydens as a scapegoat for yet another thing. As crazy as he thinks it is, this former stager feels obligated to protect the Haydens.

But for now, he's too tired to process any of this. As his breathing grows heavy and the sounds outside his window become hazy, he attempts to calculate the benefits and drawbacks of finding Mayfield's body. He could probably trace his way to it if he pushed Hadley. Back at MIND Academy, they had a rule that warned cadets about the dangers of pushing witnesses. Agent Stevenson forgets the exact point of that rule now, and he thinks this inability to remember would have been unfathomable to the eager young agent he used to be. Has he really withdrawn so much from the agency that he's starting to forget basic rules? Lying here on this futon and on the brink of unconsciousness, it's that little kernel of hope that pushes him into slumber.

CHAPTER TWENTY-TWO

Step crosses 5th Avenue, weaves through a line of construction cones, and slowly vaults the wall at the edge of Central Park. This is the most direct route from Reuben Mayfield's apartment to the Junction, as the crow flies. Only, from everything Step has ever learned about that possibly-extinct animal, the crow would never want to be in the Junction. Like a crow, Step has no place in the Junction or anywhere on the street for that matter. Haydens are uniquely built for whatever adversity they face. But not Step.

"Come on, Step," Haddy says, keeping pace and scaling the wall as well. "Can we talk about this? What are you so afraid of?"

"Nothing," Step says and shoves a path through the landscaping. "Leave me alone." The Central Park Zoo is to the right, and Step thinks the snow monkeys are whistling. They sound like birds. At least that's what Step remembers from a trip to the zoo that the Haydens took years ago.

On the path, Step takes a moment to regain orientation, giving Haddy a second to catch up. Just as she arrives, Step remembers to take the tunnel toward the pond. Just before they reach the tunnel, Haddy grabs Step's arm.

"Don't get like this," she says. "I'll tell you everything that happened. But don't get all righteous on me."

"Righteous!" Step can't believe that's what Haddy thinks. "I'm not being righteous. I'm being safe. I'm getting as far away from you as I can." The thought of enabling Haddy's craziness any longer just infuriates Step. "I want nothing to do with you or that agent back there. I don't know what you two were talking about and, frankly, I don't care."

Step heads into the tunnel beneath East Drive.

"Step!" Haddy shouts. "Wait, Step!" Her voice echoes down the tunnel, past Step and to the other end. "Just stop, already."

Step stops to turn and yell, "I almost died because of you! Don't you understand?" When Haddy freezes for a second, Step keeps walking.

Step's legs are fatigued. All this hiking around the city has taken a toll. When the pond comes into view, it occurs to Step that this is probably where Mayfield preyed on Hayden's like Nona. Who wouldn't come here to relax for a moment and try to forget the awfulness of those city streets? And then Mayfield comes along and takes advantage of that vulnerability, finding a Hayden girl with her guard down.

Just thinking about what that monster must have done to Nona, Step is glad to know that Mayfield is dead. But the fact that Haddy might know about it or that she has something to do with it makes Step confused and angry.

Haddy catches up again, and Step is too tired to keep moving. At a small outcrop of rocks that stretches into the pond, Step sits down to rest and look at the reflection of city lights off the water. Haddy sits down beside him and neither speaks for a moment.

Finally, Haddy says, "Step," and Step puts up his hand to stop her.

"I don't care why you're entangled in some crazy plot to take down the System," Step says. "I don't want to know why you're chummy with some MIND agent or why you fled to some commune run by a garbage human being who preyed on your friends... your family. I don't care how you know that he's dead. Hell, I don't even care if you did it." Step looks at Haddy. "I kind of expect that you did."

"I—" Haddy tries to interject but Step continues.

"None of it matters to me. I'm not cut out for that level of... I don't even know. Insanity? Is that the right word? I can't even think of the right way to describe the mayhem you invite and... and bring to *my* life."

A fish nips at the water's surface, and Step watches ripples distort the reflection of skyscrapers like they aren't even real.

"You know, I'm not like you," Step says. "I'm not like the others. I don't *feel* like a Hayden." It's not just that Step grew up as a boy in a girl's world. There are plenty of Hayden boys now. Not many but enough for this feeling to be something more than that.

In the hospital, Step spent hours dreaming about a world that didn't involve hustling and grinding to survive, a world without perpetual fear or the necessity to fight. Above all, Step wavered between wishing for a new life and giving up on life altogether.

There's no way to explain this to Haddy now without sounding like a fool. Retreating to some blank world, calling on some stupid wizard to grant Step the power of perseverance just to make it another day. Calling on this ridiculous, cloaked being to yield some fragment of self-respect, some shred of responsibility or accountability to anyone. But Step knows that, in the end, a Hayden has to look out for themself. Any act of kindness toward others is an act of momentary self-preservation. And it's gotten tiring.

"I don't have the grit," Step says. "I just don't have it."

Eyes closed, perhaps searching for the magical man, Step feels Haddy's arm slide across both shoulders, her warmth coming closer.

"I don't believe you," she says. She squeezes Step's shoulder. "You're one of the bravest, toughest people I know."

"I don't want to be tough!" Step fires back. "That's the point! I shouldn't need to be!"

"I'm sorry," Haddy says. "I'm not saying—"

"Stop!" Step stands up on tired legs. "You taught me how to survive, and I thank you. I really do. But I can't keep up anymore. I'm tired. What you're doing, whatever it is... it's just too much for me."

Haddy stands up and tries to take Step's hands into hers. "I'm just trying to make sense of all this," she says, giving an exhausted laugh that comes out more like a sigh. "Ever since my accident–"

"Haddy," Step says, cutting her off. "I get it. I mean, I don't. I can't imagine what it's like being fried. But somewhere along the way, it's like you decided to make it your mission to take on every last injustice. The System. Reuben Mayfield. Where does it end?"

Haddy shakes her head, saying, "I just want to help," and Step can see that she wants to say more but she can't seem to bring herself to do it.

"I'm going to go lie down," Step says. "I'm tired. And then I'm going to pack my things and find somewhere new to crash."

"Why?"

"I'm not a Hayden anymore," Step says. "Neither are you. Let's take this chance to become who we each need to be. For ourselves."

Haddy stands, dumbstruck. Maybe this is coming out of nowhere to her. Step doesn't know what Haddy has been through. But for the sake of moving on, it's not worth finding out now.

"Find your blank slate," Step says. "Let all this... whatever you have going on... Let it go."

CHAPTER TWENTY-THREE

A ping from Mom: *Have you seen what they're doing now? Stay safe!*

Attached is a video that has more than two million views since it was posted on Look@Me yesterday.

A shaky porto video shows a group of teens and young adults in hoods, their faces masked with handkerchiefs and balaclavas. Many of them have ponytails dangling from their beanies and caps. The video has a dark, hazy filter to it. The hooded cronies march down Court Street in Brooklyn, smashing car windows, throwing bricks and other objects through shop windows. Molotov cocktails arc through the air, crashing against walls and cars in massive explosions of fire. People are screaming. Babies are crying...

Reply: *Mom, this is fake.*

Mom: *It's not. I got it from Susie. She got it from Karen.*

Reply: *It's obviously fake. Look at the explosions. Have you heard any sirens or helicopters?*

Mom: *Haydens are rioting and you want me to go outside to hear sirens?*

Reply: *Have you watched the whole video? They have missile launchers.*

Mom: *Its really getting out of hand. Whos going to stop these girls?!*

Reply: *MOM ITS NOT REAL!!1!*

Mom: *Are you one of those anti-MIND people now?*

Reply: *Mom, I live 4 blocks from there. NONE of this happend.*

Mom: *Hope ur safe.*

CHAPTER TWENTY-FOUR

Lying in bed and unable to sleep, Thomas stares at a GPS pin on his porto. Within minutes of parting ways, Reuben Mayfield pinged Thomas with a GPS location on the Lower West Side with a message that read, *Deep in the subway tunnels.* If this is actually where Hadley lives, Thomas isn't sure why Mayfield doesn't just go himself. It seems more like a fetch quest than a hunt. Either way, Thomas wonders how he might get to this place any time soon. He has burned his weekly pass already to meet with Mayfield, and there is no way he would get an exception for another. He could wait until Monday to get a new pass, but some things are too important to wait. Maybe he should sneak out and suffer the consequences. Finding the Hayden responsible for bringing down the System is exactly the sort of thing that warrants truancy. Maybe this will solidify his place as first in his class, earning him a 4301 tattoo. He'll be a hero.

Frustrated by MIND's apathy toward the city's upheaval, Thomas thinks that maybe it will take a fresh perspective like his to remedy the situation. After all, he's the one that found Reuben Mayfield. Surely MIND has been looking for Mayfield too.

Thomas puts his porto to sleep and places it back on the charging pad. For the next several minutes he listens to his roommate's heavy breathing and thinks about how kids like Luke can sleep so soundly at a time like this. They're clearly ignorant to the danger out there in System City. Thomas has seen it firsthand. Thanks to his reckless, estranged sister, Thomas knows exactly what these Haydens are capable of. But there's nothing Thomas can do if he's trapped in this dorm room while less-capable agents are out fumbling around to find a culprit that they can't even identify. It's this thinking that convinces Thomas that he must do something. He must act now or his chance might pass by.

Careful not to wake his sleeping roommate, Thomas slowly climbs out of bed and stalks over to Luke's dresser. Cadets are told to keep their uniform shirt and pants hung in the closet. Dressers are for underwear, socks, and recreation t-shirts. In his bottom drawer, Luke keeps a set of what he calls "weekend clothes" for when his mother takes him out to dinner. However, instead of nice dress clothes, Luke's dinner attire includes a navy blue sweatshirt and light gray work pants. This is what Thomas is looking for. He could put on his own casual clothes, which he barely wears, but Luke's worn clothing will make for a more convincing costume.

First, the pants slip on too easily. They won't stay up. To remedy this, Thomas grabs a belt and cinches it tight at the waist until the pant legs dangle loose like two long bells, exposing his ankles at the bottom. Luke is much shorter and heavier than Thomas. So, when Thomas pulls the sweatshirt over his white sleeping shirt like a poncho, his exposed wrists emerge from the end of two short saggy sleeves. The resulting image in the mirror is of somebody who had to scrounge for their clothes and, with no other choice, came up with these. Thomas could add a few stains but thinks it probably isn't necessary. What he sees in the mirror will pass for a male Hayden, or at least some street punk. He messes up his hair and pulls on his training sneakers. He'll have to get the shoes dirtier on his walk to the Lower West Side, but he's pleased with the overall ensemble.

He grabs his porto and, on the way out the door, finds his small pocket knife that he bought at the academy trading post during his first year. Shortly after 3 a.m., nobody is up at the academy. Because it's already well fortified, there's only one security guard on duty. All Thomas has to do is be quiet going down the stairwell, listening for whether the security guard enters the stairwell on his rounds. Lucky for Thomas, the guard never appears, and Thomas is able to exit through a side door into the alley behind their dorm building. From there, his escape is mostly a matter of confidence, keeping his head down in case there are any cameras while he strides with conviction toward the nearest street.

At the sidewalk, Thomas takes in the lights and the way the buildings rise stoically into the sky. As with his walk home last night, he finds himself becoming more comfortable with the city at night. Perhaps it's because he has a real, tangible mission and he feels that he too can walk with a sense of purpose like everyone else. Only, at night, there are so few people out that he can't help but sense that he's doing something wrong.

As he passes by dark windows and shadowy alleyways, Thomas wonders if somebody is watching him. Is he out of place? He quickly consults his porto for the destination but tucks it away before he draws any attention. When he comes upon a Streetboard leaning against a lightpost, he pulls up the app to see if he can rent it. The charge appears to be low but he hopes it can make it the rest of the way. He would never rent one of these during the day for fear that he might run over a pedestrian or be run over himself. He's nearly been hit a number of times by careless people zipping by while he walks.

Now, with the Streetboard he can cover the remaining blocks much faster. As he rolls, the usually dank city air moves past him like a warm breeze. To keep balance, you have to stand more erect and ready like a statue parading quickly along the bike lane. This makes Thomas want to jokingly plant his hands on his hips like a proud superhero. Too bad he has no cape to trail behind him in the wind.

Despite a near scrape with a slippery sewer grate, Thomas arrives at his destination unscathed. There were no death defying stunts or challenging tricks along the way, but that doesn't keep Thomas from feeling like a carefree kid again. Not that he ever really lived that free and easy. But he realizes, for the sake of the mission, that loosening up a little could help him get into character.

He ditches the Streetboard and walks the remaining distance, trying to position himself exactly where Mayfield placed his pin. Only, it's in the middle of an intersection, reminding Thomas that wherever Hadley lives must be below the surface. *How do I get down there?* he wonders. *Through that manhole?* This is a fleeting thought when he smells the sewer vapors.

Thomas retreats to the curb and out of the way of traffic, so he can scan the area for an entrypoint. *Where would a Hayden gain access to subway tunnels?* Thomas immediately realizes the foolishness of this question, and he finds the nearest subway station staircase.

He descends the stairs and hears the gate accept credit from his porto. Once inside, he follows the stairs down to a subway platform that sits between two tracks. Nobody's down here at this hour and, according to the schedule sign, one won't be here for several minutes. He leans over the tracks, looking in either direction where a line of tiny lights stretches until they're no longer visible. A rat scurries past in the darkness below him. If this is the way to Hadley, then the path must be along one of these tracks. But he doesn't know which track to follow and in what direction. He chooses the southbound side and is about to leap onto the track when he hears a noise come from behind.

He freezes, leaning with one hand on the platform and a foot suspended over the track. When he looks back, nobody is there. But he gets up on the platform quickly before whoever or whatever it is appears. Once up, he stands still and waits for another noise, which comes almost immediately. It sounds maybe like feet on a gravel but not in any cadence.

Thomas slowly moves to the other side of the platform, looking for whatever is there. Nothing stands out in the darkness until the sound comes again, and Thomas can hone in on a general direction and area down that tunnel. Sure enough, he sees a figure of a person. He watches the figure, wondering if it's moving, until he realizes that the figure is walking farther down the tracks away from him.

There's no time to consider the danger he's putting himself in. If he wants to find Hadley, following this person is likely the only way. And given the trouble he'll be in when he gets back to the academy, he better have something to show for it.

Thomas tries to lower himself onto the track as quietly as possible. But when he reaches the tracks, he realizes that he's going to have to give up being quiet for moving swiftly. The figure is almost out of sight. But then Thomas sees a flash. Then another. And then a small trickle of light that goes out within seconds. Soon he starts to smell tobacco smoke. The person he's following must be smoking, and Thomas can't help but feel the lawlessness of life in these tunnels.

Not far down the tracks, the figure turns toward the wall, and Thomas can see a tiny red dot that must be the tip of a rolled cigarette. In a seemingly brazen move, the figure tugs open a metal door with a loud squeal of the hinges along with a scraping sound, both of which echo down the tunnel. Then the figure disappears.

When Thomas reaches the door, he can see spray painted tags on the door and concrete wall around it. He touches the handle and gives it a light tug to see how stealth he can be while opening it. He'll have to give it the same tug he watched the figure give it. The door lurches open with a screech, and Thomas waits for any surprise on the other side. Instead, he finds another pedestrian tunnel with caged bulbs lighting the way every twenty feet. Just up ahead, the figure stands at the ready, looking back at Thomas. He can tell the person is probably female, maybe in her teens. But they're backlit by a light just behind them.

She doesn't speak, only takes a drag from her cigarette. The smell of smoke makes Thomas feel guilty by association. He's come this far. There's no turning back. Every move he makes now is a gamble, the first of which is assuming that this person is a Hayden.

"Hadley?" he calls to her. He feels the shape of his knife in the baggy pocket of his pants. She might be able to see him. So, he doesn't remove it.

"I don't think I know her," she says. "Who is she?" Her voice isn't raspy or harsh like he expected. Nor is she threatening. It comes off as more like she's asking for the secret password.

"A Hayden," he says. "Like us." As proud as he is about this cool undercover demeanor, he can't help but feel sickened about roleplaying one of them.

She takes another puff of her cigarette before the red dot darts toward the wall in a tiny spark and settles on the floor. "First time, huh?"

"Yeah," he says, trying to find a balance between toughness and naivety. "Can I follow you? I don't want to get lost."

"Sure," she says, and starts walking again without waiting for him.

Following after her, he keeps a healthy distance of a few feet in case she makes any sudden moves. He can't open his knife in his pocket but he keeps teasing the blade open a little with the meat of his thumb, hoping he'll have a quick reaction if needed.

Along the tunnel, through another door, down a dark, musty staircase, and down another tunnel, Thomas takes note of all the graffiti. Random images pass by. Guitar, dog, shovel, hot air balloon, bicycle wheel, maple leaf. These crude paintings and marker drawings cover the walls like hieroglyphs.

Before long, Thomas emerges from the smaller, cramped tunnels onto another subway line, and he can smell smoke. The girl walks down the middle of the tracks, instead of along the side with any caution. Between this and the trash he sees strewn along the tracks, he figures this must be an old, defunct subway tunnel.

"If you're going to sleep the rest of the morning, be careful where you settle," she says. "Some of us get territorial."

Some of us? So there are others down here? How many? he wonders. In his imagination, Hadley has some tucked-away alley or nook where she nests in blankets and trash. Maybe there are other Haydens nearby in this vision, like some shanty town or village of makeshift tents. But as he follows this Hayden down the tunnel, he can see a pulsing light drawing them closer. Before he knows it, the tunnel opens up into a massive domed room where train tracks cross at the center under a campfire.

And without warning, he finds himself surrounded by more than a dozen Haydens basking in the glow of firelight. The smoke is almost too much to bear but an undercurrent of mildew and body odor makes him glad for the more tolerable smell.

The girl plops down on an old seat cushion next to another Hayden thumbing her porto screen. Thomas can see that this other Hayden has piercings and a face tattoo of a sun on one temple and a moon on the other. The two Haydens lean back against a stack of pallets.

Another Hayden is plucking strings on a guitar, somewhere in the shadows. Thomas can make out a small cover of blankets draped over what looks like a wooden frame or maybe old swing set bars. The guitar doesn't fill the room with noise, perhaps dampened by this rudimentary soundbooth.

"You gonna stand there all day?" says one of the Haydens. "You're making me nervous."

"Oh," Thomas says, and looks around for a place to settle. "I, uh–" He goes to sit on the ground where it's not too dark but not directly on the tracks.

"Not there," says a Hayden.

"Oh, sorry," he says, and shuffles a few feet over.

Another Hayden says, "Seats taken."

Thomas stands again and a few of the Haydens laugh.

"We're just messin'," one says. "Sit wherever." And as Thomas sits, they say, "Except there." And the other's laugh again.

Thomas finally sits on a wooden board that rests on an old car tire, giving the seat a little bounce. Finally settled, he looks around to see that all of the Haydens are girls. He knows there are male Haydens, and has seen them on the street. He also knows that most Haydens are girls. Yet, this doesn't keep him from feeling greatly outnumbered and out of place.

"Who tipped you to the Junction?" asks a Hayden.

"What's that?"

"Who told you we were here?"

"I don't know," he says, trying to think of an answer. "Hadley, I think?"

A couple of Haydens shake their heads like they don't know her. But one says, "Yeah, I know Hadley. She's not been down here much lately."

"Oh," Thomas says, disappointed but still overwhelmed by what he's discovered. "Do people come and go?"

"Come and go?" says a Hayden. "Of course. That's, like, basically life."

A few others laugh.

"Did you just spring from Hayden House?" asks one.

"Yeah," he says. "A few days ago. I've been sort of kickin' around."

"Kickin' around," says a Hayden, looking at another. "Talks funny."

"Do a lot of you–us, I mean–do a lot of Haydens come down here?" he asks.

"Sure," says one. "It's not really a secret. Does nobody talk about it back at HH?"

Thomas doesn't know how to respond without giving himself away. HH must mean Hayden House, and he doesn't know the first thing about that place. In his mind, that place is basically a zoo. He and his classmates joke that it's probably just a bunch of girls in cages waiting to be adopted like they're in some kennel.

"Probably not," says another Hayden. "The next gen are too scared to come down here."

"Nah," says another. "They're just young."

"We were all scared," says another. "Like this guy here." They all look at Thomas.

"I'm not scared," he says, for some reason feeling the need to defend himself.

"Sure," says one of the Haydens. She leans forward and makes a spooky face in the firelight. "Boo!"

Thomas doesn't jump but he is a little freaked out. He realizes that these girls could easily overtake him, and he worries that he won't be able to find his way out. It occurs to him that maybe some of these girls haven't left these tunnels in days. As he studies years of graffiti on the walls and ceiling, he wonders how long this place has been inhabited. What brought the first Hayden down here and what desperation draws others to return?

"So, like, what do you all do?" he asks.

"For fun?" one says and laughs.

"No," he says. "Like to live. Do you all work?"

They laugh.

"I'm a cop," says one.

"Architect here."

"Male stripper," says one of the girls.

They all have a good laugh.

"Nah," one says. "We'll do whatever's paying."

"Oh," he says, not sure what he was looking for in an answer. He didn't expect any to admit to stealing or robbing from people. He's heard that they hustle and do odd jobs. But seeing so many down here at once, and getting a glimpse at where they live, it suddenly makes him wonder if there's any stability among them. While many of these girls seem vile, he can't help but pity them a little.

From down a tunnel, Thomas can hear somebody coming, but none of the Hayden's stir. This must be normal. Into the light comes another Hayden, this one a boy. He's older than Thomas but not by too many years. He's scruffy, as expected, and looks tired. The boy nods at Thomas and warms his hands over the fire. Thomas can see a hospital bracelet peek from the boy's sleeve.

"Throw some more wood on there, would you, Step?" says one of the Haydens.

The boy looks for a piece of wood. Thomas realizes he's sitting on one, gets up, and hands it to the boy. The boy doesn't say anything, just takes it and positions the wood on the fire. He stands back to watch it catch flame. Thomas watches, too, as do others.

"Newb," one of the girls says to the boy, gesturing to Thomas.

"Okay," says the boy.

"He asked what we do for a living," says one.

"Sure," says the boy.

"Step, here, is an astronaut," says another, pointing lazily to the boy.

They laugh.

"Some of us want to be something," the boy says. "Some of us don't."

"None of us can," says one of the Haydens.

"Whatever," says another. "We can but they won't let us. Zoe can play guitar like nobody." A chaotic flurry of strumming comes from the dark. "Mel can cut hair."

"Sure can," says a Hayden that might be Mel.

"Monique fancies herself a developer," says the girl who led Thomas down here.

Beside her, the girl with the porto and face tattoos looks up and says, "Coder."

"See?" says another Hayden. "So much potential."

"What can you do?" one asks Thomas.

"Ah, nothing," he says, not wanting to talk too much.

"Future trash collector," says one, and they all laugh.

"Yeah," Thomas says, trying to joke along.

Conversation slows as the fire grows. Everyone seems entranced. Thomas is feeling the lack of sleep but there's no way he'll be comfortable enough. As the hours pass, some of the Haydens fall asleep. Some, like the boy, retreat to spaces somewhere in the dark. All the while, Thomas stays awake in case Hadley comes through. But she never does. The fire slowly dies.

Eventually, a Hayden with purple hair comes from one tunnel adjusting her small backpack. She looks curiously at Thomas as she kicks a toe at some embers while she passes the fire pit.

"Are you headed out?" Thomas asks her in a hushed voice,

hoping not to wake the others.

"What's it to you?" the girl says.

"I'm new here," he says. "Not sure how to get out."

She snickers and looks him up and down. She's probably younger than Thomas but the wear in her eyes and the way she carries herself makes her seem older. "Fine," she says. "I'll show you."

They don't speak the whole way out. Thomas is thankful. He's exhausted but he needs to remember every turn they take, every door they open. The graffiti seems to lead this way but he doesn't want to rely on that should he come back down here.

At the active subway tunnel, a train punches by just outside the last door, and the girl waits. Thomas can feel his heart rushing from the sound. When they hear the train leave, she puts a shoulder into the door to open it, and they step out into the rush of air trailing the departing train. They walk the tracks to the platform and the girl seems so casual about climbing up as commuters look on. Thomas can't help but feel a mix of shame and fear. But nobody seems to care beyond giving them space. Somebody mutters, "Haydens," but that's the extent of interaction.

By the time Thomas gets back to the academy, he realizes that he can make the tail end of breakfast. In the shuffle of morning routines, he's able to slip back to his dorm without so much as an odd look from other cadets. As much as he wants to wash off the night's funk and the stench of smoke in his hair, he opts for tossing on a uniform and quickly taming his hair with water before heading down to the cafeteria. While he knows he'll have to account for missing drills, he doesn't expect to run into commanding prefect Douglas outside the cafeteria.

"Karp," Douglas says in his best stern tone. "Where were you during drills?"

"Sorry, Douglas," he says. "I slept in."

"No you didn't," Douglas says. "You look like you didn't sleep at all." He smells Thomas's hair. "Where the hell have you been?"

"I can't say," Thomas says.

"Well," Douglas says, waking his porto to take down the official notes. "This is way more than just a demerit. I don't know where you've been but it was obviously offgrounds."

His heart races while his head is foggy from his overnight adventure. While he didn't find Hadley, he has contact with Reuben Mayfield and he knows where the Haydens hide out. Plenty of information that could possibly explain or excuse his whereabouts. But he's too flustered to calculate how he could play it.

"I'm going to have to report this," Douglas says, thumbing through a form on his porto. "And if you're not honest about where you've been, I think this could seriously sink your standing here."

"Wait," Thomas says. "What if I told you I know exactly where the Haydens hideout?"

"That's nice," Douglas says, not taking Thomas seriously. "What good is that?"

"We all know they did this to the System," Thomas hears himself saying. "And I can tell you exactly where they're gathering to plan another attack."

Douglas lowers his porto and says, "I'm listening."

Thomas doesn't know why he made that up but he needs something to get him off the hook. "Can we just keep this to ourselves for now?" he asks. "Maybe you can help me do some more recon." And maybe he and Douglas can team up after all.

"Depends on what you already know," Douglas says. "Convince me."

So, Thomas tells him every detail he learned from subway platform to campfire.

CHAPTER TWENTY-FIVE

A short commercial starts with wholesome music swelling over a scene of children at play in a nondescript city park. The sun breaks through the trees in streaks of golden light. Cut to a close up of children, in slow motion, swinging and singing. Two boys chase each other around the merry-go-round, laughing and squealing.

A voiceover says, "Enjoy your freedom and safety on us."
The MIND logo fades into view over the scene.

The voiceover continues, "Making System City safe for nearly half a century."

Fade out on a closeup of the swinging children.

—

A digital billboard advertisement above Times Square features a man in glasses and a nice t-shirt. He looks into the camera and says, "I am System City."

Cut to a man in a suit. He looks into the camera and says, "I am System City."

Cut to a woman in a pantsuit. She says the same thing.

Then a prep school boy.

A male trash collector.

A well-known female news anchor.

Cut to a shot of all of them together, saying, "We are all System City."

A MIND logo appears in the corner before the advertisement fades.

—

An advertisement on the side of a subway train with the MIND logo in the bottom corner presents a worm's-eye view of a sidewalk. Shadows stretch across the pavement, and the lower part of a pair of legs is at the foreground. The person's tattered pink sneakers have a skull and crossbones drawn on the side of one shoe in permanent marker. The letter *H* is drawn on the other. What appears to be the end of a baseball bat, scuffed with something dark, peeks into the frame, as if the subject is holding the bat at their side.

A line at the bottom reads, *If you see something, say something.*

CHAPTER TWENTY-SIX

"DON'T GET IT TWISTED: BEATING PROPAGANDA AT ITS OWN GAME."
An interview with Drs. Jenna Rosenthal and Gary Ireland
by Nadine Bates

On the patio of Full Stack, the toney East Village pancake spot that serves eponymously sized towers of pan-fried confections, I sit down with Jenna Rosenthal, associate professor of political science and media studies at City University and author of *Propaganda Kryptonite*, along with Gary Ireland, author of *Riding Alone: Propaganda in the Age of Isolationism*, as they spar for the sake of humanity and for the last pat of butter.

Nadine Bates (NB): Jenna, I'd like to start with your work on propaganda. In your book, *Propaganda Kryptonite*, you argue that propaganda's greatest weakness is the story we already know to be true. Can you elaborate on what you mean by "the story"? Or do we need to back up some?

Jenna Rosenthal (JR): Not too far. What I get at with my book is that propaganda, at its core, can only tap into what we feel, not what we know. Narrative is a common structure, among many, for propaganda. But what we feel and what we know are two very different things.

Gary Ireland (GI): Are you talking about card-stacking versus testimonial versus bandwagon, etc.? Because I think we would have to define what we mean by "story" or "narrative" for each propagandic structure.

JR: No. I'm not as concerned with techniques of propaganda. Nor is the book truly concerned with the tools–

GI: The appeals?

JR: Correct. I'm not so much concerned with the appeals themselves.

NB: Can we back up for a second and agree on the basics?

GI: Of propaganda? The basic elements?

NB: Yes. I think our readers can use the refresher. Maybe I can too.

GI: I suppose you mean it must evoke emotion, appeal to some fear or hope in its audience, have simple information, and attack its opponent.

JR: I think Hobbs more or less defines it that way.

GI: Thomas Hobbes? Please don't bring philosophy into this.

JR: I think Philosophy has a place in this discussion. But, no, I was referring to Renee Hobbs.

GI: No philosophy, please.

JR: Fine. Still, I would argue that you don't need all four elements that you describe. You can have just two–say, simple information that evokes emotion–and still constitute propaganda.

GI: That's bad propaganda.

JR: But propaganda nonetheless.

NB: So, then, if those are the four basic criteria, and a story can also contain those same elements, then how can one defeat the other?

JR: By "defeat," I assume you mean in its manipulation. That is, after all, the main objective of propaganda.

NB: Sure, yes. I mean in the battle of manipulative narratives. The battle for control.

GI: I'd argue that all narratives contain manipulation.

JR: But not always for gain. Propaganda is *always* for gain.

GI: Fair.

JR: The main point I try to make is that propaganda must be

sustained for it to keep its hold. We look back on the propaganda of the great wars or those trying to stifle civil rights or of neo-fascism. We can look back and see a clear end to the propaganda coinciding with the end of those popular ideologies.

GI: Now, that's not fair. Both military or culture wars run their course. The utility of propaganda is diminished once the struggle or conflict dissipates.

JR: At the risk of digression, I would argue that the struggle never "dissipates."

NB: Okay, okay. So, you're saying that propaganda runs a course.

JR: It runs a course but is also forgotten.

GI: But we're talking about it.

JR: Academically. Don't be pedantic. I mean that their emotional appeal is forgotten by their target audience. Their control on our emotions or way of thinking is eventually lost.

GI: Because they lose context or because the next wave of propaganda takes hold?

NB: Great question.

JR: That's a question that I try to explore in the book. Context matters for propaganda. However, it doesn't matter for all narratives. Nor does it matter for knowledge.

GI: But then how is this a fair fight? Propaganda limited by context and relevance versus evergreen narrative.

JR: That's the point. One of propaganda's biggest crutches, beyond the need for a manipulator or champion, is the need for relevant context. Narrative wins almost by accident, and it doesn't even know it's in a fight. We can learn from narrative and apply it to relevant real world context over and over. But propaganda relies on being framed in relevancy from the start.

GI: But to weaponize that narrative against propaganda, it needs a champion, somebody who stands to gain from it.

NB: Plenty of literature is written with intent to persuade or

manipulate.

JR: And plenty isn't. But, for the sake of argument, let's restrict propaganda and narrative to the same constraints that we afford all other forms of art and media. If you remove the creator's intentions, all you're left with is how the audience receives it.

NB: **I'm not following.**

JR: Take organized religion. About as dead as it's going to get.

GI: Wait. Are you saying religion was propaganda?

JR: Are you saying it wasn't? What of the four criteria does it not fulfill?

GI: Off the top of my head, how about attacking its opponent?

JR: Maybe not directly.

GI: Okay. Fine. But what about religion was manipulative for gain?

JR: Do I really need to explain that? Did churches preach their version of the gospel to simply spread the word? No. It was for money. Some might even say for power. Sure, churches would argue that without money they couldn't sustain their mission to spread the word. But this is where my argument about knowledge comes in.

GI: Are you going to say that religion wasn't knowledge so much as faith.

JR: I mean, that's part of it. But let's shift gears to more tangible science. After all, religion didn't last but science is still here.

GI: By the skin of its teeth.

JR: Because of waves of propaganda! But I'll argue that science always wins for one simple fact–it is knowledge. We teach it. We don't proselytize it.

NB: **Can you give us an example?**

JR: Sure. Take gravity. Do you question it?

GI: No. I'm not a physicist.

JR: But you believe in it.

GI: Yes. But I don't know anything about it.

JR: What do you know about it?

GI: Well, to be a contrarian, I know it's really a theory. It's not even necessarily true.

JR: First of all, scientific theory isn't the same as theory theory. Science is tested.

GI: And then it becomes a law.

JR: Still not true. Yes, Newton's law of gravity was disproved by Einstein's theory of relativity. But, to me, that only hammers home the notion that scientific theory holds the most weight. Scientific law concerns the tangible relationship between two variables, whereas theory is the how and why. The how and why is never settled. It's just continuously challenged. We test it and test it and test it. And the more it passes tests, the more we accept it.

GI: But isn't testing it the same as questioning it?

JR: Which is why I asked if *you* question it. And you don't. But you believe in it. Though, I would argue that every time you throw a ball in the air and expect it to fall back to your hands, you're testing gravity.

GI: Okay, okay.

JR: Well, the physicists who do question it maybe don't fully believe in it. The more we think about something, the more we consider other angles or sides to it. And the things that can sustain constant questioning, like relativity, will become more deeply accepted as fact.

NB: I see where you're going. Religion can't sustain itself under scrutiny without somebody constantly championing it.

JR: Right. The thing about the church was, in order to survive as a church, you had to keep talking about that faith. But the more you talk about that faith, the more inquisitive your audience might get. Unless you control the narrative. So, when the money dries up, and there's no incentive to keep talking, who then controls the narrative? And if nobody controls it, then people are left to forget their faith, thus the propaganda loses. Or they just question their faith and, again, propaganda loses to empirical evidence.

GI: Okay. So, give me an example of narrative that wins over propaganda but that isn't supported by empirical evidence.

NB: That was my next question. I swear.

JR: Did you ever turn over your shoes and give them a tap to knock the spiders out before you put those shoes on?

GI: Can't say that I have but I know people do that.

JR: Or, you have a kid, right?

GI: In his twenties now but yes.

JR: Did you ever check his Halloween candy for needles?

GI: Maybe once. I can't speak for my wife. But I know exactly what you're talking about.

JR: That's what I mean. You've heard the story. Probably never did it yourself. Nor could you even recollect a complete narrative example of it ever happening. But you *know* the story. You have its morals, themes, and relative emotions burned into your brain.

GI: Okay. Fine. I'll go along with that. But it means nothing without context.

JR: True. You're right. But isn't halloween the context? People don't check all the candy bars they buy at the store throughout the year. But some people still check halloween candy. And why is it that anyone would check candy on halloween? Out of fear.

NB: Okay. So, we have emotions evoked. But can we tie this back to propaganda?

GI: Yes, please.

JR: Of course. So, take manipulation out of religion.

GI: You mean, take away organized religion. The church.

JR: Exactly. You have no church. Nobody to hammer home cherry-picked, often whitewashed stories from a bible. Let's say a person has only heard some of those stories, maybe from a family member or referenced in a book or a movie. They hear enough to know the themes or morals of the story. That person might draw on those themes or morals to solidify their sense of right and wrong in a given situation.

GI: Or they could have simply had moral, ethical, caring parents.

JR: Yes. That too.

GI: You seem to be discounting children's stories or folktales that carry the same themes. Why can't we attribute a moral compass to those?

JR: We can. I would. But I also wouldn't argue–with the exception of Dr. Seuss's very propagandic work in the 1940s–that these stories are manipulative. Whereas organized religions weaponized biblical narrative for certain gain.

NB: In your book, you talk about a study done in the late 30s. Can you expand on that?

JR: So, a think tank does a study on bias and cultural influence in... I want to say 2036 but it might have gone over a year or two. As with any cultural study, it bled into religion, focusing partly on different religious communities within the United States.

GI: I read about this. I know this.

JR: The part that stuck out to me was when they surveyed Christian faiths. Participants were asked to identify their standing in organized religion, ranging from deeply involved–like going more than once a week to service, attending bible study, participating in church events–to merely influenced–such as people who say they were "raised Catholic" or had a "religious grandma" who exposed them to bible stories on occasion when they were very young. People were asked to relate their feelings about God on a scale from fear to love. The more involved people were in their church, the more they swung in either extreme. Whereas the least involved participants, the ones whose memory or knowledge of biblical stories were vague, fell right in the middle.

GI: As expected.

JR: Yet, also as expected, all participants had a firm sense of right and wrong in scenario-based questions, especially when the question ended with "What would Jesus do?"

GI: So, ethically, they were identical. But they're knowledge-base was very different.

JR: Yes, one group gave money to an organization whose sole

purpose was, apparently, to teach those people how to be moral and ethical. Whereas the other just sort of *knew* the very basics of those same stories.

NB: Interesting.

GI: It was a small study. But I can see the value. Yet, where do we cross the line into propaganda? I can argue that tithing is just paying your dues to a club for a sense of belonging. I'd even argue that they're paying tuition, if you look at church more like biblical education.

JR: Well, here's the tipping point for me. Those same participants were then asked about other religions. Mind you, the participants of other faiths were asked similar moral and ethical questions and identified on the same scale of engagement from deeply involved to slightly influenced. And the outcome was similar. They all had the same sense of right and wrong in any given modern-day situation. But when asked about other religions–

GI: I know where you're headed.

JR: The most deeply entrenched Christians nearly always said the others were wrong.

NB: Attacking the opponent.

JR: They all had the same basic knowledge–of right and wrong, good and bad–but for some it was twisted by a propagandist, somebody with an agenda. And when organized religion failed in the face of global catastrophe, we see now that those most deeply entrenched ended up feeling betrayed, so much so that their sense of right and wrong was fractured.

GI: They either rejected what they learned or didn't know how to apply those morals to contexts outside the propagandist's view, like what others might view or experience.

JR: People will believe what they want to believe. Yet, morals that are *known*, and not forced, are likely to be stronger than those forced by a propagandist.

NB: So, what's the moral of this whole thing?

GI: Knowledge is power.

JR: And knowledge can be twisted.
GI: So, don't get it twisted.

PART THREE

The thing about being a Hayden is that you might be homeless but you're not alone. You have people around who will help you out of jam. You have a lot of the same problems as the average drifter, like where you might sleep tonight or where your next meal will come from, but you know there are a hundred or so people within a five-minute walk who can help you for at least one night.

CHAPTER TWENTY-SEVEN

There are things I wish I could forget. Like almost everything having to do with my birth parents. You wouldn't think I actually knew them. Why should I? I'm a Hayden, an outcast, a byproduct of this country's lousy history. Take a massive economic crash and a government trying to recoup by selling off any non-urbanized land to American Indian tribes. Cram everyone into a dozen or so select cities, like this crummy place, leaving behind skeletal suburban remains where tribal colonies now grow amidst an otherwise abandoned and barren rural landscape.

Weston pauses the audio player when Trevor walks in.

"Is that Haddy?" Trevor asks.

"Yes," Weston says, embarrassed that he was caught listening to her audio files. "What do you need?"

Trevor stands quietly for a moment and then says, "I miss her. She's genuine."

"I agree," Weston says. He's been listening to Hadley's files for the last couple of days and has been marveling at the courage it must have taken to put herself out there like that, even if she was the only one who would hear it. She clearly knew that somebody might one day come across it, what with everything being in the cloud and vulnerable to security breaches.

"Anyway," Trevor says. "Renee and Laars have an inventory from the garden. They can use more manure and some tools."

Weston is still thinking about Hadley and only half listening to Trevor. Apparently it's obvious because Trevor says, "Should I come back?"

"No," Weston says, deciding that he needs to be firmer as a leader. He's felt detached for so long, and he's still trying to figure out how to treat the residents. "Make it happen then," he says.

"Make it happen?" Trevor asks. "So... I should go get their supplies?"

"Get the supplies," he says.

"Ok," Trevor says, but instead of leaving, he stays there in the doorway. "Weston?"

"Yes?"

"How do I do that?"

Weston doesn't have time for this, he thinks. Just the thought of training others to do what he used to under Mayfield makes Weston feel overwhelmed. But when he looks at Trevor, he sees somebody who has spent his whole time at the colony acting out of blind faith, doing whatever Mayfield asked, rather than understanding why. Weston thinks that if he leads through transparency and empowers residents to take on more responsibilities, then their ownership in the colony will deepen. But Weston also wonders if that's the best way to lead. Mayfield's opaque, top-down method worked for a reason. And maybe it was because nobody wanted to take responsibility.

But, Weston thinks, *is that sustainable?*

"I'll tell you what," Weston says. "Let's sit down after dinner and look at the inventory. I'll run you through what I've always done."

"Okay," Trevor says, turning to leave.

"Trevor," Weston says. "Think about what'll work best for you all. Let me know if you have any ideas on where we can improve." Weston was never able to do this with Mayfield and it drove him crazy. Mayfield was thorough and detail-oriented but didn't always have the best perspective when it came to how things worked outside the colony. Running supplies takes knowing how to best source them and what are the best times to get them and routes to take.

Trevor seems almost confused but says, "Sure. Yeah. Will do." And he leaves.

Staring through Mayfield's iWindow at the closing office door, Weston worries about whether he's doing the right thing. Part of him wants to go back to being subordinate. Maybe he can relinquish control to the watchers. After all, their MIND training is probably perfect for establishing order. But he also knows that the residents might not take well to more regimented operations.

Perhaps he's procrastinating or simply avoiding his duties as a leader, but Weston goes back to what he was doing and clicks the audio player again.

The result of that great migration is overpopulated cities with a half-assed unwritten one-child rule stoked by certain meager government incentives. You get abandoned babies—dead or alive—left at fire stations and churches. Usually girls because, you know, it's more important to pass on the family name than to spare a life. You get thousands of unwanted children roaming the streets. You get the Haydens. You get me.

He stops the audio player and thinks about Hadley. When he met her, she was so defenseless. But there was also this flame within her. She always seemed to be simmering with energy. Maybe not always good energy–like when she lashed out. But what can anyone expect from somebody who was basically abandoned on the street?

As Weston listens to these audio files, he can't help but feel motivated by her assuredness and her understanding. There's something honest and raw about what Hadley has recorded. She tells everything the way it happened. No mask. No filter. It's the diary of a girl from the street who couldn't catch a break. But it's also the story of corruption and evil. And maybe Weston feels that he's complicit just for listening to it and doing nothing about it. Or by keeping the colony going and creating a safe haven for people to flee that corruption, then he is doing something. At least that's what Weston tells himself for now.

Weston sits back for a moment and considers what it'll take to train up some of the residents to do his previous roles, who will be best at doing what, and who might show interest. While he's not sure if this is the best way to go about leading, he can't let that insecurity take hold. If anything, he has the tools and the foundation for the colony to succeed. He's also convinced that somewhere on Mayfield's iWindow he'll find a roadmap of what they need. He's just too afraid to mess up something on the screen. He doesn't know if he can close any programs for fear that he won't be able to find them again. But with so many programs open on this massive expanse of a screen, it's hard to keep track of what's important now and what might be worthwhile later, especially when he doesn't know half of what he's looking at.

For instance, he occasionally sees something move on the corner of the screen, peeking out from behind others. Short strands of text pop into view from the bottom of the small program like a messaging application. It seems like nonsense as he reads them.

Rats nest. 40.767944868386515, -73.98573822730559.

Gather falcons at 40.768068229907314, -73.98187281456427

Send for armadillo backpack.

Mayfield was good at deciphering things. After all, there are at least two programs on this iWindow that are dizzying walls of code that nobody would make sense of. But this is different. It's almost like something Weston has seen in old military movies.

He pings 2701 to meet him in the office.

While he waits, Weston thinks about playing some more of Hadley's diary but refrains. Before long, 2701 knocks and enters the room.

"Ten Fifty-two and I are finishing up the cameras," he says. "We'll need to install the monitors on your iWindow once we're done. They're not the best. We had to source them from a territory south of here. But they'll do for now."

"Sounds good," Weston says. "Thank you. But I have something else here I want you to look at."

"I really don't do computers," 2701 says. "We'll be able to install surveillance but–"

"I just thought you might understand what I'm looking at here,"

Weston says, pointing to the odd messages.

2701 points and says, "Well, right off the bat, I can tell you those are coordinates. And–" He stops and backs away.

"What?"

"Rats," he says. "That's—"

"What?!"

"Rats is code for Haydens," 2701 says. "Mayfield has a tap on MIND comms. Unbelievable." He looks away for a moment, eyes wide. "I have to admit, he was impressive."

"So," Weston says, still confused. "Rats nest means—?"

"Maybe their hideout," says 2701. "But that's not what I'd be worried about. I'd be more concerned about armadillo backpack."

"Why?" Weston asks, seeing a spark of concern in 2701's eyes.

"That's artillery." 2701 points to the coordinates. "They're talking about a weapon's shipment going to this location."

Weston looks at the message and the coordinates. It makes no sense to him what this means. But it likely matters to Haydens back in the city.

"Something big is about to go down. Glad I'm not there," 2701 says and, as if none of that matters, he goes to leave. "I'll let you know when we have those cameras operational."

"Thank you," Weston says, and he watches the door close as 2701 leaves.

System City seems so far away, and what goes on there seems so inconsequential to the colony. But Weston knows people there, and now he has information about something big that might happen. Maybe in a previous role he would have kept quiet, waiting for Mayfield to order his next move. But now he's the colony leader.

And suddenly, instead of thinking about what Mayfield would do, Weston finds himself wondering how Hadley would deal with this.

CHAPTER TWENTY-EIGHT

The news studio isn't what Agent Stevenson expected when he contacted them about an interview. Small like a hotel room and lit so brightly from such small lights, the entire space is still barely enough room for him, Max Neuland, a camerawoman, and two staff members who seem to handle everything else. Yet, here he is about to send every last bit of his credibility into question for the sake of blowing a gaping hole of truth into MIND's System failure.

The producer couldn't offer a live broadcast, which Agent Stevenson imagined to be the most potent option, but they agreed to expedite the interview, given its relevance. Agent Stevenson promised to give an exclusive, first-ever MIND agent account of everything happening behind the scenes. However, he didn't tell them that he doesn't officially work for MIND anymore.

Based on what he plans to share, Agent Stevenson isn't idealistic enough to imagine that people will take to the streets in protest. The citizens of System City have never been known for their shared passion. In fact, instead of bringing people together through familiarity, the System has done more to build mass apathy. People simply don't care enough. But what he expects to come from this interview is more transparency on how MIND operates and to, at the very least, clear Haydens of their stigma.

Moreover, Agent Stevenson hopes that MIND will not be able to touch him once this interview makes him a high-profile figure in the whole story. If people really listen to what he's saying, there will be no way for MIND to simply make him disappear.

Perched on the edge of a black metal chair topped with a fake leather cushion, Agent Stevenson practices his posture, holding it better than he has since sitting at attention at the academy. Across from him is an identical black metal chair where Max Neuland will sit. But at the moment, Neuland is flicking through his porto, reacting with loud scoffs and guffaws at something he's reading.

A large compact of makeup appears before Agent Stevenson. "Hold still," the makeup artist says. "I just need to dull this sheen."

"No," Agent Stevenson says, putting up a hand.

"Fine," says the makeup artist. He calls over his shoulders, "Lights for a shiner!" And walks away.

Lighting keeps changing slightly in position, shade, and intensity.

"Ready in four!" calls another staff member. Aside from the camerawoman and Max Neuland, the others keep appearing and disappearing through two different doors, moving things, leaving things, and hollering the whole way.

Max Neuland sits and the makeup artist finishes patting below his eyes while he moves his porto around to see it.

"Everyone seems rushed," Agent Stevenson says.

Max Neuland keeps his mouth shut while makeup is being applied. Once the makeup artist disappears, Neuland keeps looking at his porto but says, "I go live in..." he flicks at his porto for the time and says, "fifty-four minutes." Tucking his porto in his jacket pocket, he says, "But no rush. Let's get this right."

"Ready," says the camerawoman.

Max Neuland fires off a two-finger hand gesture to signal for them to start rolling. To Agent Stevenson, he says, "Don't worry. We'll edit in an intro. Let's just cut to it."

"Got it," Agent Stevenson says, though he doesn't completely understand.

As if a totally different person is sitting across from him, Max Neuland sits upright, squares off with Agent Stevenson, and says in a broadcasting voice that startles him, "Special Agent Kelsey Stevenson, welcome."

Hearing his first name takes him off guard but he rebounds and says, "Thank you for having me."

Max Neuland looks at the camerawoman and drops his broadcasting voice to say, "Keep rolling. We'll do second takes after."

He gets a thumbs up from the camerawoman.

"We're honored to have a MIND agent in our studio for an exclusive," he says in his broadcasting voice. "And thank you for your service."

Agent Stevenson nods in acknowledgement.

"Does it make sense to get your origin story?" Max Neuland asks. "Should we start from the beginning?"

"I don't know," Agent Stevenson says. "Maybe just confirm my credentials?"

"I'll queue it up in the intro." To the camerawoman, Max Neuland says, "Or in post. Keep rolling."

"Special Agent Stevenson, what can you tell us about MIND's efforts to rectify this travesty?"

"Good question," Agent Stevenson says. "MIND has the resources to address this issue in two ways."

"The dual-pronged approach that Director Arthur Klopek announced."

"Correct. That involves agents on the ground, as well as a team of cyber specialists aimed at reversing the effects of the attack and working in lockstep with field agents to apprehend the bad actors behind this attack."

"And, as we understand it, MIND is looking closely at a group of Haydens for this."

"That's a–" Agent Stevenson doesn't want to feed this line of thinking, but has to dance around coming off as insubordinate. "MIND is exhausting all possible leads."

"So, you won't confirm that Haydens are the primary suspects," Max Neuland says. "Our sources say otherwise. And I should add, the confidence level is high. Can you reveal any of these other leads? Maybe our viewers will be able to help."

Agent Stevenson would like to redirect the conversation but can't figure out a way. He could easily cut this short by explaining Reuben Mayfield's plot to take down the System and what then happened to Mayfield, but then he would have to explain how he knows this information while MIND doesn't. So, he says, "I think we need to back up a bit."

"Oh?"

"I'd like to back up a bit," he says. "I think your viewers need more context on how the System works."

"That would be fantastic," Max Neuland says, perking up. "Please spare us the technical jargon though."

"Of course," Agent Stevenson says. "As a field agent, I don't even understand all the bells and whistles."

"Very good," says Max Neuland. "Also, please know that we'll be airing a full look 'under the hood,' as they say. So, feel free to skip anything about databases and, well, the identity recognition stuff."

"That's more or less the System," Agent Stevenson says.

"Ah. Well, I guess we beat you to the punch. Then can you give our viewers a field agent's perspective? What goes on in your day to day to preserve the System from the ground?"

Agent Stevenson feels his detachment from MIND driving a rift between what he wants to say and what he thinks he should say. Can he jump right into how MIND is killing off Haydens with each and every update of the System? Will viewers understand that they, too, were at a time victims of this archaic process?

He sees no other way around it. The people need the truth.

"Okay," Agent Stevenson says. "Let's start with the Department of System Dependencies and Continuity."

"Sounds very official," Max Neuland says with a playful smirk.

"Official indeed," says Agent Stevenson.

"Almost top secret," Max Neuland says.

"Covert," Agent Stevenson says. "Almost sinister."

Max Neuland's smirk melts a little but he doesn't stop Agent Stevenson from continuing.

"My most recent role in the Department of System Dependencies and Continuity was what us insiders refer to as a 'stager'."

"A stager," Max Neuland says. "What does a stager do?"

"To put it bluntly," Agent Stevenson says, looking briefly at the camera. "A stager... A stager ensures that the System will update in a given timeframe."

"Okay."

"But the stager also makes sure that it's done so in the most secure manner possible."

"That sounds like a good thing," Max Neuland says, curious as to why Agent Stevenson is reluctant to talk about this. "Can you tell our viewers how that's done?"

"Sure," Agent Stevenson says, unsure if he can bring himself to say this to millions of people. Can he reveal one of MIND's darkest secrets? But before he considers the right and wrong of revealing it, he just says it. "We kill people."

"Sorry?"

"Every time the System updates, somebody has to die," Agent Stevenson finally says. And he continues to explain. "The System has airtight security."

Max Neuland's face is frozen, a mix of captivation and shock.

"Everyone with a chip in their head has a unique password that will allow access to the gateway for data updates to pass through. So, as a stager, I would ensure that a person is set up to provide that password."

Max Neuland touches his face nervously. He scratches his cheek with the back of his thumb and, as if realizing this nervous tic, brings his hand back down across his face.

"But part two of the staging process is to make sure that the mark–that's what we call the person who provides the latest password... We make sure they don't remember."

Max Neuland briefly looks at the camerawoman.

"We kill them," Agent Stevenson says. "And now–"

Agent Stevenson realizes that Max Neuland has looked at the camerawoman. Her face is flush as she stares over the camera. It occurs to Agent Stevenson then that Max Neuland wasn't scratching his face. He was drawing his thumb across his neck.

"Are we still rolling?" Agent Stevenson asks, looking between Max Neuland and the camerawoman.

At that moment, he gets a ping. It's from Hadley.

"We can't continue this interview," Max Neuland says. "I don't think..." He shifts in his seat. "Well, MIND is a sponsor and..."

"I'm trying to give you the truth behind all this," Agent Stevenson says. He looks down at the ping from Hadley and sees the phrase, *A shipment of weapons.*

"We can't air this," Max Neuland says.

A staff member, maybe the producer he originally contacted, comes from a doorway and says, "Kill it. Kill it. We can't run this."

"You understand," Max Neuland says. "They're our sponsor. I appreciate you sticking your neck out like this but–"

"Kill it," calls the producer.

"So, this isn't going to happen?" Agent Stevenson says. "But your viewers need to hear this."

"We can't," Max Neuland says, standing up. He pulls the microphone from his lapel. To the producer, he says, "We don't want anything to do with this, do we?" And he walks out the door.

Agent Stevenson watches as his only chance to expose MIND has just left the room.

"Thank you for your time," the producer says, and he guides the camerawoman out of the tiny studio as if Agent Stevenson has some sort of contagious disease. The lights cut out.

Agent Stevenson looks at the full message from Hadley and starts out the door before finishing it. The message reads, *A shipment of weapons and ammunition is on its way to System City. MIND is waging war on Haydens.*

CHAPTER TWENTY-NINE

There's a show at Ziggy's, and Cammy can't quite bring herself to go. Normally she would dump her work clothes, put on something comfier and grungier, and let some towering speakers blow all the stress and pressure from the work week right out of her head. She would dance with friends, enjoy a few drinks, and be the person her coworkers would be mortified to meet. Oh, the stories she could tell.

But the practical woman she has become also tells her to stay away from any place full of Haydens. She has read about the insane stupidity of old America, when guns outnumbered people and any gathering-from parades to grocery stores to elementary schools-became invitations for target practice. Long gone are the daily mass shootings but if ever there was a moment in her lifetime that mirrored the ugliness of humanity's past, it's now with all these anti-Hayden ravings from the media. Perhaps more exhausting than the hateful rhetoric is the lifetime of ducking and dodging, of barely scraping by, of constantly having to prove herself against all prejudices.

That is why Cammy finds herself in a swanky bar on the edge of Greenwich Village, sipping a drink she can't name and can barely afford. She needs the colorful lights, the flashy dress, and upbeat music to melt away the ennui of sitting alone in a hermetically sealed chamber of an office and staring through an iWindow at a blank white wall as undynamic and lifeless as her future.

When the texts start coming in from Haddy and others, Cammy's heart quickens. Her sisters are in distress. The unflinching response from other Haydens is the result of Cammy's and other OG Haydens' hard work. Haydens aren't known for longevity. Most of Cammy's peers and predecessors have fallen to crime, drugs, starvation, or poor health from living on the streets. Cammy is among a very few who remember when the Junction was founded. She participated in building a culture of inclusivity and sisterhood. To see so many replies to Haddy's ping fills Cammy's heart.

But she has to let it go. She has to leave this to the younger generation. By the looks of it, they'll handle themselves just fine, whatever the situation. Of course, it might be nothing at all. From what she can tell, something is going down at 79th near the river. Or maybe it's Joseph Brant Circle. It's probably just another stupid prank. This is what happens when you have so many bored, feral kids who are desperate for attention of any kind. Cammy can't bother with this right now or ever again.

Her cocktail has a curl of orange peel in it that the bartender had set on fire before serving the drink. Cammy pushes the orange peel deeper into the glass and swirls it with her finger. She hears the chime of another message. Instead of looking at it, she silences her porto and sets it on the bar, screen down. *The kids are alright*, she thinks and takes another sip.

CHAPTER THIRTY

In a thick of trees on the edge of old Van Cortlandt Park sits an unmarked warehouse that can easily be confused with the sanitation department buildings just south of it. One of three garage doors opens to reveal the frontend of a box truck. Behind it, a man in gray tactical gear lifts the loading ramp and slides it back into the truck. The other man wheels a dolly to the side and positions it against a wall. The two get into the cab of the box truck. A third man by the door gives a jovial wave. The passenger of the truck flips him the middle finger, and they all seem to laugh.

The truck's motor comes to life with a whoosh before settling at a low hum, and the truck rolls forward. The man beside the door punches a button on the wall and the door lowers.

—

There's nothing else Haddy could do but relay Weston's message to Agent Stevenson, hoping that he might be able to stop the shipment from within. MIND is tracking her by GPS. So, they're also probably tapping her messages. She doesn't want to put Agent Stevenson in jeopardy, but if what Weston told her is true, then an army of police and MIND agents are going to descend on the Junction this evening. Per Weston's intel, MIND's rendezvous spot is Joseph Brant Circle, a block from the most high-traffic entrypoint to the Junction.

Now, standing here several levels up and staring down the center of the Vessel in old Hudson Yards, all Haddy can do is wait for his response. He'll know how MIND works. If he can't get them to fall back, he might have a plan for Haydens to stop them.

A few levels up, some Haydens are sitting on the stairs leading to the landing across the Vessel from Haddy. The Vessel's webbed shawarma shape allows wind to sharply pass through. She can almost hear them giggling but the wind is blowing a bit too hard. She wants to warn them about what's going to happen but maybe it's best to keep them in the dark, as long as they don't go to the Junction. Haddy thinks about sending out a mass ping to tell everyone to avoid the Junction but MIND will see that.

Of course, Haddy can't help but feel responsible. They skimmed her porto for everywhere she has been in the last few weeks. They must know where the Junction is from that GPS data. She could have run or put up a fight when agents came for her in Step's hospital room. But she doesn't think she would have gotten far.

Now they have the exact location of the Junction and by nightfall will probably have the place under siege. Haddy imagines militarized police troops swarming in from the nearest subway stations like roaches as they pour down the tunnel, busting open each door in their path, and surrounding the unsuspecting Haydens that are down there. There will be nowhere to run.

A ping comes in from Agent Stevenson. *How do you know this?*

At the risk of MIND seeing this, she writes, *Weston.*

Can you give me more details?

Agent Stevenson knows they're tracking her messages. So, he must know what he's doing. *Sometime tonight. Joseph Brant Circle.*

Why there?

Haddy doesn't want to say or to confirm what MIND already knows. She writes, *No clue.*

Agent Stevenson's next ping doesn't come right away. Maybe he's planning their next move. Across the way, the two Haydens are playfully shoving each other. One acts like she's going to throw the other over the railing. Haddy wonders how many of the suicides that have occurred here are actually just kids horsing around and going too far. The Haydens start to chase each other around the Vessel. Haddy can hear their shrieks and screams when they pass overhead on her side. They seem so carefree.

The next ping reads, *Armory in Riverdale. Backpack come down HHP. Take 79 or 72 to Broadway.*

What can she do with this information? She's not a military captain. How is she supposed to fight back against MIND?

Get eyes on Joe Brant now, he writes. *Round up your troops.*

I can't stop them, she writes.

Stop the truck.

"What the hell can I do?" she says aloud. "What? Throw a bunch of us on the Hudson Parkway and stop traffic?" She imagines a group of Haydens stretched across the southbound lanes, cars backed up for miles, just to hold up some weapons truck.

A message arrives with a picture. The image is of a large, light gray box truck. It's not in motion but not a stock image either. Haddy wonders if this is of the actual truck or of one similar to what MIND will drive.

She opens her GPS and looks at the route. "There," she says, and taps where the street makes a circle on the map. She remembers that old roundabout at the end of 79th Street just after it tucks under the parkway. The roundabout encircles a strange pool of water that is fed by the river. She and some Haydens tried to swim there once until they realized that this was a dumping ground for old appliances and tires. Now she thinks it's the perfect spot to send this truck.

She decides she'll need to send out mass pings. Best case scenario, MIND gets spooked and calls off the raid. Worse case scenario, this becomes a war.

As many as can make it. Roundabout end of 79th, she writes. And then, *Lock it up.*

—

A dark red car makes its way under Henry Hudson Parkway going west on 79th Street. When it reaches the roundabout, it slams on the brakes at the sight of a Hayden hopping off the short concrete lip that separates the street from the choppy water around it. Another Hayden joins her, and the car carefully drives past them, around the circle and back out to 79th Street.

Another Hayden appears from under the parkway, and then three more arrive. They assemble haphazardly at the opening of the circle.

—

Agent Stevenson knows what he is doing, Haddy thinks. And she realizes that he must think she can handle this or he wouldn't bother helping. That's enough confidence to keep Haddy from giving up.

She writes to all Haydens, *Trouble in Joe Brant. Need a report but don't be seen.*

On it, comes the first ping.

Almost there

See you there.

More responses keep rolling in, and it's moments like this that make Haddy proud to be a Hayden. Chalk it up to a lack of accountability or boredom or a collective desire to make mischief. But Haydens are always ready to jump in without question. This reminds her of a time when a few Haydens had the brilliant idea to mess with the morning commute. There wasn't any reason but to make a few million people really really angry.

Before Haddy can even relive that glorious day, she realizes that their prank is exactly the answer she's looking for.

—

At the Central Park entrance nearest Joseph Brant Circle, three Haydens find themselves on the edge of a makeshift military encampment. Parked half on the curb, Police vans, unmarked MIND cars, and assorted black SUVs create a perimeter around the outside of the circle. MIND agents gather in a small group around the central monument. The three Haydens' view of them is obscured by trees, so they climb the Maine Monument for a better vantage point. One Hayden is able to reach the golden-statued peak for a better view of the entire scene. Along the outer circle, just inside the line of vehicles, police in tactical gear stand at attention. A captain paces before them, barking orders as they wait for their weaponry to arrive.

—

Pings start pouring in.

Hundreds of cops

Crap. Its an army down here.

What's going on? Are we screwed?

Troops right on our doorstep.

Haddy writes, *Stand by. Keep us posted on movement. They're planning a raid.*

More replies.

NO!

What should we do?

We can take em!

We're screwed

Haddy writes, *Take it easy. We got this.* She opens her GPS and looks at the route that Agent Stevenson gave her. She writes, *Need eyes on HHP. North of 79th. BOLO.* And she attaches the image of the box truck. *Report when it approaches.*

Within thirty seconds, a reply comes. *We got you.*

—

Haydens play water ball up near 108th Street, in what everyone now calls River Park because the river long ago encroached on this westside shortline and forced the city to build the elevated Henry Hudson Parkway everyone knows today.

Water ball is a hybrid, hydro version of soccer, taking place on the flooded fields of old Riverside Park. Haydens kick a ball up and down the field to score on netless goals at each end. The sun-bleached rubber ball skims chaotically over choppy waters, as players plod along splashing and kicking at this shin-high murk of Hudson runoff.

When Haddy's ping comes in, a bunch of Haydens on either team wade to the Henry Hudson Parkway and, despite their soaked clothing, scale the concrete columns to sit along the edge of the southbound lanes on watch for a suspicious gray box truck to pass.

—

Traffics moving, pings a Hayden.

Haddy checks the time but then realizes she has no idea when the weapons truck will leave, if it hasn't already. She plots the route as if she's going to drive it, and the GPS tells her it should take just under forty minutes.

Troops are lining up in rows over here. Helmets on, comes a ping from a Hayden at Joseph Brant Circle.

This might mean the truck is almost there. But with no call from the girls along Hudson Parkway, Haddy gets antsy. Maybe she'll have to create some congestion to slow things down.

Anyone see an accident at West End and 95th? she writes, talking about an intersection and exit before the one she wants the truck to take. Of course, nobody sees an accident. But the Haydens are about to create one.

Haddy taps the location of her fake accident on the GPS. A bubble pops up with options to tag it as an accident or speed trap or construction. She chooses *accident*. An accident icon of a wrecked car appears. Within seconds, that stretch of road turns orange and then red on her GPS, as several other Haydens tag the same fake accident.

—

A car swerves back onto the parkway just before exiting at 95th Street and nearly hits another car in the right lane. A few other cars that had slowed to exit onto 95th have regained speed to take the next exit and avoid the accident their GPS is telling them.

—

Got our bogey. Just hit 105th.

Haddy calculates the time it would take per block to get down Hudson Parkway and figures she has about six minutes to force this truck onto 79th Street.

She taps the offramp at 72nd and reports another accident. Only, now she waits two minutes before instructing the others. Then she writes, *Accident at 72nd offramp.*

A few pings come from elsewhere. *Police locking down 59th station. 57th too,* says another.

—

Traffic is already slowing a little by 75th Street. As the truck reaches

86th, the way past 73rd Street is already red. As the truck approaches 79th Street exit, it slows and makes a last-second decision to get off the parkway. Up ahead, there appears to be a crowd of girls, but it's too late to turn around.

—

Bogey approaching.

See some faces. Not too happy.

Haddy writes, *Stop em.*

How?

However you want, she replies. She hasn't considered what to do beyond this but when the next ping comes, she realizes that it doesn't matter. These girls are all in.

Get em!

—

The gray box truck slows to a crawl as it approaches a swarm of Haydens at the roundabout on 79th Street. The girls part as the truck idles through, but the group fluidly closes behind the truck, engulfing it. The truck stops.

The two men sit for a moment as girls of all ages close in on them. "What the hell?" says the driver, first to his mate. Then through the windshield, he yells, "Get out the way!"

A Hayden closest to the driver's side signals for him to let the window down. A tuft of blue hair springs from a knot of hair at the top of her head. It bounces as she steps up onto the rail along the bottom of the truck's door. Her face is right up on the window, and the driver leans away in confusion.

"Roll the window down," she instructs him.

The passenger side door opens to more Haydens already pushing to get in closer. A girl directly in front of the truck has both arms in the air like she's about to catch a giant ball. Her pink, star-shaped sunglasses are slipping down her nose as she says, "Aaaaaand pop!"

The sudden hiss of four truck tires being punctured can be heard throughout the crowd and inside the cab of the truck.

To the driver's puzzled face, the blue haired girl says, "We'll take it from here."

—

Those boys can run, says one ping.

What about this cargo?

Haddy writes, *Dump it in the river.*

In a moment, a video ping appears. It's a short video of Haydens dragging crates from the back of the box truck. It takes three Haydens to carry one crate to the giant well of river water at the center of the circle. They get it to the lip of the well and dump the crate's contents into the water like they're reenacting the Boston Tea Party. Other Haydens are in the background cheering, some of them holding rifles they harvested from the crates.

From another level of the Vessel, Haddy can hear the two Haydens celebrating what they must be watching on their portos.

Then comes another ping from Joseph Brant Circle. *Captains waving arms. Troops confused.*

—

From the very top of the Maine Monument, a fifteen-year-old Hayden in a track jacket and cargo pants watches as rows of troops fall out of line, looking at each other for an answer to what just sullied their mission. MIND agents are already entering their cars and attempting to pull away through the crowd of confused police officers.

"What's going on?" asks one of the Haydens from the bottom of the monument. "What do you see?"

"I see victory," says the Hayden above. She throws a fist in the air and, at the top of her lungs, cries, "Victory!" And the other two howl.

CHAPTER THIRTY-ONE

Behind the podium hangs the MIND logo, its unnecessary all-capital letters etched in a massive slab of mahogany and adorned with gold leaf that shimmers with each camera flash. The live broadcast has already begun and all cameras are running lest these news organizations miss any frame of Director Arthur Klopek's big entrance.

Pam Washington, reporter for KMND, and others are gambling with their time by filling this dead space with commentary and speculation, as their camera crews twitch at the ready to swiftly turn their attention to the stage.

"We're here live on scene in the press room at MIND headquarters," Pam Washington says. "I'm Pam Washington with KMND. Any moment now, Director Arthur Klopek is expected to take the podium for a major announcement. We anticipate good news, as reports indicate that MIND has been working tirelessly to rectify the situation." Her hand to her ear, Pam Washington says, "Oh, I'm getting word that Director Klopek is about to arrive."

—

Clarice Hayden steps out of the Food King Market on the corner of 20th and 123rd and squints against the glare of sunlight that reveals smudges on her glasses. She removes the glasses and wipes each lens on her faded blue apron before putting them back on to check her work. Through the lenses she can see two men in dark suits come into focus. They don't look like people from her College Point neighborhood but Clarice has come to terms with an influx of people searching for cheaper housing in this semi-affordable pocket of Queens. For a Hayden like her, this is the lap of luxury. Now these dapper fellas are probably prospecting for some new highrise condo building like the ones that made Brooklyn look like a seaside retirement community.

"Gonna be hot," Clarice says to the two men, thinking they'll pass on by and maybe return the sentiment. With both hands, she grabs the last shopping cart from the corral outside the store and shoves it firmly into the row, forcing the rest of the carts into each other, making room for more. Then she scans the sidewalk for stray grocery carts and sees one just a few feet up 123rd, half off the curb.

The two dark-suited men follow Clarice long enough for her to realize they aren't just passing through.

"You got something to say?" Clarice says, turning to the men. She's ready for whatever they bring. This isn't her first fight. She's built for brawling and has plenty of practice.

One man looks at his porto and says to the other, "We're early."

"Command says by any means," the other says, shrugging.

"My guys," says Clarice, grabbing for the cart to go about her business. "You best be on your way."

With no regard for onlookers, the two men grab Clarice by the arms. She shoves the cart into the street and a passing car screeches to a halt but still hits the cart. The cart redirects and rolls into another car parked along the curb, setting off a car alarm that sounds like a combination of siren and honking horn. Clarice tries to shake the men loose, lets her knees bend to drop her body weight, so the men lose grip.

The driver of the car gets out and shouts, "What the hell are you doing?!"

Clarice takes advantage of their loosened grip and wriggles free. She jabs one man across the chin before the other grabs a hold of her arm. She grabs him by the lapel, pulls him in and uses that as counter force as she brings her other fist into his face.

"My car!" shouts the driver, but nobody's listening.

Clarice gets two more punches in the second man's face before she feels her knee explode with pain and she collapses. As she lays there on the pavement, the first man kneels down on her stomach and brings his extended, metal baton down onto her neck. She fights to get it off her windpipe. The second man grabs her by the ankles, tugging to keep her still. The man with the baton quickly pulls away and his partner twists her legs to turn her over. Clarice fights this but before she can gain much stability, the baton comes across her throat again, and the man is now behind her. He forces her to stand by applying more pressure until she complies.

"Okay, okay," she says, gasping.

"Does anyone give a crap about my bumper?" the driver says, standing over the front end of his car.

The man with the baton walks backwards, guiding Clarice with the baton against her windpipe. The other man leads them past the angry driver and to a black delivery van along the curb. The baton-wielding man gets in the back and pulls Clarice in. The other man shuts the sliding door, gets in front, and they drive off.

—

The press room grows unsettled as Arthur Klopek enters from stage left with two unidentified staff members who assemble on either side of him and a few steps back.

Klopek clears his throat, just as the room settles, and says, "Good morning."

Viewers who are watching a live broadcast from their portos will see the text *Arthur Klopek, MIND Director* at the bottom of their screen. Depending on the broadcast they've chosen to watch and the camera angle that the news organization has been able to secure, the viewer will have clear vision of at least two members on the stage.

"I'd like to begin by assuring you that efforts to apprehend the individuals responsible for the System's failure are ongoing," Klopek says. He looks directly into the camera and says, "We will find you." Klopek looks at a teleprompter and then to a screen glowing back up at him from the podium. "Today marks an historic day in System City. Over the last several decades, since before I was born, our city has enjoyed prosperity through the safety and security afforded by a system designed to bring us together. Through the System, we have bonded as a community across the city. From the Bronx to New New Brighten, we are one."

—

The black delivery van pulls into a remote parking lot at the end of 14th Avenue. Behind the driver's seat, the man with the baton struggles in fits as Clarice puts up a fight, gives up, and then tries again.

Then her porto chimes.

"Answer it," the man with the baton says.

"No," croaks Clarice, the baton digging into her throat.

He applies more pressure on the baton, and Clarice gives in to panic as her lungs scream for air. He lets up on the pressure.

"Fine," she croaks and pulls out her porto. The message reads, *What does the anvil say?* "I don't–" she starts to say, and the man presses the baton against her throat again.

"Answer it," he says calmly.

Through the windshield, the driver watches a garbage scow float down the East River and its wake lap against the rocks here at the mouth of Flushing Bay. Clarice doesn't know what she's supposed to type into the porto. But she reads the message again and types the weird nonsense that comes to mind. She hits send.

"Good girl," the man with the baton says.

Clarice drops her porto, grabs his wrists, yanks them forward while driving her head back into his face. She can almost hear the crunch of his nose as he grunts in pain.

"Crap," the driver says, looking back as Clarice gets on top of the other man and starts punching him. He scrambles over the armrest and squeezes back there to grapple her. She tries to fight him off, throwing an elbow into his side, reaching over her head to grab at his hair. But then the man under her starts punching her in the stomach. She falls to the side under the driver's weight, and the two men continue to beat on her.

From outside, in the far corner of this remote parking lot, the black van squirms and rocks in the beating sun.

—

"Familiar and flourishing, our community has become a shining example for cities worldwide." Arthur Klopek wipes his mouth and says, "From the crash came repatriation. From repatriation, came new challenges of scarcity and overpopulation in cities like ours. But System City thrived. And now we are in a better place than any other city across the continent."

From their portos, viewers may not hear the murmur of news reporters in the press room. Small waves of conversation ripple throughout the room before the podium.

"We are set up for success," Arthur Klopek says, raising his voice over the crowd. "Today marks a new day. As of one minute ago, the System has been shut down."

Murmuring across the crowd intensifies. Portos begin to ping.

"In what we're calling Operation Rewind, MIND is going to steer our great city into a new generation," he says. "I'd like to introduce two of my staff members." He gestures to the two people behind him. "As of a minute ago, these two fine people have no names. At least not that you can call up in your mind."

He turns to the woman at his left, extends his hand, and says, "How do you do? I'm Arthur Klopek."

"I'm Cindy Morehouse," she says. They both smile.

He shakes the other staff member's hand and says, "I'm pleased to meet you, David Shulthise."

Arthur Klopek turns to the crowd and says, "It's that easy."

—

Across the cracked, sun-bleached pavement of this parking lot, the black van sits still. After a moment, the side door opens and a man backs out, holding the body of Clarice Hayden by its ankles. As he backs out further, the other end of the body comes with the other man whose arms are hooked under the body's armpits. The body's rear end nearly drags on the ground as they carry it over to the rocky bank. With a few swings side-to-side, they heave the body toward the water and it lands on the rocks. One of the men reaches to push the body into the water. He plants a foot on one of the rocks and slips. His entire leg sinks into the water, and he scrambles awkwardly to back himself out.

He tries again, this time laying across a more upright rock, as the choppy water laps against his thigh. He pushes the body with his hands, working the lower part, and then the upper body into the water.

The two men watch the body float for a moment, as it slowly turns in the water and inches its way farther out.

—

"Stay tuned for our plans to implement a new identification program and other exciting initiatives," says Arthur Klopek. "For the time being, feel free to introduce yourself to your neighbor." He looks into a camera and says, "We're all in this together."

Klopek exits stage left, his staff in tow, and the KMND camera quickly turns to Pam Washington. She says, "If you're just tuning in, Director Arthur Klopek just announced that the System has been shut down. For more on this, we turn to Larry Southern in the KMND studio. From the MIND press room, I'm Pam Washington. Back to you, Larry. Oh, and it's nice to meet you."

CHAPTER THIRTY-TWO

Some thought they should keep the campfire low, in case it drew too much attention, as if they were in the wide open wilderness. Others like Amber thought they should celebrate their small victory with a raging bonfire. With her duct-taped boot, she stomped on another slat of a pallet until it snapped, then pried the broken boards from the rest and threw them on the fire.

With a back to the wall, Step watched as she did this, surveying the entire group encircling the fire, while occasionally glancing down the south and west tunnels for any sign of intruders.

"I'm telling you," Amber says, "it was amazing. You could see the whites of their eyes." She looks to another Hayden who was there. "They were that close. Like, the headlight was practically touching my boobs by the time he stopped." She grips her chest and laughs. "He could have run me over like a speedbump."

"I thought they might," says another Hayden who was there when it happened.

"But they didn't," Amber says, pushing a board into the fire with her toe. "Because we kick ass."

"Sure do," says the other Hayden.

All this bravado scares Step. There's no pride in near-death experiences. Yet, Haydens seem to relish it.

"Show us what you got," says a Hayden. "What were they carrying?"

"You wanna see what I got?" Amber asks. "I'll show you."

Step watches as Amber disappears into the darkness of the north tunnel. The other Haydens are chanting, "bring it, bring it, bring it." When she doesn't return right away, chanting settles, and some of the Haydens start talking about the System being shut down.

"We're going to need to be armed when this gets out of hand," says one Hayden.

"What?" blurts somebody too far from the fire for Step to see. "We're golden. Nobody knows who we are now."

"Yeah," says another voice. "Quit buying into that MIND crap. We were never any safer under their system. In fact, we're safer now that it's over."

"The great rewind," says another Hayden in a mock official voice.

"Rewind us back a few centuries," says another. "Maybe girls like us wouldn't be stuck down here in these rat tunnels."

Some Haydens laugh until another Hayden says, "You must have skipped history lessons at Hayden House. Women have never had it good. At least we don't have some government of old dudes telling us what we can and can't do with our bodies."

"Yeah," says another. "Now we just can't do anything at all."

They all laugh to mask their grief.

Step gets up to put more wood on the fire. The north tunnel is dark. Some bulbs glow dimly far down the tunnel, but Amber isn't visible. Step squints to see better, imagining that MIND agents are waiting in the shadows to pounce. Maybe they have Amber bound and gagged already.

"I don't know. Without the System, hustling's gonna be harder," says a Hayden. "I liked breaking the ice by calling people by their names. It was kind of my thing."

"Eh," says another Hayden. "We'll be fine."

"Damn right, we'll be fine," Amber calls from the darkness. She comes into the firelight with two semi-automatic rifles pointed in the air. "Especially with these babies! Pow, pow, pow!"

She pokes the rifles in the air as she makes shooting sounds, and everyone laughs and cheers.

"These are heavy," she says, lowering them. She tosses a gun to a nearby Hayden. The Hayden catches it with an audible grunt.

Seeing these guns makes Step uncomfortable. Nothing good can come from having them.

"We dumped most of their stuff in the river," says the other Hayden who was there. "But we nabbed these beauties."

"Walked all the way back here with them," Amber says, sitting down happily with her rifle. "After they all scooted, of course."

"It was scary," says one Hayden. "I was across town, washing windows when you all were blowing up my porto."

"I didn't like that one bit," says another Hayden. "What if they come back?"

"Then we'll be ready," Amber says, looking over her gun fondly. She brings the gun to her face to look through a sight that isn't there.

Step sees this playing out already. From each tunnel will come laser sights cutting through the air like thin, long swords swiping at each other as a team of MIND agents and militarized police advance on the Junction. Haydens thinking they can scurry through the darkness will be flushed out by teargas thrown from agents wearing night vision goggles and gas masks. Those who are foolish enough to fight back—many of those in the Junction right now, Step thinks—will be lucky to only feel the shocking punch of rubber bullets. But if any of these Haydens dream that they can outgun and outmaneuver a trained army of Hayden-hating soldiers, they are kidding themselves.

"You think we can take 'em with just these two guns?" asks a Hayden. "Or do you have any more than this?"

"Yeah," asks another Hayden. "How many bullets you got anyway?"

"None," Amber says, laughing to herself. "You think I can afford ammo for this thing. It's just a glorified toy." She sweeps it across the room of Haydens making *pew, pew, pew* sounds.

They all break out in laughter like it's the funniest thing they've seen all week. But Step doesn't see the humor in any of it, not in the least.

CHAPTER THIRTY-THREE

The dorms are quiet as cadets sulk over the double blow of news from outside the academy. While many are pleased that the scramble of ever-changing names in their heads has come to a halt, it being at the expense of the System–the very thing they've all sworn to protect–has taken a toll on academy morale. Such news is especially hard to swallow after a rumored attempt to raid the Hayden's underground hideout failed against the Haydens' grassroots ingenuity.

However, none are as troubled as Thomas, whose reconnaissance effort led MIND agents to the location. Only, he never told MIND about it. Instead, Douglas took Thomas's intel to the academy chancellor, who then alerted contacts at MIND headquarters. Douglas was given all the credit, even though he fabricated the entire story, claiming that during his two-hour pass last week he had tailed a suspicious Hayden out of curiosity. Thomas might be able to blow up Douglas's story by providing better details, but Douglas would then be compelled to rat on Thomas for sneaking out to do so. It's a gamble Thomas is unwilling to take.

Thomas's roommate, Luke, is outside their dorm room holding court with other cadets. They're talking about how agents went about the raid. Each cadet has a small snippet to add to the story, as if any of them know what really happened. News media were told to stay away. MIND agents walked the perimeter of their staging area at Joseph Brant Circle, making sure that nobody was recording on their portos under the legal statute that this was a "tactical public safety mission," which is protected under provision 3856B of urban conflict law. These cadets should know that. So, nobody in this dormitory, or in any part of the academy for that matter, should know what went down beyond the news that a weapons shipment was intercepted at the 79th Street exit from Henry Hudson Parkway.

When Thomas heard that part of the story, he couldn't believe that MIND would make such a monumental blunder. His class hasn't even graduated into tactical training yet, but they all know enough from military history classes that a weapons transport should always include security as part of the convoy. Never should you drive a vulnerable unmarked vehicle alone, even outside of wartime.

Thomas finds all of it embarrassing. Beyond the brief nightly segments from non-MIND-sponsored news outlets that mention an unusual gathering of MIND agents and law enforcement partners at Joseph Brant Circle or the MIND transport being ambushed, deeper investigations have speculated on MIND's intentions with the apparent raid attempt. To which MIND's public relations department has responded with a weak justification, that it was simply "a drill." As for the amateur porto footage that captured a group of Haydens accosting the truck, "that's obviously doctored," says MIND Communications Director Alex Curry. His tune changed only hours later when the video was authenticated. But then his excuse was, "There's no evidence that the truck had anything to do with MIND." MIND's sponsorship of all mainstream System City media made sure no reputable outlet reported on the event.

Thomas pushes his way through the cadets, not getting as much as a "watch it" out of the group so enthralled in their make-believe rehash of the incident. He takes the stairwell to the ground floor and goes outside onto academy grounds for some fresh air. It's quiet during midday recess. Some preteen cadets lounge by the stairs to the dormitory, their uniform shirts open like there's any sunshine to soak up. Some younger boys are sword fighting with sticks near the statue of Ernest McQuade, founding director of MIND.

Thomas watches the sword fight for a moment when he spots Douglas, Chancellor Hairston, and two MIND agents walking toward the dorm building. The chancellor pats Douglas on the arm as if congratulating him. The MIND agents shake Douglas's hand and they part ways. As Douglas passes Thomas on the way to the dorm building, a smirk crawls across Douglas's face. Thomas would punch that face right now if he could.

"You're a snake," Thomas says in a low voice.

Douglas stops and says, "What was that?"

"You know what I said."

"I think I heard, 'My name is Tommy and I want a demerit'," says Douglas, assuming a mocking high-pitched voice.

Thomas clenches his teeth to keep himself from speaking. He'd rather grab Douglas by the collar and shove him into a wall, but that's not a wise idea.

Douglas steps closer. Over Douglas's shoulder, Thomas can see that they've drawn the attention of the preteen sunbathers. In a quiet voice, Douglas says, "You'll make a good counterintelligence agent." He leans close. "But leave the smart ideas to leaders like me."

Thomas doesn't hide his balled fists. He can feel the heat in his face. His jaw is clenched so tight his teeth might break.

Douglas's eyes look down at Thomas's fists. He says, "Those for me?"

Thomas looks across the quad at the chancellor and MIND agents not yet out of view. There's nothing he can do now that would satisfy him and not get him suspended or expelled from the academy. Douglas is untouchable.

"Didn't think so," Douglas says, and he continues into the dormitory.

The preteens are still watching. Thomas looks at them and lips a curse at them. They quickly look away.

Unable to go back inside right now for fear of running into Douglas again, Thomas tries to walk off his anger in the quad. He can't believe that Douglas stole his intelligence and used it to get the attention of the chancellor. This is surely going to jeopardize

Thomas's chance of being first in class.

This is the first time Thomas wonders if being a cadet is even worth it. MIND seems to favor idiots, he thinks. What's the point if buffoons like Douglas get rewarded? Thomas thinks it must have been another dumb Douglas at MIND headquarters who came up with the brilliant plan to send an unchaperoned weapons transport. MIND must be full of Douglases with bad ideas. They should all be purged, he thinks.

That's when Thomas suddenly has an ingenious idea. It's a long shot but not ridiculous. But to execute it correctly, he'll need help.

He pulls out his porto. To Reuben Mayfield, he writes, *I think I know how to get Hadley.*

Across the quad, the young boys with sticks have moved on to playing chase around the McQuade statue. A moment passes before Thomas's porto chimes. The message reads, *What do you need?*

CHAPTER THIRTY-FOUR

In the spirit of their ancestors, society continues to consume the past, be it through reruns or remakes or reboots or retroproductions (more commonly called *retropros*) or, now what the industry has coined, replicasts. In recent decades, and in response to public opinion, production companies have favored reality series in avoidance of the hurtle that the System's identity recognition program posed on viewers. Live theater has sustained success with fictional productions due in part to the historical need to flex suspension of disbelief. Audiences have always needed to act like what they're watching is real, even when it's a Civil War battle scene acted on a fifty-foot by thirty-foot stage framed between curtains and beneath a visible lighting truss. But the sense of immersion or capturing of reality that film and television once enjoyed was almost instantly lost the moment the System kicked on and the viewer recognized an actor not as T. E. Lawrence, but as Peter O'Toole, in the Arabian desert.

The result is a blend of two trends–reality and replication. Production companies began trying to recreate entire seasons of classic reality shows like *Survivor*, *16 and Pregnant*, and *Real World* in their original locations but with new casts. More recently came the fad of game shows. Some tried to recreate every aspect of a classic show like *The Price is Right* with replica prizes from the past. Unfortunately, when the host announced, with a coy smirk, "a new car!" that replica Plymouth Horizon with its combustion engine would not be drivable today.

More successful now are shows like *The Dating Game*. Today's recording features a bachelorette named Helena, a furniture designer whose parents kept her when complications during her mother's birth made it so they couldn't have more children. She shares this biographical note not for pity but to explain the first in a long string of luck that has pulled her through life.

Three bachelors sit on the other side of a wall, out of Helena's sight. The first is Patrice. Patrice works in synthetic solvents and lives in Bushwick. The second is Jaylon, an industrial welder and metal sculptor. He comes from Marine Park and has a studio in Brooklyn Heights. The third bachelor is Yuri, a systems architect for an enterprise software firm who lives in Tremont. The three men seem charming enough and smile for the camera.

Helena asks Patrice the first question. "Patrice, how do you do? Can you tell me how your ideal date would go?"

"Of course," Patrice says, showing interest at the sound of her voice. "I'd love to take you to Del Piero Bakery in Brooklyn. We can feed each other cannolis and enjoy a morning walk in Prospect Park."

"A morning date," she says, intrigued. "Interesting." She adjusts herself on the tall director's chair that they make all show participants sit in. The canvas feels tight and the hinged wood construction feels flimsy. "Hello, Jaylon. This question is for you."

"Hit me," he says.

"Please describe for me one of your dreams," she says.

"Like an aspiration or something I've dreamt one night," he asks.

"Either," she says, smiling.

"Well," he says, feigning uncertainty. "I have a good one."

What the other two bachelors and viewing audience don't know is that Helena and Jaylon are already a couple. The show producers have started to find "bachelorettes" who are already in committed relationships, and then surround the male suitor with two unsuspecting contestants. This way, producers can guarantee chemistry is "found."

"One time I dreamt that I was in a zipbike gang," he says. "I was on the lam from the law. My gang was a rough group."

This was a dream Helena had only a few weeks earlier. She told Jaylon about it the morning after during breakfast, and they laughed over what tattoos she must have had.

"That's something else," Helena says.

"I had a tattoo of a taco holding a sword," he adds.

"That's funny," she says. Helena's face turns red and she laughs nervously. When she composes herself, she addresses the third bachelor. "Yuri, I understand that you like to learn."

"I do," says Yuri. "I'm sort of a life-long learner."

"That's great," she says. "So, tell me something you've learned recently. Something none of us would know."

"Sure thing, Helena," he says. "As you know, I'm sort of a software tinkerer, if you will. I am very curious about that stuff."

"Aren't we all," she says, jokingly. She makes a cringing face but only the audience can see. And they laugh.

"Well," Yuri says. "Yesterday, I was reading through my data mining report."

"Oh?" she says, feigning interest, and makes a judgy face that the audience laughs at again.

"Oh, yes," he says. "It's really very simple once you set it up. All you have to do–"

"What did you learn?" Helena says, cutting him off. The other two bachelors look at each other as if to say, *Can you believe this guy?*

"It's kind of interesting," Yuri says. "They say the System's been shut off now for a day or so, right?"

"Sure," she says.

"Well," Yuri says. "I don't think it is. In fact, I know it isn't."

"Oh... kay," Helena says, looking at a show producer behind the camera.

"There's data traffic still moving in those bands," Yuri says. "I've been monitoring it for years. I know what to look for."

Neither of the other two bachelors know what to say, nor does Helena. The crowd can be heard talking, as well.

"I-I don't know what you mean," Helena says. She looks past the camera and says, "Can we break for an ad or something?"

"I'm saying that we're still fed data," Yuri says with a tone of fascination. "The System isn't–"

The Dating Game title card briefly appears on screen then quickly cuts to a commercial for dust wipes.

CHAPTER THIRTY-FIVE

Ever since word spread among Hayden House staff that a man had threatened Miss Ula Mae and the Haydens, many of the younger, newer staff members have been calling in sick. Miss Ula Mae might have been able to keep that information to herself but she believes in transparency. Instead, she thought it would be better to keep her staff informed. Growing tension around System City has already raised alarms across Hayden House. Anti-Hayden protestors have been circling the city throughout each day and night, several times stopping for nearly an hour outside of Hayden House to chant veiled threats at anyone inside who is listening.

"Pay no mind," Miss Ula Mae tells the older girls who wish to confront the aggressors.

They scream out the windows at the anti-Hayden cronies, "Come and get us!" Such taunting, Miss Ula Mae thinks, will only feed the flames.

Still, after days, the man she only knows as Ivan Laurel VI, who lied his way into Hayden House to sling threats and assault her, has not come back. As far as she can tell, these protests are no more a threat than the propaganda that litters the news. And while faint graffiti remains on the exterior walls, she believes that these girls are still safe inside Hayden House. But with short staff and the heightened alert everyone is on, Miss Ula Mae decides to skip her weekly trip to see her sister.

Night staff has already done the rounds, checking on each floor to make sure the girls are alright. Most of them are asleep or reading.

Miss Ula Mae does a sweep of her own, mostly because she enjoys seeing the girls at peace in their beds. It pains her to know that many of them leave Hayden House to find shelter in unsafe places, where they may never have such comfort.

Her rounds take her back to the lower floors, where she can hear some infants crying. The night nanny is doing her best to calm them, but when more than one baby is upset, it's hard to keep them quiet. Miss Ula Mae used to work in the infant room and would keep three or more babies happy by sitting in her chair with the baby bouncers fanned out before her. She would work their bouncers with her feet like drum pedals, sometimes to lullaby music on her porto and sometimes with her own singing.

She softly approaches the nanny whose arms are full with a rocking, fussing infant. The baby is on the edge of sleeping. Short fits of tears settle into rhythmic heavy breathing. Another girl across the room is crying, and Miss Ula Mae offers to soothe that child. She tiptoes over to the crib and lifts the little one out. Holding the baby to her bosom, she pats and rubs her back to calm her as they walk by the windows to an empty rocker on the other side of the room. She can see the protestors now assembling outside, and she goes to the chair and settles in.

With the sound of cursing, angry voices on the street below, Miss Ula Mae whispers a lullaby to the fussing child, letting her know that she's loved and safe.

CHAPTER THIRTY-SIX

Rays of sunlight reflect off the mirrored windows in front of MIND headquarters, brightening the small plaza where protestors assemble with wooden signs. Five of the protestors march in a line back and forth, holding up signs that read, *Brains aren't billboards* and *MIND your own business!* Behind them, a fellow protestor yells into a bullhorn at the mirrored windows, "You shut down the ID program. Now shut down the ad program. We know that the System is still on. We know you're still polluting our minds. And for what?"

The other five protestors shout, "Corporate greed!"

"Who needs flash loads if it leaves room for ad loads?" the bull-horned protestor shouts. "Spare our brains and shut down the System."

This new generation of activists is taking over the fight for ad-free brains now that it appears to be an issue again.

Years ago, MIND claimed to end their advertising program when William Van Dyke, Vice President of Corporate Relations, fell to his death at this very plaza. Van Dyke was in charge of securing corporate partnerships by selling "ad space" in the System. His advertising program generated so much revenue that MIND's operations and innovation budget more than doubled in the three years the program ran before it was supposedly shut down. In the early days of the program, Van Dyke found a great sense of pride in the advertisements they ran. He requested that he personally review each one before it was uploaded to the System and, subsequently, downloaded to everyone's brains. He would sit in his office, sometimes with a guest he was trying to impress, and watch each advertisement like they were sneak peeks of the latest episode of some popular porto series.

Of course, the program had its hiccups. One of the earliest advertisements for vaping pens promised its users they would be relaxed and popular if they used the product. Within days, parents reported that their children were demanding vape pens, resulting in the program's first regulation. There was no way to target particular demographics within the System. Therefore, all pushed advertisements had to be "family friendly" per this new regulation. But that small segment of public outcry birthed a movement.

Once concerned citizens learned that advertising was being forced upon their bodies, they began to rally in front of MIND headquarters. Information on the invading advertisements was not public knowledge. A public-interest group known as CABA formed. CABA, or Citizens Against Brain Advertising, ran regular surveys to suss out people's unusual and sudden cravings or desires. While not completely accurate, the survey unveiled a number of convincing results that, when presented to MIND for confirmation, led to press conferences to quell further outcry.

What started as a few dozen activists quickly grew to a few hundred protestors greeting Van Dyke and others each day in the plaza. Day after day, the activists gathered to shout at the building and harass MIND employees. The occasional clash with police led to arrests or injuries. Barricades would go up for a while and come back down when tensions seemed to rest. The protestors would return, and the cycle would continue.

Van Dyke learned to deal with his image on portos across the city. He may have been demonized by a small faction of citizens but his salary more than made up for the inconvenience of having to be chauffeured by security to most places.

Then one Thursday, the day of the week that he reserved for reviewing the latest batch of advertisements, he was presented with what amounted to ping messages on his porto. Instead of the fifteen-to twenty-second cinematic commercials that companies had produced just for a spot in his program, it was as if those same companies came to the conclusion that their production budgets could be winnowed down to nearly nothing by simply planting a message in a single line of text.

I want to drive a Mercedes EVE Class.

Cougar Drops give me energy.

Mattrest mattresses are cozy comfy.

Van Dyke felt betrayed and he couldn't convince the companies to put more into their advertisements. They were more than willing to pay for their slot in the System but there was no incentive to overproduce an ad that amounted to a simple subliminal message. Van Dyke knew all along what these advertisements were doing. But when his corporate partners stripped away the veneer for greater profit, Van Dyke could no longer play dumb. And now the part of his job that he most enjoyed was reduced to reading a dozen sentences on a single screen of his porto.

This betrayal, coupled with the daily reminder of how unpopular his program was in the public eye, began to chip away at Van Dyke. He began to drink more heavily. He was losing sleep. Week after week, as he read the single-sentence ads that would soon be imposed on everyone's brains, he started to think about them and expect them to appear in his mind. Late at night, unable to sleep, he would stare at the crown molding in his bedroom and search his brain for that single line.

Mattrest mattresses are cozy comfy.

As if it was a tattoo that he could look inward to read directly off the wrinkles of his brain, he closed his eyes to find that pathetic, simple sentence somewhere in there, night after night until he couldn't take it anymore and leapt from his office window one autumn morning. MIND announced the following week that they would suspend the advertising program. Only, they never did.

Now with the identity recognition program shut down and data apparently still being fed to people's chips, the only logical conclusion is that ads have been running all this time. So, protestors are back to marching before the mirrored windows of MIND headquarters, marching around a sunlit plaza where Van Dyke took his life.

CHAPTER THIRTY-SEVEN

Food trucks line either side of 2nd Avenue in the middle of Stuyvesant Square Park. The avenue is closed to traffic and tables are spread about for the lunchtime crowd. Haddy sits at a table with her back to a Greek-Korean fusion truck. When Thomas pinged to say that he wanted to meet, Haddy reluctantly replied out of guilt for what she did to him all those years ago. Still, she insisted that they meet in public, where, it turns out, Haddy knows at least two cooks among these dozen or so food trucks. She can't imagine what Thomas would try to pull, but it can't hurt to have allies nearby with kitchen knives.

Thomas arrives through the park along 16th Street, and Haddy tries to see if he has friends with him. But when he reaches the dining area, he's alone. He doesn't see her right away among the crowd, and she watches as he briefly checks his porto. The academy uniform gives Haddy pause, but his face is so familiar. It's almost painful to think that they're related. Sure, they never could have grown up together, not with the laws the way they are. But it hurts her to think that they share parents. Maybe she just feels guilty for what she did. Or maybe she's never gotten over the thought of him being loved more than her.

When he finally sees her, he approaches with the same stiff posture and assured gait that she remembers from the night he and his friends attacked her in Madison Square Park. But that was Paul's doing, she has to tell herself.

"Hadley," Thomas says. He gestures to the folding chair across from her.

"Brother," she says, immediately regretting it. Her instinct is to be cold and defensive. He doesn't seem fazed by the small attack but Haddy realizes it was unnecessary.

When he sits, he keeps the same stiff posture. Only, now, Haddy can see a tell. He smooths his hands over the table as he glances over each of his shoulders. She doesn't yet see a threat but his nervousness tells her to be on guard.

"Thank you for meeting me," he says, pulling his hands back to his lap as he straightens his back.

This must be something they force cadets to do at the academy, she thinks. Maybe in some etiquette class.

"Sure," she says. Attempting to lighten the mood, she adds, "I recommend the falafel banh mi."

"This won't take long," he says, licking his lips. He takes a deep breath and says, "I don't like you. Alright? I just want to get that on the table. Off my chest. Whatever."

"Sure," she says, half taken aback and half admiring his candor.

"It's not that you hurt me," he says. "You didn't hurt me. I won't let you. But I don't think Haydens are good people."

"We're not too fond of you all, either?" she says, injecting some snark to disarm him a little. Haddy can see that his leg is twitching.

He leans forward and says, "But these people," he points over his shoulder like some threat is behind him. "They're going to kill you."

"Who?"

"You know who," he says. "They came for you once. The other day. They'll come for you again."

"Those are your people, Thomas," Haddy says. She's not going to let him separate himself from the very agency he aspires to join.

He sighs and collects himself. "They're making a big mistake," he says. "I see that. It kills me that they even tried to raid your... whatever you call your subway hideout."

Subway hideout? Haddy recognizes it right away. How would he know that? The raid failed. Nobody even went below the surface, and the news never said so.

"We took care of ourselves," Haddy says.

"You got lucky," he quickly fires back. "They may have gone down there and dragged you out, thrown you in prison, or worse."

"Let them try," she says, again with the knee-jerk defense.

"They had you surrounded," he says, leaning in again. "Don't think they wouldn't have all those tunnels blocked."

How does he know? she wonders. *He must be bluffing but it sounds like he knows what the Junction looks like.*

"That crap you pulled," he says. "That's just going to make them come back harder. This doesn't end in any good way for you. Now you have weapons. Which means now they come at you with force."

"That wasn't force?" Haddy says with a guffaw. "You pricks have a weird sense of violence."

"Like I said, they're going to kill you."

"Okay," she says, leaning in. Thomas sits back as she does. "I get it. You're so tough. Big bad MIND is coming for us. Why are you telling me this if you don't care?"

"Nobody needs to die," he says. He sighs, as if exhausted.

"So noble," she says, sitting back like she no longer cares what he has to say. "Mommy would be so proud."

Thomas stiffens. His jaw clenches. He runs his hands along his thighs. Haddy can tell that he's restraining himself. "Mom's dead," he says, his eyes locked on hers.

She almost says, "Good," but practices her own restraint. Instead, she says, "I've been dead to her for years."

Thomas drops his head, gathering himself. His body language says that this little meeting isn't easy for him. He sighs and says, "Look. I want to help get you and any Haydens you can round up to safety. That's it."

"To safety? Where are we safe in this city?"

"I've arranged for three buses," he says. "They can pick you up from wherever. You choose a spot. They'll get you out of System City. Go somewhere until this all blows over."

"You said they want us dead," Haddy says. "What makes you think any of this will just *blow over?*"

"MIND thinks you all had something to do with the System going down," he says. "I don't think any of you are smart enough to pull that off. It'll blow over once they find the real culprit."

Haddy wants to laugh but knows better. Her snarky attitude won't help.

"Just take the offer," he says.

Haddy can't quite understand his angle. There's no way that he would suddenly want to help her out. "MIND approved this?" she asks.

"How else would I get buses?" he says. "This isn't just my idea, okay? There are others at the academy who want this. MIND goes to war and my friends and I will be called up. You understand? I don't want war. I don't want to kill. Even if it's just a bunch of Haydens."

Haddy can't believe they actually think the Haydens have an arsenal. This would all be surreal if MIND hadn't just tried to raid the Junction with those same weapons.

"You're training to be one of them, aren't you?" she asks.

"I'm not a murderer," he says. "You know, most of those guys just want to make this city a better place."

That's hard for Haddy to believe. From a Hayden perspective, there is little proof that MIND has any good intentions. But she also knows that this is her best option. Either things go on the way they are, escalating from a raid to war, or she takes Thomas's offer and sets the terms.

"I choose the location," she says, claiming as much control as she can.

"Yes."

"My girls are armed," she says. "If anything–"

"I know."

"The first sign of anything fishy and–"

"Understood," he says, cutting her off. She's glad, too, because she didn't have a convincing threat to follow up.

She stands up and reaches across the table to shake his hand. She has nothing to lose by this gesture. He looks at her hand, then glances around to see who might witness this MIND Academy cadet shaking hands with a Hayden. He stands. His eyes say he doesn't want to but he shakes her hand anyway. His palm is sweaty.

"I'll ping you the details," she says, and leaves without looking back.

CHAPTER THIRTY-EIGHT

Agent Stevenson has no reason to be back at Reuben Mayfield's apartment, but that's where Hadley asked him to meet. The apartment door has remained unlocked but buildings like this, with doormen and wealthy residents, aren't susceptible to petty crime. Usually just murder. That's what Agent Stevenson thinks about as he studies the bathroom again. It appears untouched since the last time he was here. That was with Hadley and her friend. Then he remembers the knife.

He goes back to check the entryway table where he left it. The knife isn't there. So, he goes to the kitchen drawer where he found it, and it isn't there either. Where could it have gone? Who was here? He doesn't remember Hadley or his friend taking the knife.

"Hello?" Hadley calls from the living room.

Agent Stevenson finds her there, this rough gutter punk of a girl standing in a lavish Upper East Side apartment, and he can't help but be struck by the contrast.

"I know you're probably the last person I should talk to about this," she says. "But I don't know who else to ask."

He wants to say no. He can't help her, even if he wants to. That's how it feels lately. He tried protecting her before and couldn't. His efforts to capture Mayfield failed. And somehow Mayfield's now dead. His plan to give a tell-all interview fell flat. Agent Stevenson can't think of a single way he's contributed to society since becoming a MIND agent, and he's certainly done no favors for Haydens liked Hadley. Yet, here he is.

"I spoke with my brother today," she says. "He's arranged for bus transport to get the Haydens out of the city."

He remembers that Hadley has a brother in MIND Academy, and already this sounds suspicious. "What does he want?" he asks.

"He says he's afraid that MIND will go to war with us," she says. "He doesn't want that bloodshed."

"It's not about saving you," he says.

"Probably not," she says. "But we don't have many other options."

Agent Stevenson thinks again about the knife that's gone missing. He scans the room with his eyes, maybe forgetting that he left it on an end table or elsewhere. The Haydens have weapons now. They can take care of themselves, he thinks. He doesn't want to consider what some MIND cadet is up to. He doesn't want to think about any of this.

"Just tell me what you want," he says, bluntly.

Hadley cocks her head, perhaps offended. "I thought maybe you could scout the pickup location," she says. "You'd know what to look for."

"Maybe," he says.

"If you hadn't helped us with that raid, we'd all be dead or in jail," she says.

"Maybe," he says again. She's probably right but he's also learned that these girls have keen survival instincts. They may be sloppy and unorganized but their guerrilla tactics are admirable.

"Look," she says. "All I'm asking is that you be at Joseph Brant Circle before pickup. Check the situation."

"Joe Brant," he says and snickers. These girls are sloppy, unorganized, and *bold*. It's almost like they're taunting MIND by doing this, which might just be his only motivation. "I'll help."

Hadley looks visibly relieved when he says this. "Thank you."

"If there's danger," he says, "and it's likelier than not, I can't help you. I can only warn you."

"I understand," she says. She sighs and looks around them in this living room.

Agent Stevenson does the same, taking in the ornate rug beneath their feet, the expensive furniture, and those pristine dark drapes.

"How awful people end up with all this," she says, more to herself.

He doesn't say it but from his experience, and from what history tells him, those who have are also the greediest, most awful people.

Hadley smiles with gratitude and says, "I'll let you know when."

"Sure," he says.

Hadley seems to take it all in as she leaves, peering at the crown molding, the wall art, and the arched opening to the living room. She leaves Agent Stevenson without another word, something that he actually appreciates.

The detective in him wants to keep searching the apartment but the realist in him wants to let it go. There's nothing left for him here. Somebody took that knife. Maybe it was Hadley's friend. Maybe not. It shouldn't matter to him. Yes, his fingerprints are on the knife. But this isn't a crime scene. There is no body that he knows of.

Agent Stevenson goes to the window to take in that multi-million credit view. He leans toward the window to see the sidewalk in front of the building, maybe catch Hadley leaving. But he can't see that far down without opening the window. Just as he stops leaning forward, he notices a man standing against a dark car parked outside the Italian restaurant across the street. He isn't somebody Agent Stevenson has ever seen before but the man has that look. Dark suit. Well groomed. His yellow glasses are the only part of his appearance that doesn't scream MIND agent. The man looks at the front entrance of Mayfield's apartment building, and his head slowly tilts upward until he's looking directly at Agent Stevenson. Maybe it's too bright for the man to see him. Maybe the apartment is too far up. Or maybe they're looking directly into each other's eyes.

Agent Stevenson doesn't move. Something or someone at the front entrance has caught the man's attention now. Maybe it's Hadley leaving. The man with the yellow glasses watches whoever it is now moving down the street. He doesn't seem in a rush as he gets back in his car and pulls away from the curb. Agent Stevenson thinks about whether he should try to follow that man, not that he'd catch up to him. No reason to bother, he thinks. Hadley can take care of herself.

CHAPTER THIRTY-NINE

A blend of Douglas's cheap body spray and Chancellor Hairston's musky cologne burns Thomas's nose in the close quarters of the chancellor's sedan. It's the first time he's smelled Douglas's fragrance, and Thomas can only assume that this is a new habit for the rising star. On the other hand, Thomas might remember Chancellor Hairston's cologne but there's no mistaking the crisp dress shirt or tasteful tie that he has on, or the wrinkle-free suit jacket that hangs over the back seat. The chancellor is ready for the press.

They're parked along the curb on Central Park South just before Joseph Brant Circle. With minutes to spare, three white buses make their way into the circle and settle in a line in front the park entrance. In the pre-dawn light, Thomas can make out silhouettes peppered around the area, no doubt Haydens being cautious as they peek from behind shrubs near the edge of the park or casually lean against a building across the way.

It's not clear to Thomas what's in this for Reuben Mayfield but he's amazed that the creep has come through, not just with buses but with drivers, as well. Maybe Mayfield wants Hadley gone just as much as Thomas does. But once Hadley's gone, Thomas can forget about Mayfield altogether. With the System shut off, MIND likely doesn't value capturing Mayfield anymore. So, there's nothing to gain by giving him up. There's only the risk of revealing that he's been harboring a fugitive.

It's been a long forty-eight hours for Thomas. After getting the details from Hadley, Thomas was able to fill in the academy chancellor about his plan. He explained that any attempt to arrest or subdue the Haydens in the city was going to lead to bad press. Furthermore, the Haydens were now armed, and escalating conflict within the city would only put the public at risk.

"You make a good point," Chancellor Hairston said. "Between you and Mr. Dorchester, we have one of the strongest classes of cadets in academy history."

Thomas had to swallow that one if he wanted his plan to take shape.

"I've arranged for buses to pick up the Haydens from the same spot as the raid," Thomas said.

"Drill," said Chancellor Hairston. "It was a drill." He had apparently gotten the memo.

"Right," Thomas said. "That same location. Three buses will pick up Haydens at Joseph Brant Circle at six a.m. on Thursday."

"How were you able to arrange for buses?" asked the chancellor.

"My father," Thomas lied. "He knows people."

"Oh," said the chancellor. "I didn't know you were connected. I'll have to thank him."

"His pleasure," Thomas said. "No need."

"Well, I can't wait to see him at the next parent weekend," said the chancellor. "And where will the buses take these Haydens?"

"Out of the city," Thomas said.

"Anywhere in particular?"

At this point, Thomas couldn't tell if the chancellor was onboard or if this was just some fun thought experiment for him. But while Thomas's plan had few unknowns, those were all parts of the plan where things could go very wrong.

"Let's just say out of sight," Thomas said.

Chancellor Hairston rubbed his hands over his mouth and stared across the room, considering Thomas's proposal. Thomas wondered if this was how he treated Douglas's news that led to a botched raid.

"You expect them to be sitting ducks?" the chancellor asked.

"What about their weapons?"

"Frankly, Chancellor, what's stopping us from asking that question now?"

Chancellor Hairston nodded thoughtfully.

"The only thing that changes is that hopefully the Haydens leave their weapons behind," Thomas said. And when the chancellor remained silent, he added, "The Haydens are going to be just as cautious as us. If they come out of hiding with rifles in hand, they should expect a firefight."

"You're very bright," the chancellor said after a moment. Thomas enjoyed hearing that.

"But I thought you were here to ask for my permission."

Thomas realized that his neck was on the line but he also knew that his plan was better than anything MIND was concocting.

Before Thomas could make an excuse for his gall, the chancellor said, "I see that everything is already in place. None of this has to do with the academy or with MIND. So, what do you want from me?"

"In order for this plan to work," Thomas said, "I need troops."

After a moment to ponder this proposal, the chancellor said, "I'll see what I can do." He smiled thoughtfully and added, "You really are very very bright."

—

Chancellor Hairston is quiet now as he keeps an eye on the buses. Thomas thinks maybe in a previous role at MIND, the chancellor was an investigative agent on stakeouts. His calm patience is something to aspire to. Instead, Thomas is quietly cursing the Haydens. While their departure time isn't as important, Thomas wants to make sure that the plan goes off without delay. Once those buses depart the circle, Thomas will be able to breathe easier. But so much of this depends on Haydens cooperating and getting here on time.

"So, we're just supposed to let them go?" Douglas asks from the back seat. "No justice?"

Thomas doesn't want to entertain Douglas's remark. Chancellor Hairston stays quiet, watching the buses. Douglas doesn't know about the armed agents that the chancellor has put in place. He may never learn about them. There's no plan to follow the buses, nor has Thomas arranged to track them. As far as he's concerned, the moment they leave the city, all those Haydens will disappear.

"I would have loved to see that raid pan out," Douglas says. He's doing something in the back seat with his body, like tucking in his shirt or leaning back to reach into his pocket, and the car rocks a little. Thomas can feel Douglas's knee dig into the back of his seat. "Imagine seeing hundreds of Haydens zip-tied at the wrists and sitting along the curb, their smug, greasy faces all sad and scared," Douglas says, with a pouty voice for that last part.

It may be a trick of the eyes, but Thomas sees silhouettes moving past the circle. Every so often one or two people leave the subway at 59th and, instead of coming to the buses, they're all headed west. Each of the three drivers has deboarded and has opened the luggage compartment on the side of their bus.

"Tommy," Douglas says. "Did you think of this operation all by yourself? That's a big boy move, right there."

The chancellor briefly glances over at Thomas with a look that says either *don't listen to that kid* or *are you going to let him run his mouth like that?* Thomas wants to say that at least he has a plan. Douglas only knows how to steal somebody else's work and then let the grown ups make the plans. Instead, he says nothing.

"Those buses look nice," Douglas says. "Can't believe we're giving Haydens a first class ticket out of here without so much as a slap on the wrist."

"For what?" Thomas finally says. "What are we arresting them for?"

"I don't know," Douglas says. "They're Haydens. Pick a crime."

"Don't be such a turd," Thomas blurts, and immediately regrets it.

Chancellor Hairston looks at him with some surprise but still doesn't say anything. The boys go quiet for a moment. A metal thermos of coffee sits between them, and the chancellor takes the thermos, slowly, unscrews the lid, and takes a long sip.

After a minute, Douglas asks, "So, do we get out and orchestrate any of this?"

"We don't want to spook them," Thomas says. "They'll know what to do."

"How?" Douglas asks.

"How what?" Thomas says. "It's boarding a bus. It's not complicated."

Douglas grabs the back of Thomas's seat to pull himself forward, and says, "How do they know that these buses are for them?"

Chancellor Hairston looks at Thomas for an answer, as well. Thomas hoped he wouldn't have to explain this part. Nobody at the academy knows that he has a Hayden sister or that he's been in contact with her. While it's very possible, Thomas doesn't know if any cadet has ever had a Hayden sibling before. It's unlikely that the cadet would even know. But Thomas has to assume that this is just Douglas's way of getting under his skin. After all, Douglas knows that Thomas infiltrated the Hayden hideout.

Suddenly, Thomas gets a ping. He doesn't get many normally and never this early in the morning. So, he knows it's either Hadley or Mayfield. Neither of which he wants to reveal to the chancellor.

Hiding his screen from the other two, he checks the message. It's from Hadley.

Location change. W. 52nd. Under the offramp. Tell your drivers.

Thomas doesn't know what to do. Why would she change the location?

"Are you one of them?" Douglas asks, obviously joking. Before the System went down, there would have been no way for Thomas to do this and hide his name. "Chancellor," he says. "I think we have a spy in our midst"

Already on edge about the plan and strained by Douglas's presence, Thomas turns and grabs Douglas's arm. "Shut up, Doug!" he yells. "When this plan is a success, you'll be kissing my ass."

"Oh, yeah?!" Douglas fires back.

"Boys!" Chancellor Hairston commands.

Thomas releases Douglas's arm. Douglas sits back and mutters something under his breath.

"Enough," the chancellor says. To Thomas he says, "What's the matter? Who was that?"

"They want to change the location," Thomas says.

"That's why none of them are here," Douglas says. "I don't know. This seems like a trap."

"I need to tell the drivers," Thomas says.

Chancellor Hairston sighs in aggravation. "I don't like this," he says.

"I don't either," says Douglas.

"Go," the chancellor says to Thomas. "Hurry back."

Thomas exits the car. As he walks toward the buses, he looks back and realizes just how much they've been sitting ducks where they are. There's nobody else around. Not many cars have passed by. People aren't out at this hour. If a Hayden had the skills, the three of them could be sniped with no witnesses.

Thomas quickens his step as he approaches the closest driver. "Change of plans," he calls to them. He waves the other two drivers over. They're in no hurry.

"Pickup spot has changed," Thomas tells the three drivers.

"Directions said Joe Brant," says one driver.

"And the directions have changed," Thomas says.

Two of the drivers check their portos. "I don't see it," says one.

There's no way the chancellor can hear them but Thomas knows that this delay looks bad.

"Look," Thomas says. "Have you been paid?"

"Yup," says the first driver.

"Double time," says another.

"Then you should be okay with a slight change of plans," Thomas says.

"Depends on what you mean by *slight*."

"West 52nd," Thomas says. "Under the greenway. Not far. Just go."

None of the drivers look happy about it but their faces just as quickly contort to indifference. As they go back to their buses, one says, "This means our ETA is delayed."

"Sure," Thomas says, knowing there is no ETA. There's no destination that he knows of. Did Reuben Mayfield give them a final location? Before Thomas can ask, the drivers are already in their buses. Doors close and motors hum to life.

Thomas trots back to the chancellor's car and gets in.

"All settled?" the chancellor asks.

"Back on track," Thomas says, trying to feign confidence.

"Good," the chancellor says. Just before he starts to go, he turns to the boys and says, "We're going to make sure these buses are off without incident. And the two of you..." He points a stern finger at each of them. "You are going to be the mature cadets we've trained you to be."

The buses pull away, and the chancellor creeps ahead, following at a safe distance.

"When this is all over," he says, "I'm going to talk to the press. I'm going to let them know the good work *both* of you have done." He guides the steering wheel around Joseph Brant Circle, keeping several dozens of feet from the last bus. "I don't need you two embarrassing this academy. Got it? You're MIND cadets. Act like it!"

"Yes, chancellor," they both quickly reply.

CHAPTER FORTY

She was right about the raid and about the weapons shipment. She knew where to send Haydens and what they should do to stop it. None of this surprises Step. Haddy has always been a leader. So, when she showed up in the Junction yesterday to ask for everyone to spread the word about a bus transport, Step listened. But Step is the skeptical type. Thankfully, so are many Haydens, and they had questions.

"Why now?"

"Who's running this?"

"Will we be safe?"

"How can we trust that this isn't a trap?"

"Where are they going to take us?"

To most of these questions, Haddy could only say how important it was that they leave now before MIND wages war. Step had to assume that Haddy's information was credible because she somehow had direct contact with that MIND agent from the apartment the other day. And while their relationship would normally give Step pause, Haddy wouldn't knowingly jeopardize Haydens' lives.

So, Step stood by Haddy, echoing her warning. "We don't have time to argue. We're not safe down here anymore. It's time to move on."

While Step understood their skepticism, the safe choice was to flee while they could. Luckily, most agreed, albeit reluctantly. In less than forty-eight hours, these Haydens were going to meet at the end of West 52nd Street, under the greenway, and say good-bye to the Junction for the last time. The eve of their departure, they had the biggest send off they could muster in such a short time. They had all the meat they could scrounge cooking on the fire in the center of the Junction. Tunnel water, which is what Haydens call their version of moonshine, was passed around. They filled their bellies with alcohol and meat, while different Haydens, including Step, took turns playing music. Smoke filled the domed ceiling of the Junction as Haydens shared bitter-sweet tales about life in System City. It was a night to remember.

—

Now, with a sleepless night behind them, Haydens begin to emerge from the tunnels with the few possessions they value stuffed in duffel bags and backpacks. Up the 59th Street Station stairs, Step can see the three buses sitting at Joseph Brant Circle. Haddy said to ignore them there. Her reasoning was that this was where her MIND contact suggested they board, making it a perfect location for an ambush. By relocating their departure at the last minute, law enforcement would have no time to assemble at the new location. As usual, Haddy has all the ideas.

Feeling the previous night's merriment and maybe still weak from the hospital stay, Step sits on the concrete bench on the edge of the fountains that surround the Joseph Brant monument. While here, should any Haydens forget Haddy's warning, Step can redirect them away from the buses.

The trees surrounding the center of the circle diminish visibility, but being at the center allows Step to see in every direction and take note of peculiarities. To the north, Haydens appear in small groups from the subway and head west, as instructed. To the east are the buses, the drivers vaping before they have to depart. Just past the buses, down Central Park South, sits a black car. The tinted windows make it difficult to see if anyone is inside. Not that one car can make an ambush. But then, to the south, Step sees a man standing by the mouth of 8th Avenue. In fact, the man is looking directly at Step, and he looks an awful lot like the agent that Haddy knows. Step gets up to approach the man but doesn't even clear the trees before the man retreats around the corner. Standing here at the center of this circle with tall buildings all around, Step suddenly feels vulnerable and decides to head west toward the new departure point.

For the first two blocks along 58th Street, Step keeps looking back expecting to find a MIND agent following. The streets are eerily quiet as sunlight slowly drowns out the glow from street lamps and buildings. The occasional car hums by. Shopkeepers roll up the front cages with a clatter of metal. The only other sounds are of other Haydens as they slog along the sidewalk laughing and goofing off. Step has always liked being out during these off-peak hours. Something about owning the city at this time. When all the good citizens are at home resting, Haydens can roam free. This is their time.

At 11th Avenue, traffic has picked up, and Step turns south to see the buses ahead turning from 57th Street. Walking along these wider avenues provides a view of just how enormous System City is. For blocks, maybe miles, buildings can be seen along either side of the street stretching into the orange sky. So many people live and work in these buildings, Step realizes. So many experiences. So many worlds. And so much of it is out of reach for Haydens.

Step wonders if where they're headed will be anything like this. Will buildings swallow the sky? Will they end up somewhere so big that, after years of living there, they may only get to know one tiny cave of a home? Will they be hated or ignored by nearly everyone around them?

By the time Step reaches the departure location, dozens of Haydens are already waiting in the dark recess beneath the Greenway off-ramp. The Hudson River laps against a concrete barrier just feet away, and the air feels wet and cool. The buses line the narrow street, while Haydens surround the caravan. It's hard to believe that everyone will fit in these three buses.

Haddy is already there and steps off of one of the buses. It's unclear if she hitched a ride or if she was here before they arrived. From the lowest step of the bus entrance, she calls to the group, "If we're all going to fit, we need to dump our luggage below!"

As she says this, the drivers open their cargo hauls beneath the buses. Haydens look at each other as they reluctantly load their bags. The seriousness and finality of the moment is beginning to sink in. Haddy talks to one of the drivers. She seems to be okay with what he's saying, whatever they're talking about. Step can't hear them from this side of the crowd.

"All aboard!" Haddy calls, almost comically. She's smiling, though Step can tell it's forced. Nobody here should be joyful. They're fleeing their home for safety. They're basically about to become refugees.

Haydens file on, and before long Step can hear some calling to reposition on the bus and make room for more. Maybe a protector by nature, always bringing up the rear, or just cautious, Step is among the last to board. Once inside, Step finds that the only spot available on the bus is the one underfoot, right next to the driver.

"I'm okay if you're okay," says the driver. "You'll need to hang on."

Up close, any suspicion that the driver might be a MIND agent in disguise is out the window. The driver's tired eyes, unshaven appearance, and sagging belly suggest that he hasn't been through much rigorous physical training.

Through the windshield, the back of the next bus slowly rises. The door beside Step closes and their bus begins to lift, preparing to head out. Behind Step, Haydens are crammed in seats and on the floor. Some sit on other's laps. They open windows for better air. The mood isn't very joyous. Some girls are talking but most everyone else is quiet. The bus in front of them starts moving and Step feels their bus lurch forward.

—

As the buses climb onto 12th Avenue, and the river comes into view to their right, Step can't help but feel that this is all surreal, like some anticlimactic ending to the life they've all led to this point. Or maybe it's just too easy. Never has anyone arranged something so elaborate for them. And yet, here they are fleeing for safety in the nicest-looking vehicle any of them has ever been on.

Skyscrapers pass by on the left as they make their way downtown. To the right, Step can see the roofs of old pier-supported buildings reaching into the river. Standing next to the driver, Step can see the rearview mirrors and backup camera. Behind them is a black car. For a moment, Step thinks it's the black car that he saw at Joseph Brant Circle. But there are a lot of black cars in System City. Maybe not with such heavily tinted windows. Step can see an elbow peeking out from the open passenger-side window.

Way in the back of the bus, some Haydens begin singing "Ninety-nine Bottles of Beer." A few more join in but it never fully catches on, and by eighty-eight bottles, the singing has stopped.

Once downtown, the driver works the bus back into the city toward the entrance to the Holland Tunnel. They exit onto Spring Street and the black car follows them. The same goes for Varick Street, and Step is starting to worry. But then the bus merges onto the tunnel entrance, and the black car passes to their left. The open passenger-side window reveals a boy watching the buses as they pass. Step almost laughs in relief, so relieved that he doesn't realize he has seen that boy before in the Junction.

A few seats back, a Hayden says in a somber tone, "Good-bye, System City."

"Good riddance," says another.

Step realizes that this may be the last any of them sees the city for a long time. Step quickly ducks to get a view out the side window. The driver cranes to see around Step's head but says nothing. In that fleeting moment, with no time to reflect on all that they're leaving behind, the bus descends into the tunnel, and Step watches those tall, beautiful buildings disappear above.

CHAPTER FORTY-ONE

From her seat on the first bus, Haddy can see a faint flicker of blue outside her tinted window. System City is no more than a jagged line of buildings across the river in the distance. The landscape has become open terrain. Cracks in the road bear weeds. Wild shrubbery, small trees, and remnants of a chain link fence surround piles of rust and sun-bleached paint in the vague shape of shipping containers as far as the eyes can see. Blue light flashes more prominently against all this as they pass.

"Here we go," says the driver. "I don't leave the city for this reason." He pulls the bus into the wide paved entrance of a long-forgotten freight yard. A security booth sits sadly by a mangled gate, its windows broken and the rest pocked with graffiti.

"What's going on?" asks a Hayden.

"Bribes, I'm sure," says the driver. "Gotta pay your taxes. I'd ask if any one of you can pitch in but…"

The driver brings the bus to a stop, turns off the motor, and awaits instructions from whoever has them pulled over. Two SUVs with blue flashing lights pull in front of the bus, pinning it between them and the bus behind them.

Haddy climbs over the girl next to her and walks along the arm rests up the aisle to get to the front.

"Just sit tight," the driver says, putting up an arm.

"These aren't local police," Haddy says. "They're MIND."

"I'm going to get hell for carting a bunch of girls without a chaperone," he says.

"No you won't," she says. "Nobody cares about us."

Outside, six MIND agents step from the two SUVs and form a semi-circle around the front and side of the bus, assault rifles in hand. In the mirror, Haddy can see more assembling around the other two buses. Haydens begin to panic. A couple of them on Haddy's bus start to scream. These girls have seen some ugliness in their lives but weapons like this will frighten any preteen into hysteria. Girls try to calm those around them who are upset, while unrest grows among the others.

"Open the door," Haddy says.

"No," the driver says.

"Let me out," she says.

An agent walks to the door and knocks. The driver decides then to open the door.

"Driver, please step off the bus," says the agent.

"No way," Haddy says, standing between the agent and the driver. "We agreed."

"Ma'am," the agent says. "Step aside. Driver, off the bus. Now."

In the mirror, Haddy can see the other drivers deboarding at the command of agents. She cautiously steps down the stairs toward this agent. "Look," she says. "I don't know what you're doing but we agreed on Centralia."

She looks at the driver, and he says, "Those were the orders."

"Hayden," the agent says. "Move. Driver, get off!" He steps back and points his weapon.

Haydens start screaming and shouting.

The other two drivers are being escorted to SUVs. They are not bound or cuffed, maybe because they're cooperating.

"What are you going to do?" Haddy asks, putting up her hands. "You going to execute us all?"

"Driver!" the agent yells.

With his hands up, the driver looks at Haddy and says, "Sorry," and steps off the bus.

"Leave your porto," he tells the driver.

"What?" the driver says, pulling his porto from his pocket to secure it in his hand. "Not gonna happen."

The agent forcefully pries the driver's porto from his hand. "Here," he calls to Haddy, and tosses the porto to her. He turns to the other agents and says, "Take him to the car."

As agents escort the driver away, Haddy can hear him say, "My boss is going to give me hell for this."

The agent at the bus door says, "Listen to me. There are armed agents at every bridge and tunnel. You are no longer welcome into System City. Any effort to infiltrate the city will result in immediate termination."

"What did he say?" asks a Hayden in the front seat.

Haddy doesn't know if she heard correctly either. "We can't go back?" she asks.

"Haydens are banned from the city," says the agent. "Indefinitely."

"No, no, no, no," she says, stepping down off the bus. The agent readies his weapon. "You can't. We agreed to just lie low for a while."

"We didn't agree to anything with you," he says, and steps to leave. The other agents are already getting into the SUVs.

"Wait," Haddy says. "We have friends back there. Other Haydens. Hundreds of them. What will happen to them?"

"You are no longer allowed back in," he says. The other SUVs are ready to go. Haddy looks back at the other two buses, and some Haydens have already stepped off. This agent gets in his SUV and looks back like he might say something. But then he closes the door, and the fleet of SUVs drives off in the direction of System City.

The SUVs get smaller in the distance. Haydens begin to deboard, asking what is happening. They all gather, as Step, Haddy, and a Hayden they call She-Ra naturally come together, holding the three drivers' portos.

"What the hell was that?" Step asks. "Was that part of your plan, Haddy?"

"Don't, Step," Haddy says, not interested in arguing.

"Don't my ass," he says. "We're out here in the middle of nowhere. Look at it! Where the hell are we?"

Weed-riddled concrete stretches in every direction to reveal toppled stacks of shipping containers, overturned cranes, and caved-in warehouses. Haddy can't believe what she's gotten them into this time.

"What are we supposed to do with these?" She-Ra asks, holding up her driver's porto.

"If this is so we can drive these buses, I'm out," Step says. "I am done."

"Yeah, Step?" Haddy fires back. "Are you going to walk back? I'm pretty sure the city is off limits now."

Step gets in Haddy's face and says, "I told you. I'm done with you." He gestures around him. "I'm done with this."

She-Ra already has her driver's porto open to the active GPS. "Cen-Central-ia," she reads. "What's there?"

There's some unrest among the Haydens watching them.

"It's okay," Haddy says. "I lived there for a bit. It's safe."

"Nothing is safe," Step says.

"It's fine," Haddy says. "We'll be fine."

"Looks like we might be better off in Allentown," She-Ra says. "I don't know though." With repatriation, there's no telling what they can expect in any location on the GPS. Names like Allentown, Easton, and Centralia are legacy names from long ago. With travel so restricted, and unnecessary in most cases, cartography and mapping have gone to the wayside.

"Looks bigger than Centralia," Step says, looking at his driver's GPS.

"No," Haddy says. "We're going to the colony. To Centralia. It's way less risky."

"We," Step says, motioning to the rest of them, "don't have to listen to you. You are the risk."

"Step," Haddy says, exhausted with having to explain every

decision. "Please trust me. I know what I'm talking about."

"You know trouble," Step says. "And I'm staying away."

Step walks back to the third bus, calling over his shoulder, "Anyone interested in Allentown, come with me!"

Haddy looks to She-Ra. She-Ra grimaces and says, "Same! Allentown or bust!" And she starts toward the second bus.

Haydens begin to file toward either of their buses. Those who haven't gotten off of Haddy's bus are asking what's going on when she steps back on.

"We're splitting up," Haddy says. "I'm taking this bus to a place I used to live. We'll be safe there. Those two buses are going to Allentown."

"What's in Allentown?" a young girl in the back asks. She's far too young to have left Hayden House, Haddy thinks, but here she is.

"I have no idea," Haddy says.

"Where are we going?" asks another Hayden.

"A place called the colony." Just saying it sounds so unreal to Haddy. It's been maybe two weeks since she left there with Paul, and yet it feels like an eternity.

"Is it nice?" the young Hayden asks.

"It's nice," Haddy lies.

Haydens make their choice and cargo is sorted. Haddy ends up with a smaller load with most of the seats taken but room to spare. Haydens are packed like sardines in the other two buses as they pull away. Step shares a look with Haddy as he drives the bus away, lurching it to each side as he acquaints himself with steering. The look he gives is nothing new to Haddy. They've bickered in the past. But if she needed him, he'd come back. So she hopes. She half expects the other two buses will end up at the colony anyway.

Haddy climbs back onto her bus and sits in the driver's seat. She sets down the driver's porto, and the bus hums to life. With her own porto, she pings Weston.

49 Haydens. I hope you're ready.

She doesn't wait for a reply. Instead, she looks back and says, "Got about three, maybe three and half hours. I hope you all tinkled."

Some of the girls giggle. Most are quiet and scared. Haddy shuts the door, looks at her cockpit, and grabs the wheel. "Here we go," she says to herself, and presses the accelerator. The bus lunges forward and she slams on the brakes to the sound of girls either laughing or screaming.

"Hold on tight!" she calls. She eases the accelerator but they still take off quicker than she expected. The bus sways like a boat on water as she spins the wheel to get the bus on the road again. Before long, they're on route and everyone is quiet. Haddy looks back in the mirror and sees girls sleeping while others are lit by their portos.

The bus's motor hums from way in back. Tires whir against the pavement. Haddy can feel the forward momentum lulling her. The GPS has them taking old highway 78, and most of the way she sees signs for Allentown that she hopes the others ignore. When exits for Allentown draw closer, Haddy braces for requests to deviate from their route. More buildings come into view. Most of them are dirty, abandoned office buildings that sit just off the highway. Shells of old restaurants and gas stations dot their route. There are countless vacant strip malls with overgrown parking lots.

Not long after they pass by Allentown, they reach their exit, putting them onto a smaller country highway that will take them to Centralia. But Haddy knows that they'll miss Centralia proper, and skirt it as they weave through the hills toward the colony.

Her porto chimes with a message from Weston. *I hope they like soup.*

Haddy smiles. She imagines Weston in an apron in the colony cafeteria, ladling soup to a line of girls. Weston was cold and callus to her before but, to a Hayden, that doesn't always mean a bad thing. She'll take cold over abusive. Just thinking about the colony makes her nostalgic and nervous, like going home after a long while. She used to feel this way returning to Hayden House after a stint with a foster family. The rules and restrictions she used to crab about would somehow feel familiar and welcoming. With Paul gone, she wonders if the colony will be the same. Could that much have changed in just a couple of weeks?

The windshield flashes with morning sunlight as the road cuts through forests of overgrown trees. For the last hour, only two zipbikes and a truck have crossed their path. No other traffic or fuss. It's a very pleasant drive. The bus floats like a cloud, winding through the hills and dipping into valleys. By the time they reach the colony, most of the girls are asleep. Haddy slowly negotiates the gravel drive that leads into the colony. A recent rain carved ruts that make the bus bounce a little, causing some girls to wake.

Groans, sneezes, yawns. One Hayden says, "Where are we?" No doubt, these girls are struck with a mix of awe and concern by the cluster of concrete buildings around them. More girls wake up and stand to see better out the windows. Haddy remembers the first time she arrived here and how weird she thought this cluster of concrete buildings was. It hasn't been that long but the colony almost seems tidier.

Familiar faces come out from the cafeteria building and dorms to greet Haddy and the new guests. Renee and Trevor appear with their "look who we have here" expressions. Laars limps with a makeshift crutch that he likely carved himself.

Weston approaches the bus door as Haddy brings it to a halt. Beside him is one of the watchers. They both look welcoming. Haddy can't even imagine what led to the watchers being part of their group now. She opens the door and starts down the steps.

"Welcome back," Weston says. A rare smile stretches across his face. As much as she would probably deny it, Haddy feels like she's home.

CHAPTER FORTY-TWO

It's been nearly two decades since Agent Stevenson set foot on the MIND Academy campus, ignoring invitations for five-, ten-, and fifteen-year reunions. He occasionally passes by it, just like he passes MIND headquarters from time to time, looking at it like ruins of a bygone era in his life. Only, the ruin is something he projects.

Upon flashing his MIND badge, the security guard at the gate directs him to an administrative building that Agent Stevenson remembers as the place you go when you're in trouble. The hall leading to the front office is much smaller than Agent Stevenson remembers, but the smells are as familiar as ever. Already he feels underdressed to be here. His hair needs a trim. He hasn't shaved in several days. These would mean demerits as a cadet.

Behind a desk, a young man, probably a former cadet who didn't make the cut to be an agent, sprays an invisible code onto the back of Agent Stevenson's hand. The code works for about two hours, until it's completely absorbed into the skin or washed off. The young administrator explains that the cadets should be in their dormitory at this time, catching up on homework before dinner or wrapping up extracurricular club activities.

Crossing the quad, Agent Stevenson thinks the trees must be taller. A short stone wall around the McQuade statue looks new. But that means it could have been built fifteen years ago. Even with these subtle changes, the path he walks to the dormitory is familiar, and makes him a little sad. Taking each of the front steps one at a time makes him feel old when he thinks about how he used to leap up them as a boy racing back to his dorm. He remembers the restrictive material of his uniform pants, how it made clearing all four steps difficult at times.

Beside the dormitory entrance is a small brown scanner. He presents his hand, and a flicker of light reads the code. A lock pops and Agent Stevenson opens the door. Immediately, a tsunami of citrus-scented cleaning products and young man body odor nearly throws him back down the steps. At once familiar and appalling, the smell forces Agent Stevenson to shorten his breath in a pathetic attempt to avoid taking anymore into his lungs.

As he approaches the elevator, the doors open and three boys run out and shove past him to get outside. None of them give him a second look, and he wonders if he was that ignorant when he was a cadet. The academy will surely break the best of them into awareness.

Inside the elevator, another brown scanner reads his hand, only allowing him access to the floor he needs. The doors close and the elevator begins to ascend. He doesn't remember it feeling so crammed. When the doors open again, an assault of teenage squeals blasts his ears. A door slams. Somebody shouts playfully and another boy yells less playfully–the threats between adolescent boys.

The room he's looking for is about midway and on the left. The door is open and Agent Stevenson finds two boys inside, one at a desk and one on a bed. The shorter of the two looks at him, a stunned, yet vacant look in his eyes. Like a baby.

"Thomas Karp," Agent Stevenson says. The short boy looks across the room at his roommate. The taller boy, at his desk, turns from his propped-up porto. Agent Stevenson has a quick glimpse of the screen before Thomas tilts it downward.

"Who are you?" Thomas asks.

Agent Stevenson looks to the other boy and, with his thumb, gestures for him to leave.

"This is my room," the boy says.

"What the hell?" Thomas says, standing.

"You," Agent Stevenson says, pointing to the boy. "Leave." Pointing to Thomas, he says, "Sit." The shorter boy stands as Agent Stevenson approaches him and gestures for him to get out of the way. Agent Stevenson inspects the bed with his eyes, and then sits on the edge.

"That's my bed," the boy says.

Agent Stevenson puts out his hand, suggesting that Thomas sit on the other bed across the room. "We need to talk," he says.

Thomas seems surer than Agent Stevenson expected from a cadet. It shouldn't surprise him, given what he knows about the boy. But it's a stark contrast to the roommate lingering at the door. Thomas sits directly across from Agent Stevenson, back straight, hands on knees at attention.

"He'll be fine," Agent Stevenson says to the roommate. "Get out of here and close the door."

One last look at Thomas, who nods to affirm his safety, and the roommate leaves, shutting out the squeals and slamming doors from the hall.

Agent Stevenson waits to speak. In training, this is what cadets will learn is a tactic to draw out guilty admissions from a subject. But Thomas doesn't take the bait, which surprises Agent Stevenson. He's almost proud of the boy, given this and what he already knows. Proud and sad for him. What he reads in Thomas is slight uneasiness. The boy hasn't asked for Agent Stevenson to identify himself. But that's likely because nobody is used to having to do so. But Thomas has probably already calculated that Agent Stevenson is somebody with enough authority to get inside MIND Academy.

Outside the door, the squeals have died down. Shadows appear at the gap beneath the door, as boys gather to eavesdrop.

Agent Stevenson nods toward the porto on Thomas's desk. "You follow the news?" he asks.

"Who doesn't?" Thomas replies.

"All this chatter about Haydens," Agent Stevenson says. "First some raid attempt, which I guess went wrong." He looks to Thomas for a reaction but the boy is impressively stone faced. "I haven't seen any official reports on this either but they say a bunch of them escaped the city a couple of days ago, apparently afraid of another strike."

Thomas shifts his weight back a little, rubs his hands on his thighs twice before settling back into the position he was in. Training tells Agent Stevenson that this is a tell. So, he presses the nerve a little more and says, "I'm impressed they were able to coordinate such a move."

Thomas feigns agreement but his eyes look toward the floor instead of at Agent Stevenson. Agent Stevenson figures that Thomas knows that the jig is up but is clinging to a shred of hope that this mysterious old man doesn't know anything. What Thomas doesn't know is that Agent Stevenson was at Joseph Brant Circle when the buses arrived. And he may be the only witness to that. Even he didn't know that Hadley had moved the departure location, probably to shake an ambush. But it also kept the media from noticing. What Thomas also doesn't know is that Hadley has already pinged Agent Stevenson about Haydens being shut out of the city.

As Agent Stevenson sits quietly, Thomas looks increasingly uncomfortable. In training, Agent Stevenson remembers their instructor comparing this moment to holding your breath. Put the guilty under water with suspicion. Their confession will be that first deep breath. Which is why, even though they're about to face their crimes, that initial feeling is close to euphoric.

Thomas looks to the shadows under the door and rubs his thighs again. He even licks his lips. Agent Stevenson thinks that if this were an older, smarter subject, he might be playing the agent. But Agent Stevenson almost feels bad for the boy. Normally, this is where an investigative agent would ask Thomas his whereabouts at a certain time and on a certain day.

Instead, he says, "I'm going to throw you a lifeline. You'll learn that what I'm doing right now, at this very moment, is disarming. I'm gaining your trust, just as I say this. I'm providing a sense of transparency, okay? That's what I'm doing when I tell you that I know the Haydens didn't escape."

Thomas shows some confusion, his nervousness fading.

"Now, understand, I'm not actually doing this for you," Agent Stevenson says. "You see, I'm not here for what you think I am. But I need us to be on the same page."

Thomas almost speaks but he stops himself. Agent Stevenson reads this as a need for clarity. But Thomas might know enough to not speak for fear he may incriminate himself.

"So, I'll just walk you through this," Agent Stevenson says. "Because I would want that if I were you."

Agent Stevenson leans forward, putting his elbows on his knees like they're going to plot something together. Thomas's anxiety seems to dissipate as he mirrors Agent Stevenson's posture.

"I got to thinking about how you knew the location of the Haydens' hideout," says Agent Stevenson. "I'm guessing you had nothing to do with that raid. It was botched from the get-go. But I bet you were the one who gave up the location."

The subtlest nod from Thomas suggests to Agent Stevenson that he's correct. The boy just wants credit.

"But how?" Agent Stevenson continues. "How did you know? I've been around longer than you and dealt with Haydens all my life like anyone else. I know their scams and hustles. Can't walk a block without feeling like you'll be hit up for food or credit."

Agent Stevenson pauses again, thinking he can draw out Thomas. But the boy is impressive.

"You see, the real tip for me was the other day at Joseph Brant," he says, looking for a glimmer of surprise in the boy's eyes. He can see Thomas briefly suck in his bottom lip, clasp and then unclasp his hands. He does this just once, but it's enough. Still, the boy maintains eye contact. "I ran the plates on those buses," Agent Stevenson says. "They're not MIND vehicles. They're charters."

A slight shade of concern on Thomas's face suggests that he's following.

"So, I talked to the charter company and, wouldn't you know it... those buses were paid for by somebody with a single name–Paul. But you know him as Reuben Mayfield." Agent Stevenson sits up, runs his hands down his thighs, fingernails down like he's scratching, then settles back into the forward-leaning posture, as if waiting for some gossip. He asks, "So, where is Reuben Mayfield?"

Keeping eye contact, Thomas opens his mouth but then looks to the side, draws a breath like he might speak, and then stops himself. Something in his eyes changes, like he's aged and matured right before Agent Stevenson's eyes. He's no longer Thomas but somebody else.

"What do you really want with me?" Thomas finally says.

"That's it," Agent Stevenson says. He sits up again, thankful that the charade is over. "I just want Mayfield. You know where he is and, as far as I can tell, you have no use for him."

"Who the hell are you?" Thomas asks.

With a mix of shame and pride, Agent Stevenson takes a deep breath and unbuttons his shirt to reveal the tattoo. With a cold, absence in his eyes that Agent Stevenson would never have expected, Thomas looks at the tattoo and then looks away and snickers to himself.

"Eighty-eight," he says. The boy bows his head, conceding that this old man at least made the cut. But he's amused, and Agent Stevenson is brought right back to commencement, at the ping of disappointment in being almost at the bottom of his class.

"So," Thomas says, as if signaling that the conversation is over.

"So," Agent Stevenson says. "Harboring a fugitive, lying to your chancellor, and to others. These are not qualities of a MIND Academy cadet. Or have they dropped all that stuff about honor and integrity."

That's how he gets Thomas. He can see it in the boy's eyes now. He's finally touched that nerve. But the boy keeps up his facade. "So, what now?" he asks.

"You're going to give me Mayfield," Agent Stevenson says. "Whatever that means. Give me the location. Set us up. I don't care. But you're going to hand him over. No tricks. Don't try to be clever. You don't know what that man has done."

"No?" Thomas says, trying to act more knowledgeable than he is.

"No," Agent Stevenson says, no doubt showing it in his eyes. "This is serious."

Thomas appears to understand but still, he resists. "Or else?"

Standing up and buttoning his shirt, Agent Stevenson grimaces and says, "Or else I talk to the chancellor, and you can kiss this all good bye." He gestures around them. "You seem to forget who I work for," he lies.

"You really don't seem like a MIND agent," Thomas says, shaking his head. "Who got to you?"

"Honestly?" Agent Stevenson says. He walks to the door and opens it. Five cadets nearly fall into the room. He looks at Thomas and says, "Your sister did."

Agent Stevenson waves his hands, scooting the boys away from the door. They scamper in each direction down the hall. When he looks back at Thomas, he finds a boy staring at his feet, wondering what he's gotten himself into.

"A little advice," Agent Stevenson says. "You're gonna need to show more integrity and honor if you want to be top of your class." From the hallway, he turns again and says, "But maybe you're agent material just the way you are."

CHAPTER FORTY-THREE

Clouds move slowly across the sky, giving residents short moments of reprieve from the sun. It isn't very hot out but the work they're doing is strenuous as they level a stamp of land to prepare for a new building. Weston found plans on Mayfield's computer that detail future colony growth. While it's a rough schematic, Mayfield was accurate enough with measurements to plot each building's foundation to fit into the colony's geographically-restricted footprint. Weston remembers Mayfield talking about a twenty-first century eccentric who built his own castle in southeast Pennsylvania. The man's name was Henry Chapman Mercer. He built his home, Fonthill Castle, almost entirely out of poured concrete. This apparently fascinated Mayfield, and he clearly thought he could do the same on a small scale with each of his colony buildings.

Weston watches as long-time residents work side-by-side with the young Haydens who arrived just days ago. The scene looks like some big brother, big sister program. Everybody is working together. Some are digging while others chip at dirt and rock with pickaxes. Others run water and snacks to the excavation crew. Some residents tend to the garden, while others move dirt, stone, and clippings in wheelbarrows.

While he would love to take credit for building this commune, Weston is happy to be part of its thriving future. The influx of nearly fifty new residents has posed challenges but, thanks to a willing community, much of the work is met with little fuss. Add to the mix the expertise of 1052 and 2701, whose knowledge in logistics and security have helped create efficiency and peace of mind. Weston has also learned to lean on people's soft skills, like Renee's and Trevor's humor. Morale has never been higher.

If only Weston could ease the worries of some newer residents. A few of the preteen girls, as young as eleven, don't understand why they've been kicked out of the city. Weston doesn't understand either. Thankfully, older Haydens like Hadley have been able to comfort the younger girls.

Yet, Weston believes it will be a topic of conversation for many more weeks. Girls keep asking questions like, "Why are we hated so badly?" and "Why doesn't anyone understand us? We're human like anyone else."

Watching them each day, Weston admires their dedication and willingness to contribute. Not that he should be surprised. He watched it with Hadley when she first came to the colony. Her resistance to conform melted away when she realized what it felt like to belong. But now that he's listened to all of Hadley's diary, he understands the Hayden perspective a little more. In fact, now he feels guilty for the anger and contempt he previously showed her. He realizes that the emotional growth he's experiencing is entirely her doing. And when she stops for a moment to stand beside him as they watch the others work, Weston lets her know how he feels.

"I'm sorry for the way I used to act," he says. "I was angry. Ignorant even."

Hadley looks at him and smiles. He admires her strength and ability to know when to speak and when to listen.

"Walk with me," he says. The two stroll around the colony perimeter, observing the progress made on the new building plot. "I, uh, listened to your diary," he says.

She looks at him curiously and says, "I don't know what you mean."

"You recorded yourself, I guess back when you were here before," he says. "It's really, I don't know. Honest."

Her face contorts as if pondering what he's talking about but then seems to understand, as her cheeks turn red and she laughs. "I know what you're talking about," she says. "How did you–?" Before she can finish the question, she realizes the answer.

And they both say, "Paul."

"I was just trying to make sense of... I don't know," she says. "All that stuff. Being fried. And you know."

"I do know," Weston says. "I get it now. And I'm so glad you shared that."

They walk past the bus, which is acting as temporary sleeping quarters for several of the new residents until the next dormitory building is finished. When they reach the garden, they stop to watch a couple of Haydens learn how to safely harvest the root vegetables without damaging them. Weston always assumed that girls this age, preteen and teen, would complain about doing this work. But, as he learned from Hadley's recordings, Haydens are a tough bunch.

"You know," he says. "I can't stop thinking about everything you all have gone through back in the city, and how awful people are to you." He feels ashamed for what he's about to say but he knows it's important to get off his chest. "I know how much I probably agreed with them before. And I'm sorry. But if they just heard your recordings, the way you tell it–"

"It's okay," Hadley says. "We're okay now."

"Sure," Weston says. "But aren't there others back in the city?"

"Of course," Hadley says. "Hundreds more. But they'll manage. They have no choice."

Weston doesn't want to accept that. As much as it's their only option, he can't seem to let it go. "I just think if people heard your story, I don't know... maybe they'd understand like I do."

"Maybe," Hadley says, watching Haydens work hand trowels into the soil.

They stand here for a minute. Weston feels the heat of the sun on his neck and takes a long breath of sulfur-laced air.

"These recordings, are they like audio files?" one of the

gardening Haydens asks. She's young like most of the Haydens here but she has tattoos on each side of her face, one of a sun and the other of a moon. She looks up at Weston and Hadley. "Are they just files on that computer in there?" She kneels on one knee and drives her trowel into the dirt.

"What computer?" Weston asks, knowing full well what she's talking about.

"I'm sorry," she says. "A few of us got lost and wandered in there. I'm kind of a nerd about that stuff and... forget it." She goes back to digging.

"You're Monique, right?" Hadley asks.

"Yeah," she says. "That's me."

"I remember you," Hadley says. "A programmer or something?"

"Coder," Monique says. "I mean, I'd love to be one someday."

"What did you want to know?" Weston asks.

Monique stands and brushes herself off. "What you have on that computer... that code. I read it. That's a command line interface to push files into... well, you know."

Hadley and Weston look at each other with the same thought. Neither knows a thing about how Mayfield did it but they both know that he uploaded a virus to the System using that code.

"All that stuff predates me," Weston says. "But maybe you want to take another look?"

"Sure," Monique says. "But I think I understand well enough already." She looks over her shoulder and then leans in to talk in a hushed voice. "That was like the System, wasn't it? I saw some code commit language in there. I'm just saying, if what you're talking about is an audio file... I mean, I bet we can compress it or make a transcript and zap that up there, no problem. Think of it like flash loading a porto series."

Weston can't believe that this ridiculous idea he thought of a moment ago might actually be possible. Unfortunately, Hadley doesn't share his eagerness to give it a try. Instead, she looks at him and laughs skeptically.

"Sure, whatever," Hadley says, snickering to herself. "Have at it."

"You'll be famous," Monique says.

As the three of them march to the office, Weston's excitement grows with every step. He thinks it's a shame that Hadley isn't as hopeful as he is. But she had to live all that awfulness. Weston gets to learn from it, just as everyone else will, he hopes. She grew from tragedy, became stronger. But Weston is changed by her words. The residents used to joke that Weston was a stiff, practically dead inside. Renee once called him a walking cadaver. Others called him an obedient zombie. Looking back, Weston can't deny that. Much of his job required that he be alone, act alone, stay unattached. But that's all over now, and he hopes that the others will see him differently over time.

When they reach the office, Weston and Hadley step aside to let Monique sit at the iWindow. She immediately starts sorting applications and windows.

"Don't close that," Weston blurts, forgetting that she knows more than he does about what she's looking at. Monique shoots him a glance that says exactly that.

"Where are the recordings?" she asks.

Weston points through the back of the iWindow at the folder.

"I have more than that," Hadley says. "I don't know how much is there but I'm sure I recorded more after leaving with Paul."

"Paul?" Monique asks.

"He's not important," Hadley says, pulling out her porto. "Can I shoot these last ones to you?"

Monique looks around for a way to pull files off a porto, maybe some sort of wireless linking application. Weston is impressed by how quickly she navigates the iWindow. She taps an icon and a small box opens. A few taps on the iWindow, another few taps on Hadley's porto, and the files appear on the iWindow. She drags them to the folder.

"Will this take long?" Hadley asks.

Weston thinks about what's going to happen when everyone suddenly has Hadley's story in their head and they understand all that these poor girls have had to endure. He imagines the city suddenly coming to a screeching halt, a collective drawn breath of surprise, and the understanding that everything they've come to know about Haydens, the System, and the world they live in is built on lies. And all Hadley must be thinking is that this is taking too long.

"No," Monique says. "Well, I'm going to compress the files first. I've already run the transcript. It's rough and punctuation is kind of janky. But it can't hurt, I guess. The raw audio files are bigger. So, they'll take longer to package."

"Like how long?" Hadley asks.

"A minute?" Monique says, still swiping at the screen.

Weston gives Hadley a look that says, *she's good*. Hadley nods in agreement, even as she gives a doubtful smirk.

"The thing that held up Paul," Hadley says, "is that he needed a password. I don't know if you'll be able to get in."

"Like this?" Monique says, pointing to a line in the code that reads *Enter user: hot air balloon*, followed by a line that starts with *Enter password*. But it all looks like another language to Weston.

"Will that still work?" Weston asks.

"Don't know," Monique says. "We'll find out."

"It'll work," Hadley says. "Why else would they want each of us dead afterward?"

Weston remembers this from her diary, how MIND set up people to die after they were prompted to enter a password. Or, in Hadley's case, the murder attempt failed and her chip was fried, apparently no longer giving her access to the password. None of that would be necessary if the password didn't still work. None of it was necessary at all, Weston thinks.

A couple of swipes and a drag of the finger, and Monique says, "There. Done."

"Done?" Weston says, thinking that can't be it.

"Done done?" Hadley asks.

"Done done," Monique says, sitting back in the leather chair, a proud smile on her face. She sighs, wide eyed with glee as she looks at the code on the iWindow.

"I guess all we can do now is wait," Weston says, thinking how any minute now, it'll be like everyone in System City has awoken from a bad dream.

"I hope it works," Hadley says, with a doubtful tone.

"Who's Paul anyway?" Monique asks. "This is his computer? It's nice."

"It was," Weston says. "He basically built the System."

"What? Really?!" Monique's eyes grow wide with amazement as she seems to see the iWindow before her in a whole new light. "He's a genius, you know."

"He was a piece of hot garbage," Hadley says.

Monique looks to Weston, who nods in disappointed agreement. Monique's face goes slack with betrayal but she doesn't question her fellow Hayden.

"Dang," Monique says, sitting back again, suddenly uninterested in the iWindow before her. "Mega bummer." She sighs and says, "Never get to know your heroes."

CHAPTER FORTY-FOUR

Most viewed Look@Me videos of the day.

A dog yawns, emitting a noise that sounds vaguely like the wind up of an air raid siren, and the video cuts to old footage of a small town in middle America just before a tornado touches down.

—

A montage set to a ragtime piano tune. A bride is about to feed the groom some cake at an outdoor wedding, when a passing bird dive bombs directly into the cake. Two people stand on the roof of an old Chelsea Piers building in high winds when a gust wipes them into the choppy river. A tree falls across a tennis court, and the two players stare at it from either side, until the server commences anyway and the ball disappears into a thick of branches.

—

Just over a dozen protestors march outside of MIND headquarters, waving signs and demanding the end of the advertising program. Two teenage boys stand in the foreground mocking them and act like they're crushing the protestors' heads with their fingers.

—

Shot after shot of different sets of hands over different pots of boiling water in different kitchens snapping fistfuls of spaghetti, amplifying the bubbling sound of water and the satisfying crunch of dry pasta.

This is what people seem to care about today.

CHAPTER FORTY-FIVE

Red and swollen, as if he just crawled from a buffet meat carving station, Preston Blake sits before his microphone and licks his chapped lips. "Welcome back to *What's the Matter?* I'm your host, Preston Blake, and here's what's the matter."

He takes a sip from a bottle, wipes his mouth, and positions the bottle before the camera.

"This episode is brought to you by Platypus Punch Energy Nectar," he says, choking back disgust. "All the nutrients and vitamins a man needs to be a man."

He adjusts his MIND Over Matter hat.

"So, what's the matter? you ask. I'll tell you what's the matter." He pulls the microphone close, licks his lips. "It's been the same thing for the last, what, three weeks. But it keeps getting worse. Just keeps piling up like some giant heap of... of... dung! Let me read it for you. I know you've already seen it."

He picks up his porto and squints.

"MIND Director Arthur Klopek announces the System is shut down," he says. "Let that sink in, my dear listener. Because of these little goblins. Goblin girls. I'm going to call them that from now on. The goblin girls. The name *Hayden Hussies* gives them too much credit. These goblin girls have made it so that soon... I'm not saying tomorrow... but in the near future, we'll all be carrying some form of identification like some twenty-first century traveler."

He acts like he's wearing a jacket and pats imaginary side pockets.

"Oh, oh. Sorry, sir. I must have forgotten my passport," he says, shooting a look at the camera. "A passport! Think about that. Do *you* want to be responsible for carrying something else? Don't lose your ID card. Don't forget your passport or else you're in big trouble, mister."

He takes another drink from his bottle of Platypus Punch, winces, and puts the bottle down. He turns it so the label is visible.

"I don't know about you, but I don't plan on traveling any time soon. Where is there to go? What do I need a passport for? But here we are letting these goblin girls put us in this position." He pulls the microphone toward his face again. "Need I remind you that these are the little gremlins that cracked the code? They're already in our heads. Who knows what they're telling us to do."

He removes his hat, puts it on the table next to the bottle. He looks off somewhere and fixes his thinning hair.

"Oh, oh," he says, squaring up to the microphone. "I'm sure you've heard the latest, speaking of traveling. Can you believe those little goblin girls got away? Who knows how many escaped. Not all of them. But we just let them run off, probably to plot their next attack on our bodies. My body, my rules, right? And here they are breaking in like little cyber burglars. Do you want them in your head?"

He grabs the microphone like he's choking it. He looks into the camera.

"They're invading your head right now! Did you let them in? Because they're already trying to control you. What are you prepared to do, listeners? What are you willing to do to stop them?"

CHAPTER FORTY-SIX

By the end of their first couple of days, two bus loads of Haydens have come to an agreement–either you like Allentown or you absolutely hate it. Step falls into the "absolutely hate" category. Much of the downtown is occupied by the Delaware tribe. Shops and restaurants seem to thrive in that central area, but farther from the city center, it's clear that the tribe's population is still not enough to fully occupy the municipality, leaving areas to ruin.

Upon arrival, the Haydens sought the central-most point of town, judging by the tallest buildings they saw. What they found wasn't anything like System City but it wasn't entirely bad, either. Like System City, Allentown's streets run in a grid but its downtown is far smaller, leading to neighborhoods of single-family detached homes in every direction. Step finds the green yards to be romantic, like pictures from long ago. But within half a mile, the blocks are overgrown and unkempt. Homes are in disrepair or abandoned. There are no clear boundaries to the city like System City's rivers. Instead, you have to know not to go beyond 15th Street, where entire blocks might be open green spaces with rolling hills and no public transportation. The farther you go, and not far at all, the more vacant stores and ruins of commerce can be found.

Step would not call their reception hostile. The tribe, in general, was rather welcoming but skeptical. No doubt many of the Delaware traders had heard stories about underground teenagers from System City, and it was the younger among them that posed the greatest resistance. In the end, the tribe allowed the Haydens to seek shelter west of town on the campus of old Muhlenberg College. There they found ransacked dormitory buildings with musty and moldy mattresses, broken windows, and plenty of rodent inhabitants. But it was good enough for Haydens.

During their first full day, Step and others explored north into the neighborhoods to scavenge for supplies. They broke up into groups of four, each taking sides of a street. Moving from house to house, the Haydens found kicked in doors or broken windows where they could enter homes and gather any silverware or tools that hadn't already been pillaged long ago.

But each time they returned to campus, they would find curious residents from Allentown waiting outside their dormitory building. That night, the Haydens gathered in a lounge on the first floor of their building when many of the girls couldn't sleep. Outside, they saw headlights from cars in the parking lot across the way. Somebody was watching them, and the Haydens needed to stay vigilant.

After the second night, when several young Haydens were approached coming back from a neighborhood south of campus, just past a small lake, many of the Haydens had decided it was time to move on. The girls had made a mistake in trying to take a shortcut through the dark grassy land around the lake, and a group of teenage boys came out of the shadows and chased them. The boys were lucky to not catch them and even luckier for stopping short of campus, as they had no idea who they were dealing with. Once the Hayden girls shared news of their encounter, a dozen older Haydens marched from the dormitory building, armed with knives and pipes to find those boys. Among them was Nona with a box cutter she was more than willing to use. After fifteen minutes of searching, heavy rain drove the Haydens back to shelter.

That's when Step and several others decided to cut their losses. The next day, they scrounged their meager credit to get the buses charged, and they campaigned for the group to move on someplace south. A debate erupted and, in the end, just under half of the

Haydens agreed to leave.

Now, back on the road, Step looks up in the mirror to see a bus full of Haydens that he has unofficially committed to taking care of. Nona sits in the front seat, and Step sees her as second in command. She's much older than Step but also much quieter. The girls look up to her but have no idea what she's been through.

The road they take goes south through small country towns, farmland, and rolling hills. Step can't decide if life on the road is better or worse than trying to make a home somewhere new. But each passing day will prove to be a challenge either way. He has seen old stories about Philadelphia, its historical importance in the birth of America. But what they find may turn out to be worse than Allentown or more hostile than System City has become.

Not thirty minutes out of Allentown and several Hayden girls begin to complain. Step isn't in the mood to turn back but it's better to know now than when they've reached a new place to settle.

"What?" Step calls back to the girls. "What's the matter?"

"My porto is dead," one girl says. "I can't get anything on it now."

"Mine too," says another. "I mean, it's on but I guess it doesn't have a signal. Is that a thing?"

Step looks at the bus driver's porto resting on the dashboard. It's still on and the bus's onboard porto is still on. They're still linked. But when Step's porto awakens, the GPS app shows a blank screen. Nona gets up and kneels beside Step.

"Did they cut us off?" she asks.

"I don't know if they can do that," Step says. "I don't even think they know who we are to be able to do that."

"Maybe we're just out of range then?" Nona says. "Weird."

"Maybe," says Step. And suddenly it feels like they've traveled to another world.

The bus is quiet again as their new reality sets in. What are they going to do if they don't have their portos to keep them occupied or to help them navigate and communicate? Several minutes pass before anyone says a word. But then a Hayden shouts, "King of Prussia! Look!"

Sure enough, up ahead comes a sign for a place called King of Prussia. A land of royalty. Perhaps a land of prosperity.

"I'm going to be the queen of Prussia," announces one Hayden.

"No way. I am," says another. "Show me the king!"

The entire group erupts in laughter, joking about what they'll do with their portion of the family riches. Step has no idea what King of Prussia is or what it will hold for them, but the GPS is dead and there's no telling where they would end up otherwise. At least for now, the girls are in good spirits.

Like that, it has been decided. Step takes the exit toward King of Prussia. Onward they go.

CHAPTER FORTY-SEVEN

The babies are asleep when Miss Ula Mae checks on them. Miss Lisa, the night nanny, sits in a rocker across the room and gives Miss Ula Mae a look that says, *Can you believe it?* Never have the little cherubs all gone down so peacefully.

Floors above, girls are winding down for the night. Most of the teenage Haydens are allowed to look at videos or listen to music on their portos for a little while longer, just as long as they use earphones. Jealous preteen girls sneak some video time on their portos but the policy is that they're only allowed to read ebooks before bed. Though, this is difficult to police without seeing every screen.

The rest of the Haydens are in various states of unconsciousness by the time Miss Ula Mae finishes up her rounds and retires to her basement apartment. As she walks through the door, she says, "Porto screen on," and her porto instantly links to the porto screen on the wall. She uses her porto as a remote, bringing up the tail end of the nightly news. There's nothing unusual going on except the report of a double homicide in Brooklyn, which is immediately followed by a feel-good story about MIND sponsoring a fun run around Highland Park. Footage from last year's fun run shows boys and their parents smiling as they walk and run past a beautiful landscape of mature trees and old headstones of Cypress Hills Cemetery. Another shot shows a kids play zone on the edge of a golf course.

There's a knock at the door and Miss Ula Mae answers. It's Miss Darla checking in before leaving for the night.

"Some of the girls complained about water pressure," she says. "I tried it too. The water stopped working. It's too late to check if it's the whole block."

Yet another thing to deal with, Miss Ula Mae thinks. "I'll contact public works," she says. "These old buildings."

"Good night," Miss Darla says.

"Thanks," Miss Ula Mae says. "You too." She closes her door.

Miss Ula Mae keeps the porto screen on while she fixes a bowl of cereal. She brings the bowl to her chair and sets it beside the bowl from last night, its milk stiffened around the edges. She settles into her chair and picks up the bowl again. She takes a couple of bites, wipes her chin, and sets the bowl back down. Her eyes getting heavy, she leans back in her chair, chewing the cereal while absently watching the porto screen now showing a commercial for mattresses. Before the commercial is over, she dozes off.

She doesn't hear noises from outside, not out front or in back of the building. A chain clanks slowly against the front entrance door handles. A lock clicks closed. A dumpster is quietly pushed in place to block an alleyway exit. Miss Ula Mae doesn't hear the hushed encouragement of angry men or the crash of glass. Nor does she hear the whoosh of flames inside the front hallway or in the back recreation room. Some of the girls hear it, as do the staff. But it still takes more than three minutes for them to figure out what is going on. By then, they'll see the glow of flames from below their windows. They'll smell smoke, maybe hear the entryway ceiling crash to the floor.

In those three minutes, the alphabet rugs in the recreation room become a pool of flames spreading in every direction. Plushies and plastic toys feed the fire, helping it across the room to wooden shelves of more toys and blankets, as flames climb the walls and lick at the ceiling. Rolls of canvas covered in colorful handprints line each side of the front hallway. They carry the flames along the corridor and to the dropped ceiling that soon catches fire.

By the time the fire alarm goes off, and the sprinklers dribble any remaining water from their pipes, it's too late. Miss Ula Mae jolts awake and rushes to her apartment door. She can feel the heat before she's halfway across the room. When she opens the door, the smoke is so thick and hot, it forces her onto the floor. Shouting and screaming come from upstairs. She hears coughing and gagging. Girls cry for help. She can no longer see. Her lungs fill with hot smoke. Her eyes feel like they're melting. Banging noises and screams from upstairs are the last thing she hears over the roar of the fire, the piercing alarms, and her own violent coughing, until she finally loses consciousness on her living room floor.

CHAPTER FORTY-EIGHT

Given the meager light that comes into her slit of a window at this hour, it might as well be ten o'clock at night, instead of the morning. Cammy can hardly keep herself awake as she stares through her iWindow at the occasional passing blur of a human figure moving among the Mattrest, Inc. cubicles outside her office door. This is what her days look like now, watching strangers be bored from a distance.

With Frances Boylan and the rest of her team several floors up, Cammy thinks she might as well be working from a bar or from home. Frances pings her maybe three times in a given day to update a spreadsheet or arrange meetings, all of which amounts to about an hour of work per day if Cammy takes her time. When back on her team's floor, given the central location of her desk, most of her duties came in passing. Usually Edna Boylan or Uncle Larry would ask Cammy to do something they didn't feel like doing, like cleaning up a presentation slide deck or preparing a document for client signatures. While menial, these tasks at least added up to a moderate day's work and provided opportunities for Cammy to socialize with her team.

Now, if Cammy thinks her job is pointless, she need only look out her office door to find others with whom she can commiserate. That cluster of cubicles outside her door encompasses some of the most vacant, uninterested people Cammy has ever witnessed. Her interactions with this group of junior attorneys, paralegals, and administrators amounts only to nods and smiles in passing. But, through observation, Cammy has gathered all she needs to know about their workday.

Since most of their projects rest not in liability or civil suits but in the rinse-and-repeat processes of mergers, acquisitions, and buyouts, their mechanical and repetitive work takes little time or effort, leading each member of the team to take up covert pleasures during their many idle hours on the clock.

Cammy doesn't know who they are. Instead, she's given them names in her head. Todd sits closest to her office with part of his iWindow visible from her open door. Todd is a paralegal with long black hair that covers a neck tattoo, which reads *BSK* in bold letters. Cammy doesn't know what it means but she sees it regularly now. Nearly every day he lounges back in his chair, hair pulled into a ponytail, earphones in, as he watches grainy old wrestling videos. Images of hulking men in strange costumes flash across his iWindow as they throw and slam each other around an arena. The only sounds are squeaks from Todd's chair, his occasional snicker or grunt, and the crunch of whatever snack he brings that day.

Kara is a junior attorney and, judging by the vinyl wrap of puppies at play on her cubicle wall, is also a dog lover. She sits one cubicle farther from Cammy's office and plays video games on her porto. Next to her is Quinn, another paralegal. Quinn has a nervous habit of peering over his cubicle wall for, Cammy guesses, their boss or some other associate attorney. But when Quinn isn't twitching like a squirrel, he's knitting. With upright posture to spot passersby, Quinn has a half-done sweater or scarf draped over his lap and works it with knitting needles beneath his desk.

It saddens Cammy to think about the facade of decorum that these people put up as they sneak a taste of their meager pleasures. Despite knowing they'll have little to do that day, these people rise each morning, put on their stiffest, drabbest clothing, and come to an office where they pass time by any means they can pull off. She knows it's not their fault. Instead, Cammy questions the necessity of such workplaces. Who dreamed up such a sterile, lifeless environment to slowly kill people with malaise? And for what?

Rather than stay in her office and watch these folks waste the day away, Cammy decides to visit her team upstairs. As expected, the Mattrest, Inc. group is hard at play when she walks past their cubicles. Only Quinn pays her any mind.

When she reaches her floor, Cammy finds that her desk remains empty with no sign that she ever spent time there. If she didn't know any better, she would think it's awaiting a new inhabitant. She approaches Frances Boylan's door but can hear people arguing inside. It isn't professional, or at least the subject matter isn't about work. She can hear Sydney and Edna bickering. It must be some family-related issue.

Instead of knocking, Cammy moves down the hall to Ronald Trapper's office, where she finds him lounging on his leather couch, mug of coffee in one hand and his porto in the other. If he's not here reading briefs, he can be found on a park bench across the street with a travel mug of coffee and a brief on his porto. If he's not in either of those two places, he's usually reading a brief while walking from one to the other.

Cammy knocks lightly and Ronald Trapper raises just his eyes, looking at Cammy above the frame of his glasses.

"Hey, kid," he says.

"Ron," she says, stepping in. She glances down the hall to see if Frances's door opens. "I was thinking since the System is down now and we're all, you know, sort of nameless—"

"Ah, Cammy," he says, resting his porto on a side table. "I understand. We miss you up here. But I can't make any decisions without the Boylans' say so."

"I understand," Cammy says, though she doesn't know why they haven't already thought to bring her back up. She's especially annoyed that Frances isn't eager to have her back. "I just think we're past all that now."

"Sure, sure," he says. "Like I said, I'll run it by the Boylans." He gets up to lead her out of his office in his gentle fatherly way. "Let's circle back on this one, okay? I'm sure once we have IDs or whatever

MIND is thinking, then everything will be square."

He leads her into the hallway and then fills his doorway, a move she's seen others do before as a way to signal that the person they're talking to isn't getting back in that office.

"Thanks, Ron," she says, though she's not happy with his response.

"No problem, kid," he says, backing into his office. Before he closes the door, he says, "Sorry to hear about your friends."

"Sure," Cammy says, shrugging off the comment. "Thanks." She ignored the pings from Haddy and the others about meeting up somewhere to leave town. Rumors have been circling that a bunch of Haydens ran away to avoid another raid. Cammy doesn't want anything to do with that stuff anymore. It's just a bunch of Hayden mischief, as far as she's concerned.

But as Cammy walks back to the elevator, she has a sudden recollection about her fellow Haydens not just being persecuted but also murdered. It's a strange thing to recall so suddenly. One by one, they're being murdered. *Why am I having this thought now?* she wonders.

As she questions this memory, it occurs to her, somehow again, that Haydens have been pawns in MIND's access to the System. *What? How do I know that?*

Cammy doesn't remember hearing this or learning it from anyone. Only, somehow she thinks that maybe Haddy told her. It's all foggy but when she thinks about it, the fact that Haydens have been killed in order for MIND to access the System is just a well-known fact. *Right? We all know this, don't we? But since when?*

Cammy is confused as to why she's only now remembering this. *Was that what Ronald Trapper was talking about a moment ago? And why now?*

Back at her floor, Cammy heads past the cluster of cubicles and hears two voices from the break room.

"It's crazy," says one voice. "The place is just a pile of ash and rubble."

When Cammy looks in the room, she sees Kara and Todd talking by the toaster oven. The smell of burnt quiche fills the room.

"I don't think any of those Haydens made it out," says Kara. "The fire was huge."

They both turn to see Cammy in the doorway. If she thought before that they didn't know she was a Hayden, their wide eyes and stumbling voices say otherwise. Or maybe they're just rattled by an unexpected social interaction.

"Oh, hey," says Todd. "You're the new person, right?"

"What's this about a fire?" Cammy asks.

"Nothing," Todd says.

"You said the Haydens didn't make it?" she says. She can feel her heart beating harder. "What happened?"

"I was just–" says Kara. "We–"

"It's all over the news," Todd says.

"I'm sorry?" Kara says, almost like a question.

Cammy can't believe something might have happened to her sisters without her knowing. She rushes back to her office, porto in hand as she flicks through the news. That's when she comes across the images. A pile of rubble where Hayden House stood. Smoke plumes as high as buildings around it. The red glow of still-burning fires in that rubble. Cammy feels sick, her stomach turning. She chokes back the urge to vomit. Her head goes foggy.

She scrolls a bit further for more details, even though the pictures tell it all. The next article is an opinion piece about anti-Hayden hate speech and what to do about a divided city. The lede reads, *Can we co-exist? What will it take?*

Cammy can't bring herself to read on. Her breath is short, her heart racing. *Those poor girls,* she thinks. She looks around her office for something to calm her but all she finds are bare white walls. Her iWindow glows faintly with the Boylan, Bolyan, Trapper, and Boylan logo–*BBT&B* in ornate lettering. The image of a collapsed Hayden House flashes in her mind. The thought of all those girls inside.

They didn't ask for this, she thinks. *We never asked for any of it.*

Those girls, as Cammy imagines, were huddled together around their cots. They were holding each other, comforting one another. Sisters who had each other's back until the end. And here Cammy is in some whitewashed cell. For what?

Cammy grabs the iWindow by its quarter-inch thick glass and whips it against the wall. It smashes with a flash of light. The cord whacks against the side of the desk. She grabs the cord, still attached to the iWindow's metal base, and uses it like a ball and chain to smash a hole in the sheetrock wall with a loud growl.

She turns and seizes her chair by the armrests and screams into the plush seat as she lifts into the air. With her seat hoisted above her head, she sees Quinn peeking over his cubicle wall. She brings the chair back down as if body slamming it into her desk. The wooden desk barely shows the impact. So, she lifts the chair and tries again with more force. This time, Cammy lets go and the chair bounces out the door and against Todd's cubicle.

Cammy steps toward the wall and punches it three times, denting the sheetrock with her fist, dots of blood smeared on white paint. She turns to the door and kicks it open even further, smashing the doorknob into the wall. The chair is settled on its side, and Cammy steps out to grab it again. That's when she sees everyone from the Mattrest Inc. group watching. Todd and Kara are in the breakroom doorway. Quinn is still tucked behind his cubicle wall. Others are standing outside their offices surrounding the cluster of cubicles. Everyone is there to see what all the commotion is about, what has disrupted their monotony, what this Hayden has done now.

Almost out of breath, arms heavy, and her face hot and wet with tears, Cammy looks around the room at all their stupid faces. As if discharging the collective cries of all the girls who lost their lives in that fire, Cammy releases a low growl that grows into a scream that spends every ounce of her breath. And, still, these people will never understand.

CHAPTER FORTY-NINE

Several Haydens have been crying on the bus all day. Younger girls have made forts in their section of two seats by draping coats, sweatshirts, or blankets across headrests. Inside these makeshift rooms, they hold each other and weep. Haddy spent some of the morning on the bus, sharing memories of Miss Ula Mae and hearing other girls' more recent stories. None of them can believe that she is gone and Hayden House has been destroyed. Yet, nobody questions who do it. The city did it. The System took their lives.

The other non-Hayden residents are doing their best to be supportive. Haddy can tell that they are sad for these girls. Even Laars, who used to hate Haddy, has asked if they will be okay. Some of the girls busy themselves with chores, hoping to take their minds off the news. And when they take longer than normal to haul a wheelbarrow of dirt to the pile at the back of the colony, or get distracted by their thoughts, the other residents on the job remain patient.

In the late afternoon, Weston suggests that they make a bonfire so that the girls can share more memories with the group. The residents pair off and spread out into the hills around the colony in search of sticks and larger pieces of wood, which they throw onto a pile where they usually have their campfires. By nightfall, the pile is so high and wide that it takes up the entire area where people would normally sit. Haddy gathers a bundle of dry twigs and leaves and sets it on a cookie sheet from the kitchen. Using the flint and steel from around her neck, she ignites the pile of dried kindling and fans it into a sizable flame. She then walks around the bonfire, scraping small bundles of lit kindling into places around the base of the wood pile, where twigs and pine needles catch fire. Eventually, the individual flames reach each other, creating a ring around the edge that slowly works its way into the core of the pile.

The orange glow from within the smokey pile of wood reminds Haddy of the news images she saw of Hayden House. Her stomach has been in a knot all day but she hasn't been able to cry. She can't, not in front of the girls. For their sake, Haddy has to be a source of strength. Several of the girls have joined her to watch the bonfire grow. As the flame builds, she can see in the glow on many of their faces that they will get through this. As always, they have each other.

Before long, the entire pile of wood is engulfed in glorious flames that reach into the sky. More Haydens emerge from the bus, wrapped in blankets and coats that they use to wipe away tears. Their eyes are transfixed by the enormity of the bonfire. Other residents appear. Weston and the watchers join, making a place for themselves among the Haydens who sit on rocks and stumps. Renee comes up alongside Haddy, puts an arm around her and gives Haddy's shoulder a firm squeeze. Nobody says a word. The only sound is of the rippling roar of the fire and crackle of wood. Haddy wonders how Step and the other two buses of Haydens are handling the tragedy. Are they gathered around a fire like this, wherever they are?

This gathering and the fire, it all reminds her of the Junction. But instead of looking up to find a constellation of graffiti across a concrete dome, the speckled night sky stretches into infinity in every direction. There is no surface above them. No streets or city. Nothing that keeps them in hiding.

From a cluster of girls comes a short laugh, a single guffaw. "Holy cow," says the voice. It's Monique. Her face lit by her porto, she looks up and says, "Look. Look at this." Other girls crowd around her, looking at the screen. They, too, start laughing. Smiles spread as more faces look at the screen. "Amazing," a girl says. They're crying again but smiling.

Monique says, "You have to see this." Weston and the watchers lean in for a view. Weston smiles and the watchers nod approvingly. The younger watcher looks satisfied. Weston waves Haddy over.

Girls part to let Haddy through, and Monique holds up the porto for Haddy to see.

"Look," she says. "Look what you did."

Haddy takes the porto. The tiny screen shows drone footage from System City. The still smoldering remains of Hayden House are lit by spotlights as emergency crews and citizens climb through the rubble in search of survivors. The drone moves toward the street to show a crowd gathered around the site, their portos held high, as the glowing screens wave above their heads in vigil. The drone pulls farther away to reveal a sea of glowing screens extended down the street and around the corner in each direction. There are way too many portos to be just Haydens in that crowd. There must be thousands. Farther still, more and more glowing screens come together in the streets. Dots of blue light keep appearing, as if pulled by some magnetic force.

"You did that," Weston says, now standing beside Haddy.

She blinks and the tears in her eyes distort her view of the vigil onscreen. She wipes the tears away and is suddenly overcome with all that has happened. Everything she spoke about, from being fried to struggling on the streets, has all come to this moment. The sadness she feels at the sight of her home in ruin and the hope that rises from seeing more and more tiny blue lights as the drone passes overhead– Haddy gives in to these feelings. She sobs so heavily that she can no longer hold the porto. Weston catches her when her knees go weak. He eases her to a seat on a log behind them, where the rest of the girls come close and place a hand on her. Her sisters are here for her, and she feels every last one of them.

CHAPTER FIFTY

Agent Stevenson sits on the steps of a brownstone on East 91st Street, sipping a coffee and watching a group of protestors march past in the street. They're passion and frustration can be heard in their voices as they shout, "Down with MIND! Down with MIND!" This is one of many groups around the city that are rallying followers to demand that MIND answers for its crimes. Agent Stevenson can't help but feel proud of what is happening, and he would happily join them, if he didn't have other business to take care of.

His porto says 3:16 p.m., which is one minute later than Thomas has arranged to meet Reuben Mayfield just around the corner. Agent Stevenson chose to wait in this spot because it's between the meeting location at 92Y and Mayfield's apartment. Agent Stevenson suspects that Mayfield has been hunkering down somewhere in this neighborhood.

After another minute, Agent Stevenson gets up and heads toward 92Y, passing his car parked on Lexington Avenue. Before he reaches 92Y, he already sees Mayfield pacing beneath the front entrance awning. Agent Stevenson couldn't have chosen a better spot than a historic fitness center favored by the elderly. Mayfield, in his green tracksuit, fits right in.

When Mayfield sees Agent Stevenson approaching, he stops pacing. His face isn't as disappointed as Agent Stevenson hoped.

"Well, well," he says. "You flipped Mr. Thomas, did you?"

It is unlikely that Mayfield thought to run, yet Agent Stevenson is ready for a chase.

"I wondered about this location," he says. "I have a place nearby. But you already knew that."

Agent Stevenson steps toward Mayfield, expecting the man to make it difficult. "Turn around," he says, pulling heavy duty zip tie cuffs from his back pocket.

"Not necessary, Agent Stevenson."

"Turn around," he says again in a harsher tone.

Two ladies coming from the front entrance gasp when they see Agent Stevenson forcefully securing the zip ties around Reuben Mayfield's wrists. It feels so good to do this, he thinks.

"Ladies," Mayfield says, greeting them as if it's just a normal everyday occurrence.

Agent Stevenson ignores them, grabs Mayfield's arm, and spins him around. "Come with me."

He escorts Mayfield to his car and stuffs him in the backseat, making sure to be as rough as possible. By the time he comes around to the driver's seat, Mayfield is sitting up behind the passenger seat. The car's onboard porto shows two links, Agent Stevenson's and Paul's. Agent Stevenson looks at the extra name on his onboard porto and smiles to himself. He finally has Mayfield.

They pull away from the curb.

"You have been after me for how long now?" Mayfield says. "How many years?"

Agent Stevenson doesn't respond. Instead, he minds his driving, checking the rearview mirror for familiar vehicles. He wouldn't be surprised to find people tailing him.

"You know," Mayfield says. "They need me. The System needs me."

Agent Stevenson inspects an SUV a few vehicles back in the mirror. It's nothing. Then he looks at Mayfield, watching him drive. The next light is green but traffic is backed up. A group of protestors marches by in the intersection.

"Do they really need you though?" Agent Stevenson asks.

"They do not have a choice," Mayfield says.

Agent Stevenson studies the line of cars behind him. He wonders if Mayfield suspected something and arranged for help.

"I believe MIND headquarters is south of here," Mayfield says.

Agent Stevenson watches the protestors march. Their signs read, *Down with MIND* and *Let us think 4 ourselves.*

"You know," Agent Stevenson says, "They tell you that if you're ever abducted, never let your abductor take you to a second location."

He looks at his prisoner in the rearview mirror but Mayfield looks away. Once the protestors pass, traffic starts moving again. Agent Stevenson has a destination in mind but he takes random turns to make sure that nobody is following.

"You must know by now that nothing will come of this," Mayfield says. "In fact, I am certain that any discipline you face will far outweigh the mere slap on my wrist. By all means, though, hand me over to MIND."

Agent Stevenson keeps going in the opposite direction of MIND headquarters, traveling farther north until he reaches the bridge to Randall's Island. He can see that Mayfield notices this, and a flash of concern comes over the prisoner's face.

"Do you know what the Haydens have done to me?" Mayfield asks. "I would open my shirt to show you. It was horrific. I will never forget that terrible moment." He looks out the window, no doubt feigning dismay. "The authorities will be none too pleased to learn what those girls have done."

"Those girls are long gone," Agent Stevenson says. "I'd have let them off the hook for worse." He sees that Mayfield doesn't react. So, he says, "You know, Reuben, I used to be a stager. You know what that is, I'm sure. I was pretty good at it. Not that there's much to it when they don't see it coming." He can see a glint of concern in Mayfield's eyes. But when they make eye contact in the mirror, Mayfield forces a smirk.

The bridge he takes leads to a tangle of concrete ramps on and off the island. It's hard to believe that such a place housed any form of outdoor recreation other than driving. Agent Stevenson navigates around the last offramp until they're approaching a road that encircles an enormous field where several baseball diamonds used to host little league games every Saturday. Those fields are gone now, washed away by encroaching water from the East River. Beyond a swamp of driftwood and trash, the road bends around toward the farthest edge of the island. There sits a lone squad car, right where the water has swallowed the road and they can go no farther. It's a natural dead end.

They pull up beside the squad car, and Agent Stevenson says, "These guys don't give a damn about what you can do. All they care about is what you did to those girls." Outside, two officers step from their vehicle. Their jackets ripple with the wind off the East River.

Agent Stevenson gets out, comes around the side of the car, and pulls the door open. He hooks a hand under Mayfield's arm and gives him a tug. Mayfield gets out.

"I shall be out before nightfall," Mayfield says.

"Right," Agent Stevenson says. He pats Mayfield's jacket pockets to find his porto. He pulls the porto from the pocket.

"That evidence?" one of the officers asks.

"This is Mayfield's lifeline," Agent Stevenson says. Like one of the pitchers that once performed on the field behind him, he winds up and launches the porto into the East River. They all watch the water where the porto disappeared.

"Hell of a throw," one officer says.

Agent Stevenson points to the enormous wall that is their only view of Rikers Island just across the water. "You see that over there," he says to Mayfield. "You'll call that home very soon."

The officers laugh. Mayfield has no words.

With a poke of two fingers between Mayfield's shoulder blades, Agent Stevenson shoves the prisoner toward the officers. "You have his record," he says.

"We do," says an officer.

"If you need anything, let me know," Agent Stevenson says. "And if MIND contacts you, give them my name."

"Will do," says the officer. He takes Mayfield by the arm and helps him into their vehicle. The two officers get in. Agent Stevenson can see Mayfield's face through the tinted glass. That usual air of confidence is missing from Mayfield. He nods to Agent Stevenson the way a chess master might to a worthy opponent in defeat. Then his face goes slack and morose.

The car backs up and turns around. They drive away, leaving Agent Stevenson in that remote edge of the island. From here, the buildings of Manhattan seem so small in the distance. He's practically in another world. He forgets sometimes about these pockets of System City, the ones left to die.

As he watches the car grow smaller down the road, he sees another vehicle coming down the same road toward him. He immediately knows who it is. Agent Stevenson looks toward the swamp where children used to run bases. Behind him is the river, and to his left is the stream that connects them at a dip in the road.

As the black van draws near, Agent Stevenson turns to look at the river. He pulls a long breath of wet air into his lungs and listens to the van come to a stop behind him. He hears the side door open. He closes his eyes, exhales, and thinks about the colorful main street of Hackettstown, how lovely it would be to spend the rest of his days in a place like that. No System, no MIND, no Haydens. He could be whoever he wants.

"Ready when you are," says a voice.

Agent Stevenson sighs and turns around. The agent with the yellow-framed glasses hangs halfway out of the van. Agent Stevenson has learned that the man's name is Agent Wilcox. With nothing worth saying, Agent Stevenson climbs into the darkness of the van, and the agent with the yellow-rimmed glasses closes the door. The van does a u-turn and leaves behind Agent Stevenson's car. Inside is his porto. Neither of which he will see again.

CHAPTER FIFTY-ONE

Ivy clings to a tinted glass awning that extends over a walkway leading to the front entrance of Macy's department store. The red star of the store's sign is sun bleached, and the plastic white letters are broken with bullet holes. Step slowly navigates the bus around this massive structure, weaving through the trees and shrubs that sprout from what used to be a parking lot. The building itself seems bigger than Central Park. As he drives, Step hears Haydens read signs from the sides of the building–*H&M, Nordstrom, Lord & Taylor*. Beside what appears to be a three-story atrium, a sign reads, *King of Prussia*. But unless the monarch is some squatter, it's unlikely that a king will be found inside.

This appears to be the heart of town. Dilapidated corporate parks and ransacked strip malls make up the rest. There is no need for Step to stop the bus. Everyone agrees that they should move on. On their way in, several of the girls remarked about a river. So, Step decides they should follow it south in hopes of finding, at the very least, a mill town to settle for a night. A green sign reads, *Schuylkill River*, and the girls debate how it's pronounced. *Shy-kill, Skewy-kill, Shooy-kill.* If only their portos worked, they could settle this argument, but the silliness of their guesses makes for a better time.

Step has trouble keeping the river in sight, as he takes the closest roads he can find. Before long, they cross over the river into a town named Conshohocken with the steepest hills any of them have ever seen. Crisscrossing the river, the Haydens see signs for places named Gladwyne and Bala Cynwyd, more names that spark debate about pronunciation. As they move south, buildings become denser. There are old elevated train tracks. These are promising signs. In an even hillier town named Manayunk, brick facades of row homes spill into the street where they drive. Step takes it easy as the bus lumbers over the rubble.

Soon the river bends, and Step can see highrises in the distance. A city. A big city, maybe as big as home. A few of the girls spot the buildings, as well.

"We're losing it, we're losing it!" shouts one, as the road bends around a rocky outcropping that cuts off their city-view.

The bus clears the outcropping, and another girl shouts, "It's back!"

"Oh no!" says another girl, playfully. The bus passes beneath a tall, stone railroad bridge. Vines hang from the ceiling of the short tunnel, as if they might be entering a jungle.

"There it is, there it is!" shouts a girl, and several clap with excitement as they emerge again.

It's an overcast afternoon. The sun breaks through gray clouds, occasionally dazzling the Haydens with a shimmering glare off otherwise brown river water. In the distance, with or without the sun, the city, which signs indicate is Philadelphia, seems somehow illuminated. The closer they get, the more Step thinks it's a mirage, like the ghost image of a city skyline.

Step thinks about everything they've ever heard about Philadelphia, which isn't much. It used to be called the City of Brotherly Love. Old white guys signed a piece of paper there that somehow gave their country independence. There was something else about a broken bell.

The Haydens lose the city again to trees and rolling green hills. They also lose the river. Yet, there are no other roads to take but this one. So, Step stays the course until they come upon an ornate building on a hill. A sign calls it a museum of art. The architecture reminds Step of the Metropolitan Museum of Art in System City. Only, this building is painted white. Even the terracotta roof, which one would expect to be clay red, is painted bright white. To their left, another building with layers of modern-style balconies, is painted white.

More cars appear on the road now. Traffic is picking up as they get closer to the city. Step steers the bus around a curve in front of the museum and ends up on a wide parkway that suddenly presents to them downtown Philadelphia. A flat, mirrored glass building reflects gray clouds. Other buildings similar in height shine with blue glass. They all peak from a dense crowd of moderately tall skyscrapers that stretch for a couple of miles in each direction. All of these buildings share a similar trait. Whatever isn't a window has been painted white.

Step is amazed, as are the other Haydens with their faces pressed against the windows to take it all in. Buildings of just about every architectural style from the last three centuries reflect brilliance from their white painted facades, so much that there seems no need for streetlights. From row homes to condominium buildings to office buildings, every structure reflects the same heavenly glow. It's almost difficult to look at.

The street they're on cuts through the city's grid in a diagonal, bringing them directly to a castle-like structure with what appears to be a statue at the top. Step negotiates the length of their bus through much denser traffic, and settles it along a curb just across from a plaza outside the castle-like building. A sign suggests that this is city hall.

"Maybe the king lives here?" says one of the girls.

Step looks to Nona to see if they should get out and scout their surroundings. Nona shrugs and says, "Why not?"

One by one, they step off the bus and onto a bustling sidewalk that instantly reminds many of them of home. Before them, a staircase leads down into a wide opening in the sidewalk. A sign reads, *Regional Rail Lines, Suburban Station.*

Step and Nona share a look.

"I bet there's a nice place for us somewhere down there," Step says, thinking pragmatically.

Nona smiles, a rare sight. "Why, though?" she says, so matter of fact that Step is taken off guard.

Why would we crawl back underground? Step suddenly thinks. *Who are we hiding from?*

"Look!" shouts a young Hayden. Across the street, small streams of water shoot from the plaza floor in patterns. When the street is clear, the girls rush over and begin to play and splash like the children they could never be before. Their screeching and giggling makes Step smile.

Step and Nona cross over after the girls and take in the sights around them. People shuffle by, ignoring them. No sideways glances or muttered threats. It appears that they're standing in the center of the city. While not nearly as tall as System City, all these white buildings stretch in each direction like an unpainted canvas to discover and make their own.

Maybe this is the clean slate I've been looking for, Step thinks.

Step watches the girls dance and play in the fountain and wishes Haddy could be here to see this. As Step thinks about her now, it's suddenly clear that she'll be alright. They will all be okay. Step doesn't know why that comes to mind. Maybe it's distance or time or absence, but everything Haddy has done seems to make sense now. With eyes closed against the brilliant glow of buildings, Step lets the girls' carefree laughter fill his ears and heart. *Everything will be different from now on*, Step thinks. It doesn't take a wizard to see how far they've come.

ACKNOWLEDGEMENTS

Once again, thank you to Nate Ragolia and Shaunn Grulkowski at Spaceboy Books. There is no better home for this story.

ABOUT THE AUTHOR

Greg Shemkovitz is the author of *Remind* (Spaceboy Books) and *Lot Boy* (Sunnyoutside Press), among other stories and essays. He lives in Atlanta.

ABOUT THE PUBLISHERS

Nate Ragolia is a lifelong lover of science fiction and its power to imagine worlds more hopeful and inclusive than the real one. His first book, *There You Feel Free*, was published by 1888's Black Hill Press in 2015. Spaceboy Books reissued it in 2021. He's also the author of *The Retroactivist* (2017). His most recent book, *One Person Can't Make a Difference* (2022), was featured on Tor.com's Can't Miss Indie Press Speculative Fiction list, and was translated into Italian for Ringworld Sci-Fi in 2023. He founded and edited *BONED*, a literary magazine, and also created two webcomics. Nate is also a husband and a dog dad.

Shaunn Grulkowski has been compared to Warren Ellis and Phillip K. Dick and was once described as what a baby conceived by Kurt Vonnegut and Margaret Atwood would turn out to be. He's at least the fifth best Slavic-Latino-American sci-fi writer in the Baltimore metro area. He's the author *Retcontinuum*, and the editor of *A Stalled Ox* and *The Goldfish* for 1888/Black Hill Press.